# DEADRAIN

OTHER BOOKS BY ANTHONY GIANGREGORIO

**THE DEAD WATER SERIES**

DEADWATER
DEADWATER: Expanded Edition
DEADRAIN
DEADCITY
DEADWAVE
DEAD HARVEST
DEAD UNION
DEAD VALLEY

**ALSO BY THE AUTHOR**

DEAD RECKONING: DAWNING OF THE DEAD
THE MONSTER UNDER THE BED
DEADEND: A ZOMBIE NOVEL
DEAD TALES: SHORT STORIES TO DIE FOR
DEAD MOURNING: A ZOMBIE HORROR STORY
ROAD KILL: A ZOMBIE TALE
DEADFREEZE
DEADFALL
DEADRAGE
SOUL-EATER
THE DARK
RISE OF THE DEAD
DARK PLACES

# DEADRAIN

ANTHONY GIANGREGORIO

## ACKNOWLEDGEMENTS

Thanks to my parents, and especially to my wife, Jody. Without her continuing support this book could never have happened. Also, thanks to Marc for his help polishing the final draft.

## AUTHOR'S NOTE

While Virginia is a real place, I have taken fictional liberties with cities and towns, so if you live around there don't go looking for anything that sounds familiar. Besides, you might not like what you find.

## AUTHOR'S NOTE 2

This book was self-edited, and though I tried my absolute best to correct all grammar mistakes; there may be a few here and there.
Please accept my sincerest apology for any errors you may find.
This is the second edition of this book.

Visit my web site at undeadpress.com

## DEADRAIN

Copyright © 2009 by Anthony Giangregorio

ISBN        Softcover  ISBN 13:  978-1-935458-11-1
                       ISBN 10:  1-935458-11-6

This book was printed in the United States of America.
For more info on obtaining additional copies of this book, contact:

www.livingdeadpress.com

# CHAPTER ONE

HENRY WATSON SAT inside the abandoned furniture store and watched the rain falling outside the glass windows.

A squirrel hadn't quite made it out of the rain when the clouds had finally let go of their payload and Henry calmly watched as it now twitched in its death throws out on the sidewalk in front of the store.

He thought to himself how at one time watching an animal suffer like that would have broken his heart. But now, in the world he found himself in, death was an everyday companion.

Snoring behind him made him glance over his shoulder at the man and woman sleeping softly on a display bed in the middle of the room.

Beside each of them, within arms reach, was a firearm. The man had a twelve gage shotgun and the woman a small .22 pistol.

Both weapons had their safeties off and a bullet in the chamber.

Henry then turned and continued to watch the street outside, looking for signs of movement. So far his watch had been uneventful; except for the squirrel, that is.

The street was empty of life as he scanned up and down it. Not that he would expect to see anything, mind you.

A stray newspaper flew at the store window, the bold black print declaring: **U.S. RAIN WATER CONTAMINATED! IS THIS THE WORK OF TERRORISTS?"**

Then the paper was caught in another updraft and flew off down the street.

As for the street, it looked like it had been through a war. Blackened cars and burned buildings decorated the landscape while trash blew in the wind and collected against the skeletal remains of automobiles.

As long as it was raining, he knew they were safe inside, for you see if you got caught out in the rain, you died, and even the dead usually stayed undercover.

About three months ago, a bacterium had gotten into the water supply in a small town in the Midwest and the contaminated water had caused the town's population to change into bloodthirsty ghouls.

Henry, along with his two companions, Jimmy and Mary, had made it out of the town alive and had then headed north to escape the infestation.

But what the small group didn't know at the time was that the bacteria had infected the clouds as well and when the contaminated water had evaporated into the surrounding clouds; those same clouds had then drifted off across America.

When the rains began two states over, no one understood what was happening as people changed into murderous, flesh-eating ghouls (zombies if you prefer) and by the end of the week half of America was contaminated.

The military stepped in, but it wasn't long before, they too, became infected. Then it was every man for himself as the country's infrastructure soon collapsed in on itself.

Now, the only law was of survival, blood and bullets the new currency, and he and his companions had learned well.

Before everything had gone to Hell, he had been a computer programmer who had just lost his job due to outsourcing. Now he was a mercenary who roamed what was left of America, trying to find someplace that perhaps wasn't infected.

He had hope; that was all he had.

When the country collapsed, the cell phones and landlines were the first thing to go, so he had no real idea exactly how much of the country was infected.

Hell, he didn't even know if the whole world was contaminated.

Sometimes they would come across other travelers who would share stories of how it was in other parts of the country. But they all said the same thing.

The dead had taken over and the living was now running for what was left of their shattered lives.

Henry set his jaw as he stared at the dead squirrel, his jaw taut as he remembered.

Well, he wasn't running and neither were his companions. They would take back this country even if they had to kill every walking corpse in America.

\*     \*     \*

His eye caught movement off to the side and he backed away from the window so as not to be seen.

A zombie (or as Henry had nicknamed them, deaders) came shambling down the street and stopped in front of the store window. More than half of its face was missing, the mottled gray and green skin hanging by a few pieces of gristle. Its left hand was nothing but a blackened nub, the bone protruding like a broken tree branch and its clothes were covered in filth and dried gore and blood.

As the human shaped monstrosity looked down onto the sidewalk, it spotted the dead squirrel twitching fitfully and bent over to retrieve it. Its missing hand tried to retrieve the small carcass and it didn't understand what was wrong. Finally, some small part of its rotting brain realized it needed to use its remaining hand. Reaching down, it grasped the squirrel with skeletal fingers and then began to consume the squirrel as it stood out in the rain.

If Henry had his way, he would have walked outside and blew the abomination away, but he knew one gunshot would attract any others from a two block radius. So he stayed hunched down and watched. If the creature didn't threaten him then he would let it live for another day; so to speak.

As the zombie chewed the head of the squirrel off, Henry studied the condition of this particular ghoul in more detail.

It had been dead for a while as he could clearly see the skin had dried tight against its skull and its gums showed plainly as it took another bite of its meal.

The hair on its head was falling out and as it shifted slightly, Henry could see it was missing an ear.

Despite all this, it was still in pretty good shape compared to some of the others he'd seen in the past three months. With its meal finished, the ghoul moved on and Henry watched as it turned the corner and disappeared from view.

He raised himself back up and walked back to the window and sat down again, continuing his watch. He checked his wristwatch and saw he only had another fifteen minutes or so until he would wake Jimmy to relieve him.

That would be good; he was exhausted from their long hike from earlier in the day.

If it hadn't been for the rain, they would probably have continued on for a few more hours until sunset, but once the clouds started rumbling the companions knew they needed to seek cover fast.

If you got caught in the rain, it was all over. Within a matter of seconds you would feel faint and then you would pass out and die.

Moments later however, the bacteria would kick-start your brain and bring you back to life, although when you revived you had an unrelenting craving for meat; preferably human.

Henry thought back to times when he had seen children attacking their parents and husbands attacking wives and vice versa.

He shook the memories away; they were useless and just took up space in the cupboard that was his mind. More minutes passed quietly by as the rain continued to fall, the sound once soothing and now only a portent of doom.

Checking his watch again, he saw his fifteen minutes were up, so he got up and walked over to the bed and gave Jimmy's foot a gentle shake to wake him.

Before Henry could shake his foot more than once Jimmy bolted upright with his shotgun in his hand, waving it around the room, looking for trouble.

"Easy there, Jimmy, everything's fine," Henry whispered so they wouldn't disturb Mary. "It's your watch, that's all."

"Huh? Oh shit, Henry, why'd you have to wake me up right now? I was having the most beautiful dream."

"Yeah, which one was it, the one when you're a rock star or the one where you find an open McDonalds?"

"It was the McDonalds one, and man was it sweet. Big Macs as far as the eye could see. It was so great."

"Well, I'm happy for you, but how 'bout taking over for me so I can get some rest?"

"Yeah, yeah, take it easy, old man, I got you covered," Jimmy said as he jumped out of bed.

Henry was horizontal before Jimmy even had a chance to fix his clothes, and within a matter of minutes, was snoring softly. Next to him he had laid his 9mm Glock down, and had then slid his sixteen inch panga from its sheath on his hip, just in case there was trouble.

Jimmy smirked at the picture Henry presented and then walked out front to continue watch.

As he walked to the window, he tucked his AC/DC shirt into his green and black camo pants. Then, after a good stretch, he plopped himself down into Henry's chair and stared out the window.

The rain had slowed down and was becoming just a drizzle, the rainwater dripping off the store awning.

Jimmy could see the slight green tint the rainwater had thanks to the bacteria in it.

About a month after they had escaped the first infected town, they had found themselves low on water and close to dying from dehydration. That's when Mary had said they should try boiling the rainwater to see if it would kill the bacteria. Maybe the rainwater wasn't as concentrated as the town's water supply had been.

They were desperate and had nothing to lose, so after they had boiled the water three times, Henry had volunteered to taste it.

To say he was relieved when he didn't feel faint was an understatement. Then the companions had drunk their fill and had quickly boiled more to stock up for later.

Now, as Jimmy watched the small river in the gutter, he thought back to his life before the world went to Hell.

He had been a janitor at a small chemical company in his home town. Nothing great, but it paid the bills. At least until his boss had turned into a raving zombie and tried to kill him.

He had left that job behind and at the time he didn't realize it but he was leaving his old life behind as well.

Then he'd hooked up with Mary and Henry and the three of them had been watching each other's backs ever since.

As Jimmy watched the deserted street, the sun had set for the night, casting the area in a pallid glow only amplified by the wet surfaces. With a heavy sigh he placed the shotgun across his lap and tried to get more comfortable.

Sitting quietly, he checked his watch and frowned when he saw he had at least two more hours before he could trade with Mary and go back to sleep.

Looking into the night sky, the dark clouds hiding the moon and stars, he sat and daydreamed about rock stars and hamburgers.

# CHAPTER TWO

MARY AWOKE TO Jimmy continually shaking her shoulder.

The furniture store was shrouded in gloom, and at first she didn't know where she was. Wiping the sleep from her eyes, bitter reality flooded back to her and she gazed up at him.

"Morning, Jimmy," she smiled wanly. "What time is it?"

"It's about five thirty; time for you to take over so I can grab some more shut-eye."

"Oh, uh sure, okay," she said, still a little groggy. She raised herself to a sitting position and rubbed her eyes some more.

Next to her, Henry was sleeping soundly, and when she stood up from the bed he turned over in his sleep and started snoring again.

Smiling at the picture he made, she got up and walked over to the front window where Jimmy had returned after he knew she was awake.

Walking up behind Jimmy, she placed a hand on his shoulder.

"Just let me pee and then I'll relieve you, okay?" She said as she walked off to the bathroom.

Entering the bathroom, she pulled down her pants and peed as she looked around the tiny room.

On a small table, about twelve inches square, sat a pile of Playboys and Penthouses. She set her gun down on the sink and picked one up and casually thumbed through it to pass the time until she was finished. Inside the magazine was a tall blonde with large breasts who was posed so she would look alluring, yet innocent.

Mary thumbed through a few more pages and then put the magazine back.

Standing up and fixing her clothes, she looked at herself in the mirror.

She turned to look at her breasts from the side as she pushed out her chest; then she let her breasts drop down to their normal position again.

Leaning close to the mirror, she tried to fix her light brown hair, but as she hadn't showered for at least a week she quickly realized it was hopeless.

Standing erect, she tried to wipe some dirt off her cheeks and then retrieved her gun. Despite all these supposed flaws, she was still beautiful, and any man would welcome her to his bed with open arms.

Accepting there was nothing more to do with her appearance, she went back to join Jimmy.

Jimmy was already standing, waiting impatiently, and as she walked up to him he sneered and saluted.

"You have the watch, sir," he said. "I'm going back to bed." Then he walked back to his bed and collapsed onto the mattress.

Mary watched all this with amusement and sat down in the chair Jimmy had vacated, then gazed outside.

She was heartened to see the rain had finally stopped and within the hour the sun would be rising on another day in Hell.

She watched a few birds as they picked their way around the puddles of light green water.

Over the past few months, since everything went to Hell, the animals had learned to avoid the tainted water, and on their travels Mary and the others had spotted sparse wildlife.

A few times they'd had to kill a few animals for food, but usually they were able to scavenge what they needed from small town stores as they made their way across the shattered remains of America.

When everything had fallen apart and the survivors in America had decided their government wasn't going to save them, that they were on their own, a lot of people had barricaded themselves into small towns across the United States.

With makeshift fences compiling anything from barbed wire to two and three cars placed on top of one another, the small towns across America had become small fortresses where strangers weren't welcome and ghouls were shot on sight.

As the three companions made their way north, they had come across some of those forts, but they had also come across some towns where the people were friendly and would welcome you with open arms if you would share some of what you'd seen on your travels.

Most of these people would always want to hear about how the big cities were doing, as that was where most of the undead had congregated after the government fell and the living people had abandoned it for more open pastures. These places where the dead ruled were nicknamed the *deadlands*, and if you found yourself there your life expectancy could be measured within minutes, if not seconds.

Although not all of the walking dead stayed in one place. Many of them would roam across the land looking for fresh meat. These had been nicknamed *roamers* by Henry and the name had soon stuck with the rest of the group, as well.

Roamers would usually travel in groups of at least four or more and they were usually quicker than their slower brethren who stayed in the cities.

But no matter how fast they were, they couldn't outrun a bullet, Mary thought, gently running her finger over the trigger of her small handgun.

Then she caught movement out of the corner of her eye from down the street and she quickly ducked down behind the window frame.

A group of seven roamers were shambling up the street. Every now and then one of them would peel off from the group and check inside a building as its partners would wait. Then, finding nothing, it would emerge and the group would continue on. They were about seven or eight buildings away and at the rate they were moving they would be upon her and her friends in about five minutes or so.

Slowly backing away from the dirty window, she quietly ran over to Henry and gave his leg a shake. He stirred fitfully, but didn't wake up, so she shook his leg again, a little harder than before. This time she was rewarded when his eyes opened and he looked up at her; his vision snapping into focus the second he saw the worried look on her face.

"What's wrong?" He asked as he raised himself to a sitting position and pulled his Glock closer.

"We've got a group of roamers heading towards us. It seems like they're checking buildings as hard as that is to believe. We've got less than five minutes before they get here," she said in a calm voice.

Henry noticed her disposition as she gave her report, but he didn't comment on it. Since he had met the young woman standing before him, he had noticed her slowly becoming harder and tougher over the past few months. While she was still a kindhearted soul, now wouldn't think twice about blasting another human being, whether alive or dead, if said person was threatening her.

Henry stood up and grabbed one of the pillows he'd used for his head and threw it at Jimmy. The pillow landed squarely on top of the younger man's face, and after only a slight pause, Jimmy stirred and sat up.

"Shit, Henry, I just got back to sleep. What's wrong?" He asked in a hoarse whisper while he rubbed his face and eyes.

"We've got a group of roamers heading towards us, got about five minutes at most. Lock and load, just in case. Mary, check the back door on this place, I want to know if we have another way out if we need it. Should have done that earlier, guess I'm getting sloppy."

"Shit, Henry, why don't we just blow the fuckers to Hell and leave it at that?" Jimmy asked as he jumped out of bed and got himself squared away.

"Because ammo doesn't grow on trees, that's why. If you can kill them without wasting bullets, then do it... but don't take chances just to save a bullet."

Jimmy nodded and went off to the front window to see where the roamers were.

Mary returned from the back of the store with a frown across her lips.

"The back doors locked tight. We could probably shoot the lock off, but you know how much noise it would make," Mary told him, looking up front to see Jimmy crouched low to the floor.

"Yeah, but at least we can if we have to. Come on, let's get to the front with Jimmy and see what's gonna happen next.

Mary nodded and the two of them walked to the front where Jimmy was still crouched low with his shotgun sitting on top of his lap.

Jimmy motioned with his head as the group of roamers continued coming their way. All the companions could do is wait and hope their building would be passed over by the ghouls.

As the roamers moved closer to the furniture store, Henry wiped sweat from his forehead. He was always like this before a fight. It was the waiting that always drove him crazy.

The roamers were now standing in front of their building and Henry heard Jimmy curse under his breath when the point ghoul turned and walked directly toward the furniture store door, shambling like a drunk who had just left a bar after last call.

As the door opened, a small bell rang, sending a playful tune across the interior of the furniture store. At one time it would have alerted a salesman a potential customer had entered the store, but now all it did was signal trouble for the three companions.

As the ghoul stumbled into the store, its dead eyes slowly gazed across the room of dust covered furniture. Then it turned to the front window where the three companions had hunkered down to try to stay hidden. As the dead man's eyes opened wider upon his discovery of the three humans, Henry stood up and aimed his Glock at the pale and slack-jawed face.

"We're closed," he stated, as he pulled the trigger of his gun, sending a bullet across the width of the room where it disappeared into the dead man's left eye.

For a fraction of a second after the bullet entered the zombie's head, everything was quiet. Then the back of the skull exploded outwards and covered the brown couch behind the corpse with gore and brain matter.

As the walking corpse fell to the carpeted floor and remained still, Henry looked over to the door to see the other roamers charging into the room. The bell connected to the door continued to ring as the ghouls pushed through the ingress. They flooded into the store to get at the prey within, jostling one another like a bad parody of a Three Stooges movie, their wailing moans filling the store.

When they had all entered the room and were now ready to attack the three companions, the roamers seemed to pause when they saw what was standing in front of them.

Instead of a few cowering humans that they could easily tear apart and kill, they had three people with weapons drawn and legs spread apart in preparation to fire.

The hesitation the roamers felt was only momentary and they charged the three companions.

"Let 'em have it!" Henry snapped as he shot the ghouls on the end of the line.

Mary and Jimmy proceeded to start shooting, too, and within moments, the roamers were dead, or at least out of commission on the blood-soaked, carpeted floor of the furniture store.

Jimmy walked over to one of them as it twitched feebly on the floor. Almost casually, he picked up a marble bust of some Greek God and dropped it onto the ghoul's head. The weight of the marble flattened the head and the body stopped moving while blood and gore leaked out from under the statue where it was quickly soaked up by the rug.

"Come on, we need to go now. If there are others around they surely heard all that gunfire," Henry said as he moved to the window to check the street.

"I'll get our packs," Jimmy said, then stepped over the corpses and went off to the back of the store to retrieve their gear.

Mary stayed with Henry and watched the corpses just in case one wasn't dead. Upon Jimmy's return, the three of them shrugged themselves into their backpacks and slipped out the door.

As they moved quickly down the deserted street, they could now spot other shadowy forms as they came out of hiding, attracted to the sounds of battle.

With guns ready, the three of them moved off down the street until they passed the last building, then they continued down the deserted highway.

Maybe the next town would be better.

As they slowly walked on the yellow line in the middle of the desolate highway, the sun had risen to its full glory and it cast its rays down on the three companions.

At least they could take solace in the fact it was going to be a beautiful day. Meanwhile, behind them, in the shattered city, the newly awaked dead wailed to the same sun, frustrated they had missed their chance at the companions.

## CHAPTER THREE

PAUL WILLIAMS WALKED along the one foot, wooden plank that trailed along the inside of the town's barricade.

The tall, ten foot fence consisted of cinder blocks, old cars and piles of scrap metal. Anything the town's people could get their hands on in a short amount of time.

The barricade went the length of the town's borders from the north to the south and east to west.

It had to.

It was the only thing keeping the small population in the town of Pittsfield, Virginia alive.

When the outside world had gone to Hell, the town of Pittsfield had been in the same boat as everyone else in the United States. The rain had infected nearly half of the town before anyone realized what was happening.

In the next month or so, the populace had banded together and eradicated all the infected ghouls inside the town's limits and had then built their barricade separating them from the outside world.

Early on they realized the rainwater could be boiled clean, and with newly built enclosed greenhouses, were able to produce food for themselves, along with cattle for milk and cheese.

Paul smiled as he gazed out at the deserted highway. They would be all right as long as they worked together.

Movement out of the corner of his eye got his attention and he stopped daydreaming and looked out onto the shoulder of the road.

A group of ghouls had wandered into the area and were now only about fifty feet from the wall. Paul frowned while he watched them shamble across the dead grass as they made their way towards him.

There were five of the poor bastards, Paul saw, and their state of decay differed from corpse to corpse.

The first one in line was little more than a skeleton covered with skin as it shambled across the plain of grass. Its teeth were exposed and the skin of its face had grown tight against the skull. The eyes had receded into their sockets and one of its ears had fallen off due to decay.

The others in the group looked no better and as Paul watched, he noticed the last one in line was carrying something. As the dead man stumbled closer he, was able to make the object out better and he was disgusted to see it was a human head, female by the looks of it.

The face on the head was frozen in agony as it swung from side to side from the ghoul's hand like a gym bag.

Paul felt sympathy for the severed head as he imagined the horror the woman must have suffered in her last minutes on earth. But nothing could be done about it now.

Paul reached down to his hip and retrieved the two-way radio on his belt.

"Hey, Boss, I got me a bunch of walkers heading to the front gate, over," Paul said into the radio.

The radio sent back static for a moment and then a deep voice came through the speaker.

"Yeah, you need help? Over," the voice asked.

"Nah, I got it. Like fish in a barrel, over."

"Okay, but you holler if you need help, over."

"You got it, Boss, over and out."

Paul then reattached the radio to his hip and unslung the rifle from off his back. Setting the barrel of the gun on an outcropping of metal on the barricade, he lined up his first shot.

With the ghoul's head in his sights, he squeezed the trigger, sending a bullet straight into the side of the head.

The bullet struck it just in just in front of its left ear and the corpse stumbled and lost its balance. The force of the bullet threw its head back, twisting in the air, and the body followed as it pitched forward, then rolled onto its back and remained still.

The others in the group seemed to hesitate for a moment as if they realized what was happening.

Paul frowned, he'd been seeing this more lately. It was as if the zombies were becoming more aware of their surroundings. As if they were evolving.

Paul ignored all this and set his gun sights on the next one in line. Firing, he hit the dead woman in the throat. The woman started to gurgle but still she continued toward the wall, so Paul quickly readjusted his aim and fired again.

This time his aim was true and the woman fell to the ground with the top of her head missing.

Paul shot the remaining three ghouls in quick succession and then shouldered his rifle again and picked up the two-way radio, clicking the mike to speak.

"Hey, Boss, I got them all, situation fine, send the cleanup crew whenever you want, over," Paul said into the radio.

After a burst of static, the voice came through loud and clear.

"Good job, Paul, they'll be by shortly, over and out," the voice said.

Paul placed the radio on his hip and continued along the walkway again, feeling good about what he had accomplished.

That was five more walking corpses destroyed that could never harm his friends or family.

* * *

Sam Foree placed the two-way radio back down on his desk and he glanced out his office window at the small town of Pittsfield.

He could see the residents of the town walking back and forth on errands only they knew of, some with a hurried gait.

From his window, the town looked normal, like every other town across the United States. While he watched the postcard picture through his window, it was hard to imagine what was going on outside the borders of his town and across America.

But situations like what Paul had radioed in had a way of slamming reality back into his face.

He let out a weary sigh and raised himself to his full 6'1, one height. He was a big man as well as tall, with broad shoulders from his days as a roofer.

His brown skin was an even darker shade thanks to his time on a thousand rooftops, and the slight stubble on his previously shaved head reflected the sun's rays as they shined into the room.

For the tenth time that morning, he rubbed his hand over his scalp. He hated the feel of the stubble on his head but hadn't had the time to shave again. One of the first things to disappear in the new America was vanity.

He shrugged into the holster he'd retrieved from the coat rack in the corner of the room, grabbing the tan Sheriff's hat, as well.

Placing it on his head, he always felt a small tinge of guilt.

The mayor and sheriff had been one of the first casualties when the rains had come and most of the deputies were just kids who couldn't run a yard sale, let alone a police department.

So when things had gone to Hell, Sam, a natural born leader, had jumped in and taken the reigns of power.

He smiled to himself as he stepped onto Main Street and headed down the street, thinking back to that chaotic day a few months ago.

When everything had gone to crap and he had started ordering people around, they had just fallen in line and obeyed him. Most people were happy to let someone else shoulder the responsibility, and that's what he had done.

Now, he was the unofficial leader of the town and the residents knew he didn't take shit from anyone. About a month ago one of the residents had started making noise about the way he was running things, wanting to start a mutiny and take over.

When Sam had gotten wind of it, he'd immediately gone to the man's home and dragged him out kicking and screaming. Then he had brought him to the city limits and told him if he didn't like the way he was running things, then he could get the hell out.

At the time there had been at least a dozen ghouls gathered around the wall, and once the man saw his fate if he was kicked out of town, he quickly recanted. The cowed man was now a firm supporter of Sam and would do whatever he asked.

Sam rounded a corner and then continued further down the street. He needed to grab a couple of guys for body disposal duty and then he was planning on getting some breakfast.

With a smile on his face, and an extra step in his walk, he continued on his way, happy with the way his life was going and the plans he had in the works for bigger and better things.

# CHAPTER FOUR

THE SUN WAS high in the sky as the three companions made their way down the lonely blacktop of the once busy highway.

While Henry walked on point, he was thinking back to a few miles behind them when they had come across a group of abandoned cars.

The cars had been intertwined in a mass of twisted metal and steel, and from what the three of them could see, most of the cars had been on fire.

When they had looked inside the burnt husks of metal, they had seen the skeletal remains of the passengers. One of the wrecks had been a mini-van and when Mary had peeked inside, she had immediately turned away.

Henry had taken a look to see what had disturbed her and had only grunted at what he'd found.

In the backseat of the van had been a car seat with the remains of a small child still strapped inside.

Henry, too, had turned away, the bitter tableaux tough to see.

True, it was terrible, but there was nothing that could be done now so he'd started to walk down the highway again with Jimmy at his side when he realized Mary wasn't with them.

He turned to see her still standing by the van with her hands on her hips.

Henry stopped walking and turned to look at her.

"What's wrong?" Henry asked simply.

"What's wrong? There's a dead baby in that car, we should bury him," Mary said as she motioned to the van.

"How do you know it's a him?" Jimmy asked.

Mary ignored him.

Henry sighed. "Mary, we've been through this before. We can't bury every corpse we find, there's just too many," he said, trying to reason with her.

When the companions had first started finding bodies on their journey, Mary had felt it was their duty to bury them in the ground out of respect. But when they started finding them by the hundreds, Henry had to make her stop, as it was a waste of valuable time and energy.

She had agreed and for the past few months had been fine… until now.

"Maybe we should at least bury the baby," Jimmy said as he glanced to Henry.

Henry sighed, two against one. They were a democracy so it was pretty much settled. He might as well just accept it so they could get the job done and move on.

"Fine, all right. But just the baby," he said as he walked back to Mary.

Mary's face filled with happiness as she moved to him and kissed Henry on the cheek.

"Thank you," she said and then she was off, with Jimmy helping her.


Twenty minutes later, the three of them were standing over a tiny grave on the shoulder of the highway.

Mary looked at the two men and said: "Thank you both, it just didn't seem right to let him stay there like that. At least now he's at peace."

"At least someone is. So, now that that's done, can we go please?" Henry asked.

Mary nodded and the three of them started down the highway again.

About an hour later a small one-story building came into view in the distance. When they were closer, they could make out a roadside sign standing out in front of the building.

"Mom's Diner, real home cooking," Jimmy said as he read the sign. "Do you think Mom's still around?" He asked the others as he kicked a rock off the road that had gotten into his path.

"We'll soon see," was all Henry said as he walked on.

"I don't care. I could use a break anyway," Mary said from the end of the line.

As the three of them approached the diner, it was painfully apparent Mom probably wasn't there. Almost all of the front windows were broken and the screen door was hanging on by only one hinge as it slapped in the gentle breeze.

Henry was the first one to the door and so was the first inside, with the muzzle of his gun aimed forward while he scanned the small diner.

The diner smelled of rotting meat and urine, but otherwise seemed safe.

He waved the others to follow him in, and with weapons drawn, they entered the diner behind him.

"Seems okay," was all Jimmy said as he sat down on one of the counter chairs, spinning in a circle like a kid waiting for an ice cream cone.

"Hey, Mary, how 'bout rustling us up some grub?" He joked as he spun back and forth on the stool.

"Ha, ha, very funny," Mary said as she walked deeper into the diner.

"Wait a sec', Mary, don't go into the back until we have a chance to secure it," Henry advised as he wandered around the diner.

There were dirty dishes on most of the tables, as if the customers had departed during mid-meal. A few tables still had money sitting under mugs or plates as if the waitress was going to be by any second to collect the bill.

Henry walked around behind the counter and froze at what he saw.

An older woman lay months dead on the floor. There was a nametag on her chest, but there was too much dried blood to make out the name clearly.

Jimmy came up behind him, and when he saw the desiccated corpse, he grinned at Henry.

"You think that's Mom?" He asked.

"Could be, doesn't really matter now, does it?" Henry asked.

"No, suppose not," Jimmy said and then walked past Henry to check out the back of the diner.

When Jimmy walked through the hanging beads separating the front and back of the diner, he had to pause for a second and let his eyes adjust to the gloom.

After a moment, he then proceeded to do a little exploring. Spider webs were everywhere as he moved through the back room. There didn't seem to be anything relevant and he was about to go back up front when he heard a soft scraping sound coming from the far back of the room.

He was about to call to Henry and Mary when he heard it again. Curious, he quietly walked to the rear of the room, pushing spider webs out of his path with the barrel of his shotgun.

Once at the back, he saw a door was closed with the words bathroom stenciled in black across the door.

"Oh, no, you don't, not again," he said; remembering something that had happened a few months ago in an abandoned gas station the companions had stopped at for the night.

Backing up slowly, he turned and headed to the front of the diner to inform Henry and Mary what he'd discovered.

\*    \*    \*

"I don't see why we have to do anything," Henry said, chewing on a piece of jerky from his backpack. "If it's locked up then leave it be."

"Yeah," Jimmy said. "But what about the next poor bastard who comes through here? Do you want them to get attacked?"

"Your talking hypothetical here, Jimmy. It's possible no one else will even come through here. Why should we waste bullets on it if it's not threatening us?" Mary asked while she sipped from their meager supplies of water.

"Well fuck you both very much. If you don't want to do anything about it, then I will."

"Look, Jimmy, I don't agree with you, but you're a big boy. If you want to do something, then do it," Henry said blandly.

"Fine, I will." Then Jimmy stormed off to the back of the diner.

After a minute or so had passed, Mary looked at Henry like a mother talking about her child.

"Would you at least go watch his back? He might get into trouble and I don't want anything to happen to him," she pleaded.

Henry sighed and nodded yes.

Picking his Glock off the counter, he casually walked to the back of the diner to help Jimmy, but when he got there unfortunately he was already too late to help.

# CHAPTER FIVE

FUMING WITH ANGER at being ignored, Jimmy walked to the back of the diner and once again gave his eyes a moment to adjust. Then he went back to the bathroom door and stood perfectly still, listening. It was quiet at the moment, so he raised his hand to the door and knocked on it.

"Hello, is anyone in there?" He asked in a squeaky voice he didn't want to admit was his.

The scratching on the door grew louder and he jumped back, startled, but when the door showed no signs of opening, he walked back to it.

He knocked again, and when the scratching began again, he didn't jump away.

Instead, he cocked his shotgun and moved his left hand to the doorknob.

Grasping the knob tightly, he took three quick breaths to psych himself up. When he was ready, he pulled the door open and jumped back, expecting a bloodthirsty zombie to jump out at him.

But that was not what he found.

Instead of facing, a blood-thirsty, animalistic, animated corpse, he found himself gazing down at the most pathetic zombie he had ever seen.

In life the ghoul had to be pushing ninety, and as it stumbled out of the bathroom, it still used the aluminum walker it had used in life.

Its pants were down by its ankles, dragging on the ground, as it shuffled out of the bathroom an inch at a time. When it took more than a minute for the ghoul to cross a foot, Jimmy realized the danger was minimal and lowered his shotgun. Amusingly he thought that if he smoked, he would have had plenty of time for a cigarette as the senior citizen ghoul slowly made its way across the room.

After a few seconds more had passed, Jimmy realized he might as well end this charade, so he walked up to the geriatric zombie and slammed the stock of his shotgun into the old guy's forehead.

The brittle bone collapsed under the force of the blow and the ghoul fell back into the bathroom where it landed back on the toilet, now forever taking its last dump.

Jimmy closed the door with his foot and then saw a sign on some boxes to the side of the door. Picking up the sign, he hung it on a small nail set about head-height on the front of the door.

OUT OF ORDER it said.

Jimmy smiled to himself.

That just about said it all.

He turned to go back out front when Henry walked into the back room.

"Everything all right?" He asked, surveying the room.

"Yeah, thanks for coming, but it was a false alarm," he said as he pushed by Henry to join Mary out front.

Henry stood there for a moment and glanced at the closed bathroom door with the sign on it. Then with a shrug of his shoulders, he turned to head out front, wanting to join Mary and Jimmy.

*     *     *

When Henry joined the others, he saw they were hunkered down over a map.

"It seems if we keep going down the highway the next town is Pittsfield," Mary said, looking up as Henry joined them.

"Pittsfield, never heard of it," Henry said as he sat on a stool next to the others.

"I wonder how they fared after all the shit went down," Jimmy asked in a rhetorical question.

Henry answered him anyway. "We'll find out soon enough. I'd say we'll be there before nightfall if we keep a good pace."

"It'd be nice to find a car that works just once, my feet are killing me," Jimmy complained as he walked around the counter again.

Shuffling around for a while, he came up with a few things of interest. He quickly made them disappear into his pockets as he went to explore some more.

Henry looked at Mary as she studied the map. She had become the daughter he had never had and he cared for her deeply. Even with her face covered in road dust, she was still beautiful.

She looked up and caught him staring and gave him a smile.

"What? What are you looking at?" She asked him.

"Nothing," he smiled back. "Just thinking of the roads we've traveled together."

She placed her hand on his and looked into his eyes.

"You've done good by us, Henry. I don't even know what I would've done without you," she said. Her eyes looked like she was going to start crying so he stood up and kissed her on the forehead. Then he changed the subject.

"Come on. Lets see what that idiot is up to and then we can go," he said as he rounded the counter.

Mary followed and the two went to the back to find Jimmy.


Jimmy was in absolute Heaven.

Buried under a bunch of empty boxes had been a box of candy bars that been unnoticed until now.

He had one in his mouth already, and with a big smile on his face, was shoving the bars into his pockets; then he picked up the box and was about to go back out front when Henry and Mary walked in.

With his mouth covered in melted chocolate like a clown's makeup, he smiled at his two friends.

"Look what I found," he garbled around a mouthful of chocolate.

Henry started to laugh and soon Mary caught it, too.

With the two of them laughing, Jimmy just stood there.

"What?" He muffled around the chocolate bar. "I like candy." The two of them just continued to laugh.

# CHAPTER SIX

THE THREE COMPANIONS had been on the road for hours, the diner far behind them.

While they walked, they would frequently slow down and look into derelict cars scattered across the highway.

Sometimes there would be corpses inside, long dead and other times they would be empty, as if the owner had stopped to take a piss on the side of the road and had never returned.

Although some had keys in them, the gas tanks and batteries were always dried up.

Not that it mattered anyway. No sooner would the companions find a vehicle that worked, but within a matter of a few miles they would have to abandon it due to some form of wreckage on the highway.

The metal islands blocking the roads were like sandbars in shallow water. Just when you had your sail up and were moving... Bam, you'd hit a sandbar and would jar to a halt; probably damaging your vessel in the process.

Henry slowed his pace as he walked by an old Honda.

It was sitting on the side of the road with a flat tire and a rotting corpse lying next to it, a lug wrench still in its skeletal hand. Inside the car, sitting in the passenger seat, was the remains of a woman, her purse still clutched in her hands protectively.

Henry thought he could piece together what had happened.

This man had gotten a flat and had to pull over and change it. Probably sometime before he was able to accomplish his task, he was attacked and killed.

Probably from a walking corpse, but then again it could easily have been other humans who decided they wanted what he'd had. Then the attackers had killed the woman, as well.

Either way was irrelevant now. Henry watched the gentle breeze blow dust into the corpse's face; then he had to turn away.

The three continued on and walked by a small panel truck that Henry felt the need to investigate. The side of the truck had the words, Sheehan Construction, splashed across the side in bold black letters.

Stepping up to the driver's window, Henry looked inside to see the desiccated corpse of a man sitting behind the wheel.

Opening the door, the body fell out and landed at his feet, nothing more than a puff of dust from the loose soil to mark its landing.

Henry stepped back and covered his nose as the smell from inside the cab assaulted him.

"Wow, that's ripe," he said, waving his hand in front of his face.

"Anything worth taking?" Jimmy asked from a few feet behind him.

"Nah, empty except for him," Henry said as he nudged the corpse with his boot.

"What about the back?" Mary suggested from the middle of the highway.

Henry shrugged. "Sure, why not."

Reaching inside the truck, he pulled the keys from the ignition, and with a jingle, carried them to the back of the truck.

"Jimmy, watch my back," Henry told him, trying a few different keys until one slid into the lock with a soft scrape of metal.

Jimmy nodded, understanding.

While the truck should be empty, in today's America if you let your guard down for even a second it could end up being your last.

With his shotgun in his right hand, Henry reached out with his left and squeezed the button on the door.

Pulling it open, he was pleased to see it was indeed empty. He let out the breath he didn't realize he was holding and peeked inside the truck.

There was an assortment of tools and supplies scattered around the floor, but nothing of real interest to Henry.

Mary had come up behind him and poked her head inside, as well, curiosity getting the better of her.

"What's in there? What's that?" She asked, pointing to a two-foot box that was partially covered by a blanket.

"I have no idea. Tell you the truth; I didn't even notice it until now, good eyes, Mary."

She smiled at the compliment. "Thanks, it's all the carrots I eat."

"Oh, that's bullshit. I've heard eating carrots has nothing to do with helping your eyesight," Jimmy spat, jokingly.

"You know, Jimmy, my mother used to say if you don't have anything nice to say then shut the hell up," Mary quipped back.

Jimmy was about to retort back when Henry spoke up. "All right already, enough, please. I swear, sometimes you two are like brother and sister. Jimmy, come here and help me with this. Now I'm curious what's inside," he said as he pulled the blanket off the box.

Jimmy moved closer, climbed inside the truck and grabbed the side of the box. Together, the two men dragged the wooden container to the edge.

Then, with the agility of youth, Jimmy hopped back to the ground while Henry used a screwdriver to pry open the lid.

With a clatter and a puff of dust, the lid popped off and fell to the metal floor.

Looking inside, Henry took one look at the contents and started to back away.

Jimmy saw his movements and looked inside.

In the box, in neat little rows, one on top of the other, were sticks of dynamite.

"Whoa, that's great, dynamite! Just think of the damage we could do with this!" Jimmy yelled as his eyes took in the treasure.

"Get the hell away from there, you idiot. That shit could blow at any second!" Henry yelled.

"What? What are you talking about? Looks fine to me," Jimmy said, reaching inside to pick up a stick.

"No, wait!" Henry yelled. The terror in his voice was enough to make Jimmy hesitate.

"Dude, what is the big deal?" Jimmy asked.

"Jimmy, do you see those drops on the sides of the sticks? They look like dew drops."

"Yeah, what about them?"

"Well, those drops mean the dynamite is sweating…and listen to this, Jimmy. They're sweating nitroglycerine."

"Oh my God," Mary said as she put her hands to her mouth and stepped back another few feet herself.

"Jimmy, for the love of God, do what Henry says," she pleaded.

Jimmy just nodded and stepped away from the truck. As an afterthought, he slowly closed the panel truck's doors, as if that might save him if the dynamite went off. With sweat now covering his brow, Jimmy slowly stepped back, somehow thinking if his footfalls were too heavy that could set the explosives off too.

Within the space of a few tense heartbeats, Jimmy had backed up and was now standing next to Henry.

"Wow, that was close. I think I just shit my pants," Jimmy said to himself.

Henry looked at him and stepped back another step.

Jimmy noticed this and frowned. "Relax, old man, I was speaking hypothetically."

"Uh huh. Good to know. What do you say we move on?" Henry said, turning to start down the highway.

Mary nodded yes and smiled, Jimmy just shrugged.

Together, the three started off again, leaving the panel truck behind.


The sun was just beginning to set when they spotted light in the distance.

The three of them stopped in the middle of the highway and looked off into the distance to see small flickering lights.

"That must be Pittsfield," Henry said, watching the tiny lights flicker like fireflies.

"You think they're friendly?" Jimmy asked.

"We'll see soon enough," Henry said as he started walking again.

Mary caught up to him and asked: "I wonder how they fared so close to the capital. Richmond had a large population."

"Like I just said, we'll see soon enough," Henry said, continuing to slog along.

After another hour of walking, with dusk falling across the austere landscape, the barricade of cars, stone and metal came into view. They could see that the lights they had seen from a distance were torches flickering atop the ten foot barricade, and as they moved closer, they could see at least two men were on watch.

When they were no more than fifty feet away from the wall, a voice called out from above.

"That's far enough, strangers, what do you want?" The voice said. The face was shrouded in shadows, but the rifle barrel was in plain view as the light from the torches danced on the metal.

"Ah, hello there, we're just some travelers looking for shelter for the night," Henry said.

"Is that all of you, just the three?" The voice asked.

"That's right, just the three of us," Henry repeated.

The voice was silent for a moment and then it came back again.

"I'm sorry, mister, but we don't have any room for you. Our resources are already stretched to the breaking point."

Henry frowned in the dark as he tried to keep the anger he now felt out of his voice.

"Okay, fine, but can we have passage through your town to the other side? If you haven't noticed, you're blocking the only thoroughfare in the area," Henry said.

The rifle barrel pointed across the open area of grass to the right of the barricade.

"Just follow that ridge for a few miles and you'll come to another road. Follow that road and it will take you past our town. Then the road will meet up with the highway in another couple of miles."

"Are you fucking serious? We're not going that far out of our way just because you..." Henry stopped Jimmy from saying anymore with a firm hand on his shoulder.

"That will be fine, sir. I thank you for your time and we'll be on our way," Henry said as he gently shoved Jimmy off the road and across the field.

When they were out of earshot, Jimmy stopped Henry and yelled at him.

"What the hell was that about, old man? Now we have to walk for miles thanks to those assholes."

"Yeah, and what exactly were you going to do to get us in there? They had the high ground and could have blasted us to Hell and back whenever they felt like it. At least they let us go. Better to walk a few extra miles than to end up eating dirt," Henry said as he glared at Jimmy with his jaw clenched tight.

Jimmy waited a second, and before he could answer, Mary put a hand on his shoulder.

"He's right, you know. They had us where they wanted us. They could have killed us and taken our weapons. At least they let us go," Mary said soothingly.

Jimmy sighed as the fight went out of him.

"Yeah, I guess you're right, it just sucks, you know?"

"Yeah, Jimmy I know," Henry agreed. "Let's go, we've got a little ground to cover before we set up camp for the night."

Jimmy nodded and then the three started off across the dried plain of grass.

About an hour later, Henry called a halt. It was pitch black around them, the moon and stars shrouded by the clouds overhead.

There was no way they could see what was waiting for them across the plain, so he decided it was time to set camp for the night.

Within a matter of minutes, they had gathered enough wood for a small campfire.

Henry dug a small hole in the ground for the fire so the light wouldn't be spotted from a distance. It was so dark the smoke wouldn't be a problem.

As they sat down and ate rations of jerky and bottled water, they looked up at the night sky.

Jimmy was taking first watch and had wandered away as he patrolled the area.

Henry and Mary sat quietly together until Mary broke the silence.

"Hey, Henry," she asked quietly. "Do you ever think we'll find someplace where the infection isn't so bad? You know, a place where we could live for good."

Henry watched as the light of the fire reflected off her eyes. She looked like the fires of Hell were burning inside of her.

"I truly don't know, Mary. But what choice do we have? Even if we stayed at one of the town's we've visited, sooner or later we'd have to go. You see how the people look at us. We're outsiders. They always want us gone as fast as they can get rid of us. The world has changed and charity to others isn't part of it anymore." He tossed a twig into the fire, the flames lapping at it greedily.

"I admit some of the town's we've been through have been nice, but I could always feel the tension from the people there. As if they were counting the minutes until they could get rid of us."

Mary stared at the flames almost as if she was in a trance. Then, in the dim light, Henry saw her nod yes.

"I know what you mean, Henry, I've felt it, too."

"Okay then, have I answered your question?" He asked.

"Yes, I guess so, I can't say I like the answer, though," she said.

"I know, honey, neither do I. What do you say we get some rest?" He asked her.

"Sure, that sounds good," she replied, yawning.

The two of them stretched out to sleep, secure in the fact Jimmy had their backs.


Henry was dreaming about his dead wife, Emily.

In the dream, she was alive and happy. They had just purchased their first house, and as they walked through the front door with the keys in his hand, she turned and kissed him hard on the mouth.

"Oh, Henry, I love it, it's so beautiful," she said, dancing through the kitchen.

"I know, hon', me, too," he said as he walked behind her.

He looked at the living room carpet and then pulled her to him with a sly grin.

"Come here, you, I want to christen the living room," he said as he pulled her close and then picked her up and carried her onto the carpeting.

She kicked her feet as if she didn't want to go, but Henry could tell it was all a show.

He gently laid her down and the two of them made love in their brand new house for the first time.

Then, like most men, he found himself drifting off to sleep. A moment later he felt his shoulder being shaken and when he opened his eyes, he came back to reality.

He looked up into Jimmy's face. He could barely see him, the darkness now enveloping the area completely now that the fire was out.

"Hey, man, it's your watch," Jimmy said from the darkness.

Henry nodded, then figuring Jimmy couldn't see him, said: "Okay, Jimmy, just let me take a piss and I'll take over for you."

"Sure, Henry, take your time, just as long as you hurry," Jimmy said with a wide grin lost in the shadows.

Henry smiled in the dark, too.

That Jimmy, always with the wisecracks.

He raised himself to his feet, and after a moment to gain his equilibrium, went off to pee. Three minutes later he returned and slapped Jimmy on the back.

"You're relieved, my friend, go get some sleep," Henry told him.

Jimmy looked at his shoulder where Henry had slapped him.

"I hope you washed your hands," he said. Then, before Henry could reply, he walked off.

"Relax, Henry I'm just yankin' your chain," Jimmy joked.

Henry just stood still in the dark. Then after a minute, he started off on a tight patrol surrounding their campsite.

Luckily it was an uneventful night, and as the sun slowly began its rise, he could see at least it was going to be a beautiful day.


Mary stirred on the ground and looked up at Henry as he stood over her.

"Why's it light out? I didn't stand watch," she said; her voice hoarse from sleep.

"That's okay, Mary. I wasn't tired so I just took your watch, too. You don't mind do you?" Henry asked her.

"What do you think?" She snickered. "Thanks, Henry, that was nice of you."

"Don't mention it," he said, giving Jimmy a gentle nudge with his boot to wake him.

Jimmy moaned on the ground and buried his head in his arms.

"Come on, man, five more minutes," he pleaded.

"Fine," Henry said. "But you better get up when I come back."

Henry walked off to the top of the gentle hill they were on. In the dark, they had no idea what was in front of them, but as the sun rose into the morning sky the way was now perfectly clear.

About a thousand feet away was a road. The same road the guard had told them about the night before. All they had to do was follow it and by the afternoon they would be around their detour and on their way.

Then Henry caught movement on the other side of the road.

As he squinted in the morning glare, he could make out about ten people or so coming from the shoulder of the road.

He waited patiently as they moved closer, and when he was able to see them better, his heart skipped a beat.

"Shit," he said, "roamers." And they'd seen him.

He turned and ran as fast as he could to the others. When he was only fifty feet away, he whistled high and long.

Jimmy had heard that whistle before in the past few months. If Henry was whistling in the middle of nowhere, where anyone could hear, then they had trouble.

Like a coiled spring, he jumped up and was on his feet just as Henry ran up to him. Mary had heard the whistle, too, and was just now arriving from where she had gone for a morning bathroom break.

"Come on, boys and girls, we need to move now. There're at least ten roamers headed our way!" Henry spit out as he ran up to the two of them.

"Shit, really?" Jimmy looked around at the open plain they were on. "Where the fuck are we gonna go?"

Henry set his jaw as he looked at the two of them.

"We're not going anywhere. I say we take them on and go straight through them," he said. "What do you say?"

"I say, why not. I mean, we have nowhere to run, right? What choice do we have?" Mary said, looking at Jimmy.

"Shit, you know my answer. I'm always up for an excuse to kill a deader, and you both know that," Jimmy said as he looked at Henry.

"Yeah, that's what I figured. All right then, let's move; they'll be here in a few minutes," Henry told them, retrieving his backpack from the ground.

"They'll be here sooner than that; look," Mary said, pointing to Henry's back trail.

"Shit, they moved faster than I thought. Okay, people, let's get it together...and be careful," Henry said, moving off to the side of the others to give them a clear field of fire.

The walkers shambled down the slight incline, picking up speed. Mary and Jimmy fanned out so the roamers had to split up.

Three went after each of them with an extra one going for Mary.

Henry was the first to shoot, but as his gun echoed across the plain it was soon followed by Jimmy's shotgun and Mary's 22.

Henry's first bullet took a ghoul in the shoulder. The dead woman swiveled on her waist from the force of the bullet, but then regained her balance and continued on. Henry swore under his breath. He knew it was the head or nothing. Now he had wasted a bullet that he could never get back and there could come a time where that one bullet was the difference between life and death.

He lined up his second shot and took the roamer in her face. As she fell to the ground, he ignored her, and focused on his next target. He lined it up and slowed his breathing, then squeezed the trigger.

The bullet struck its mark exactly where Henry wanted it to and the back of the second roamer's head blew out and sprayed across the grass. The corpse dropped to the ground, dead again before it even realized it. Then Henry calmly lined up the last ghoul in his area, and with an almost casual pull of the trigger, sent a lead package special delivery into the zombie's brain pan.

As the corpse fell to the ground, Henry had already forgotten about it and was checking on his friends.

Jimmy was doing fine. He had waited for the two walkers to get a little closer so as to maximize the stopping power of the shotgun.

When the first ghoul had come into range, he had fired from the hip, sending the shotgun's payload directly at the dead man's neck. The spray severed the head from the body, and as the head fell to the grass, the body kept right on going.

Jimmy sidestepped it and the headless corpse actually continued on for a few more feet until its muscles realized there was nothing to tell them what to do. Then the corpse fell over, landing with a soft rustle in the grass.

Jimmy didn't even notice, already lining up the other two roamers.

He noticed they were walking close together, so decided he'd save himself a shell and do them both at once.

Running at them, he swung sideways and held the shotgun high on his shoulder. Then, when he was only a few feet from them, he squeezed the trigger. The payload went straight at their heads and caught both ghouls at the same time.

Faces disintegrated in a splatter of bone and gore as the two corpses fell to the earth, entangled in each other's limbs.

Before they hit the grass, Jimmy was already moving to check on Mary, but as he took in the scene in front of him, he already knew he would be too late to help her.

# CHAPTER SEVEN

MARY HAD FANNED off to the bottom of the slope as the roamers came at her. She frowned when she saw the fourth one turn and go after her, as well.

Figures, she thought, she was the one with the smallest weapon and she had to get the most walkers to play with.

She brought her .22 up to eye level and lined up the first ghoul in her gun sights. She squeezed the trigger, and a moment later watched as the body pitched to the ground with a bullet in its eye.

As quick as she could, she lined up the second body and fired. The bullet struck its cheek, but ricocheted away from the brain. Although the face was a bloody mess, the zombie still continued toward her.

Trying to stay calm, she fired another round at its head, this time hitting it in the forehead. The corpse slumped to the grass and remained still.

She let out a breath, two down and two to go. The only problem was they were moving faster than she would have liked. She continued to backpedal over the uneven ground so they wouldn't overtake her.

She really wished she could have gone back in time just a few minutes when she had agreed to take these roamers on, but it was too late now, so she sighted the next one and fired the .22. The bullet struck the ghoul a grazing blow across the side of the head, taking its right ear off as the bullet flew by it and disappeared in the slope behind the walker.

Mary continued to back step as she tried again to shoot the ghoul. Meanwhile, the last one had gone wide around her and was now coming up from her side. She knew she couldn't hit both in time so she continued with the one she'd nicked and hoped Henry or Jimmy would be there to help with the other one.

Slowing her breathing the way Henry had taught her, she lined up the third walking corpse and fired. The small .22 bullet hit the ghoul in the nose and then continued on into its brain, where it bounced around; turning the brain to mush.

The zombie fell to the ground, but Mary was already turning to the last one, and as she raised her gun, she knew she wouldn't make it.

She squeezed the trigger at the same time the dead man lunged at her, only managing to shoot him in the upper chest. The man didn't even flinch as he pushed her to the ground, his teeth going for her throat. She tried to push the jaw away but the ghoul had once been a large man and he still had most of his body mass.

As his brown and bloody teeth prepared to sink into her throat, she did the only thing she could.

She jammed her gun into his mouth, but due to the odd position she was in, the gun went in so that the top was in his mouth instead of the barrel.

As she tried to fight the dead man off, she instinctually squeezed the trigger of her gun. The bullet shot out of the barrel and went across her face, just barely missing her nose. Then the bullet caught a piece of her left arm and lodged in the dirt beneath her.

She screamed with the pain of the gunshot, her nerves telling her brain what had happened, and she felt herself feeling faint as shock set in.

Her arm felt wet and she was getting weaker from blood loss with each passing second, and just when she thought it was over for her, Henry came charging at her with a yell. Tackling the dead man and throwing him off her.

She just lay there, trying to catch her breath, while Henry rolled off the man, put his Glock to the ghoul's head, and pulled the trigger.

The back of the head disappeared in a spray of blood and brains, the body falling to the ground, neutralized.

Now Jimmy was next to her and when he saw the blood on her arm, he immediately ripped off his shirt and tied it into a hasty tourniquet.

She looked up as the two of them looked down on her, then before she could say anything, she felt herself slipping into the darkness.

She tried to fight it, but knew it was hopeless. As the darkness overtook her, she could only hope Heaven was where it was supposed to be.

Then she knew no more.


Jimmy stared down at Mary as Henry cinched the tourniquet tighter.

"Oh, shit, Henry, is she gonna be all right?" He asked, the panic obvious in his voice.

Henry adjusted the tourniquet until he was satisfied and then glanced up at Jimmy's worried face.

"I honestly don't know, Jimmy. She's lost a lot of blood," he said, standing up.

His hands were warm and slippery from Mary's blood as he tried to clean them on the grass. He was pretty sure the bullet had hit an artery on its passage through her arm. But he could take solace in the fact that one of the ghouls hadn't bit her.

Although a person wouldn't turn into a zombie if bit by one of them, the sheer amount of bacteria and viruses in the walking dead bodies was enough to kill an average man in less than a week; unless antibiotics were administered almost immediately. Unfortunately, with the condition the United States was presently in, that would be highly unlikely.

Jimmy broke Henry out of his thoughts.

"I said, what are we gonna do?"

Henry mulled it over for a few moments and then looked at Jimmy.

"There's really only one thing we can do. We're going back to Pittsfield, and by God this time they're gonna help us," he said coldly.

Jimmy saw the determination in Henry's eyes and nodded. "Okay then, let's get to it."

With their course decided, the two men got to work on a stretcher for Mary. After finding some suitable branches from some nearby trees, they used the clothes from the dead roamers to manufacture a makeshift stretcher.

Henry looked down at it and smiled at Jimmy.

"It doesn't have to look pretty, it just has to work."

Jimmy nodded slightly in agreement and together they gently placed her on to it and picked her up and headed off across the grassy plain again to Pittsfield.

They didn't know what kind of welcome they would get there the second time around, but Henry knew if they could help, then by God Himself, he would make them.

## CHAPTER EIGHT

PAUL WILLIAMS WAS on watch again, and his eyebrows went up in surprise when he looked up and saw two men walking over the grassy plain toward the barricade, with what looked like a stretcher with someone on it.

Keeping his weapon ready, he patiently waited while the men traversed over the rugged ground.

When they were in earshot, he called out to them.

"That's far enough, fellas, state your business."

"State my business? I'll tell you what my goddamn business is. Last night my friends and I came here seeking shelter and we were told to fuck off. Early this morning we were attacked by a large group of roamers and my friend was shot.

She's pretty bad and we need help for her. So either let us in or shoot us now in cold blood because we're not taking no for an answer."

"What's a roamer?" Paul asked as he looked down from the shelter of his barricade.

"What's a roamer?" Henry yelled. "It's a friggin' zombie, you stupid bastard. Now, open that goddamn gate so we can get our friend some help."

"Damn straight," Jimmy added.

Paul mulled it over for a few seconds and then decided to call it in.

"Gimme a minute, guys. I'm gonna call this in to base and tell them what's up."

"Yeah, son, you do that," Henry said with a grimace.

Every second of the clock was a second Mary didn't have.

Getting on the radio, Paul called Sam. When Sam answered, he told him what had happened and then waited for a reply.

While this was going on, Henry and Jimmy waited impatiently in the barren street. Henry noticed a few splashes of dried blood on the pavement, residue from a past fight. Whether the owners of the blood had been living or undead was unknown, and at the moment, he didn't care.

Both men were fingering their weapons nervously as they waited for an answer from above. If the man on the barricade said no, then there was going to be blood spilled, the only question being whose it would be.

After only a few minutes, which seemed like hours to Henry, Paul stuck his head over the barricade.

"My boss says you can come in, but you have to relinquish your weapons," Paul said in a tone that said there would be no discussion on the matter.

"Fine, just open the damn gate and help my friend," Henry said, walking closer to the entrance.

Paul's head disappeared, and for a moment Henry wondered if it had all been for show. Then he heard the rumble of an automobile engine, and when the gate went up, Henry could see it was attached to a small car by metal chains.

Henry and Jimmy quickly entered the barricade with Mary between them, and once they were inside, the car backed up and the heavy metal gate settled into its slot again.

Henry and Jimmy were immediately surrounded by three men, including Paul, and as they stood there, Paul motioned for them to place the stretcher on a small cart that was off to the side. Henry wondered if it was a golf cart as it certainly fit the bill.

But as Henry and Jimmy walked over to the small vehicle, Henry could make out the shield and crest of the town of Pittsfield on the side of the cart, and when he saw the small, blue light on the top of it, he figured it was once used by meter maids.

After they had set Mary down, Paul politely asked for their weapons. After the two warriors handed them over, he motioned for them to get into the cart.

Then Paul hopped into the driver's seat and turned on the cart.

The cart shot forward and only Henry's grip on the stretcher prevented it from falling to the ground. Another security man ran alongside them as they traveled the quarter mile to the town itself.

When they entered the town, Henry was impressed to see how clean the streets were. Some of the towns they had been to were nothing more than hovels, where you had to wade through piles of trash to get from place to place.

This town looked like it had come from a drugstore postcard of yesteryear.

Driving down the middle of the street, Henry and Jimmy noticed the townspeople as they moved with purpose on the sidewalks, all wearing clean, well kept clothes. Once you were here in the town, you would never imagine what was going on just a mile away on the other side of the barricade.

The cart slowed and stopped at a small, one-story brick building. There was a sign hanging from a post that said: Doctor Maxwell Robinson HOURS from 10-2.

"Here we are." Paul said, climbing out of the cart.

Henry and Jimmy hopped out as well and picked up Mary. Then the two of them carried her into the building while Paul held the door.

Once inside, Henry's nose was immediately assaulted by the odor of antiseptic. As they carried Mary further into the building, Henry was impressed by the state of appearances.

The room he was in was clean and tidy with a small table in the waiting room for magazines. Henry would bet anything the most recent magazine would be dated about three months ago.

As he was led into a small room off the waiting room, Paul motioned for them to set Mary down on the table, then he bid them farewell with a polite reminder that there was a guard at the front of the building, waiting on them.

"You have nothing to worry about, pal. We're not going anywhere without our friend," Henry told him.

"Of course you aren't," he said with a smile. "I'll be back later to retrieve you when you know your friend is better. The boss wants to meet you, too."

Then he left the building.

Jimmy followed Paul to the door, and as it opened he peeked outside, and sure enough, there was a man with a rifle standing on the stairs. He saw Paul talking to the guard for a moment and then the door swung closed.

Jimmy returned to Henry.

"The guy's telling the truth, there's a guard out front," Jimmy said.

"Doesn't matter, we're not leaving without Mary," Henry said. Then he looked up as a small man in his late sixties or early seventies entered the room.

"Good afternoon, gentlemen. My name is Doctor Robinson. How may I be of service to you?" The little man asked as he fixed his small, wire rimmed glasses.

"Hi, Doctor, our friend Mary was shot. I think an artery was hit, we need your help," Henry informed him.

Dr. Robinson stepped over to Mary and checked the tourniquet. The second he released it a stream of blood shot out. He quickly tied it back down and looked at the two men.

"My, you were right. It is an artery that's damaged."

As he held her wrist in his hand, he looked at the two men.

"Her pulse is weak, but steady. Whichever one of you put this tourniquet on did well. You probably saved her life."

"What do you mean by probably, Doc? Is she gonna make it?" Jimmy asked.

The Doctor pushed them out of the room as he called for his nurse.

"My son, I learned long ago that there are no certainties in medicine. But your friend looks strong. I promise you I'll do my best. Now, please, let me get to work, your friend doesn't have the time for us to talk," he said.

Henry and Jimmy went to the waiting room and sat down. Henry caught one quick glimpse as the nurse carried in the instruments the doctor needed to operate and then the door closed.

Although every fiber of his being wanted to be in there with her, he knew he had to just sit and wait.

As if Jimmy had read his mind, he looked up at the clock and said: "Shit, man, I'd rather face a hundred roamers than just sit here waiting for something to happen."

Henry just nodded, the two of them starting their silent vigil for Mary.

## CHAPTER NINE

AFTER THE FIRST hour of sitting in the waiting room, Henry felt himself nodding off, as the night before and the morning's activities finally caught up to him.

As he drifted off to sleep, he dreamed of Mary.

In his dream, she was wearing a yellow summer dress; her hair blowing gently in the wind.

After a moment he realized he was on a cliff overlooking an ocean. Mary walked up to him and placed her hand on his cheek.

"Mary, I'm so sorry you were hurt. I promised you I would never let anything happen to you."

"It's all right, Henry," she smiled. "I'm going to be fine. You have to have faith."

"Faith? In what? Certainly not in a God who would let what has happened to the world happen."

"That's beside the point. You have to have faith in yourself...and your friends," she said, seeming to float around him like a wisp of smoke.

"Hell, Mary, all I do is have faith these days. What's left?" He asked her as she seemed to drift away. "Wait, come back! I'm not through talking with you!" He called as she drifted out of his reach.

"Just believe in yourself and you'll be fine," she said, seeming to disappear into thin air.

Henry stared at the spot where she had just been and pondered what she'd said.

At first he thought everything was all right, but then the spot Mary had left coalesced into something else, something nightmarish and evil. He had the vague sense he was staring into the depths of Hell and a chill ran down his spine.

Then he heard Jimmy calling his name and he woke up to see Doctor Robinson and Jimmy standing over him. Pushing the feeling of dread suffusing him, he glanced at the clock on the wall and was shocked to see over two hours had passed since he'd sat down.

"Wow, I guess I fell asleep. How's Mary?" He asked to whoever would answer him.

"She's going to be fine." Doctor Robinson said, taking off his glasses and polishing them on his new, white smock. "She's sleeping now and I want her to stay that way. The artery was torn from the path of the bullet, but I was able to repair it. She needs to rest and should be fine in a couple of days. In the mean time, you have been requested to see the man in charge. Someone will be here to escort you there in a few minutes," Doctor Robinson said and then turned to leave the room.

"Hey, Doc," Jimmy called to him.

The little man turned around and looked at him. "Yes?"

"Thanks again. You saved a good woman in there," Jimmy told him.

Doctor Robinson smiled. "That's good then, because as you know, good people are in short supply these days." Then he exited the room.

Jimmy looked at Henry and smiled. "Lucky bastard, you got to sleep through the whole thing while I've been wearing out the damn floor."

Henry looked remorseful and looked at his boots.

"Sorry, Jimmy, it wasn't planned, I swear," he apologized.

Jimmy was about to reply when a guard walked in and waved them to the door.

"I was told to bring you to see the Boss," he said in a matter-of-fact tone, stepping back to let the two deadlands warriors exit the building.

"Sure, why not. I don't seem to have any other pressing engagements at the moment," Jimmy joked as they walked through the door and onto the street.

Once outside, they were greeted by another golf cart. The guard motioned them inside and the two of them climbed on.

The cart took off with a jump and they were on their way.

As the cart drove down the street, Henry noticed how people would jump out of their way with what looked like fear in their eyes, and how the driver didn't even try to slow down to avoid them.

If the pedestrians didn't move fast enough, Henry was pretty sure the driver would have hit them.

While he watched, his assumption was about to be proven correct when an old man tried to get across the street. The man looked to be in his late seventies or early eighties, and as the cart continued down the middle of the street, it was clear to Henry the man wasn't going to be able to move fast enough.

Henry looked at the driver and saw nothing but ice in his eyes, his face impassive.

Henry waited until the last second and then grabbed the wheel of the cart. The front tire came within inches of the old man's ankles as it veered away and then crashed into a bunch of trashcans set on the curb for trash pickup.

The cans went everywhere and the trash spilled onto the street.

"What the hell's wrong with you? You could have killed that poor guy," Henry asked the guard.

For just a second, he thought the guard was going to say something, but instead he backed up the cart and proceeded up the street for their rendezvous with the man in charge.

As Jimmy looked over his shoulder, he saw the people who were in the area surrounding the trash pile immediately dive into it and begin to clean it up. While he watched, he saw their faces. They were terrified, moving as fast as physically possible to clean up the mess and fix the cans.

In a matter of two minutes the cans were back where they were and no one would ever know what had just occurred less than five minutes ago.

Then the cart turned a corner and was out of sight, but just before it was, Jimmy saw the old man wave to them in thanks.

Then he was gone.

Jimmy filed what he'd seen in his head so he could tell Henry about it later when they were alone.

The cart pulled up to what was obviously the police station and the guard motioned them to get out, then pointed to the main doors of the building.

Henry and Jimmy both did as requested, walking up the steps to the station.

Opening the doors, they stepped into the building and once inside, took in the simple floor plan of the room.

It looked like any police station you might see in a small town.

There was a small wall no more than waist high with a swinging door that would allow you to enter the bullpen where five desks sat. All the desks were perfectly organized, and as the two men looked to the back of the room, they saw three rooms with bars for the front walls.

Obviously the cells were for lawbreakers, Henry thought.

Off to the right of the front doors was a door with the words SHERIFF stenciled in white. Below that were some other words, but they had been peeled away and now there was only a faint outline due to the sun fading the glass on the door.

A man walked out of the back room and noticed Henry staring at the door and said: "If you're trying to read the words that are missing, it was my predecessor's name. Hi, my name's Sam Foree and I run this town," he said as he held out his hand for each of them to shake.

Henry also held out his hand and as Sam took it he said: "Hello, I'm Henry Watson and this is Jimmy Cooper. Are you the one we should thank for helping our friend?" He inquired while Jimmy shook hands with the big man.

"Yes, I believe I am. You made quite an impression on Paul today. He was the man on watch when you came in earlier," Sam said, motioning them to follow him into the Sheriff's office.

"What happened to the man who had his name on the door?" Jimmy asked as they sat down.

"Well, Jimmy, can I call you Jimmy?"

Jimmy nodded in consent.

"Well, Jimmy, the original Sheriff bought it when the outbreak first started," Sam said as he sat down behind the only desk in the office. "I took the reins of power out of necessity because no one else to want the job."

"The things we have to do in life, ay' Sheriff?" Henry asked as he sized up the tall, black man. He couldn't get a handle on this guy, so he figured he would just take it slow. He just hoped Jimmy would keep his mouth reined in, as well.

"Please, Henry; just call me Sam. Sheriff was my predecessor's name, not mine." He smiled as he sat up in his chair. "I have to tell you, I didn't let you into my town out of the kindness of my heart."

"Here we go, and now comes the catch," Jimmy said with a frown.

"Jimmy, please, let's give our host a chance," he said politely. But when Jimmy saw Henry's eyes they said: Shut the hell up before you get us both killed.

"That's quite all right, Henry, really. As matter of fact, it's not far off from the truth." Sam said, leaning over his desk.

"I have a little problem I need attended to and I don't have enough able men to do it. I heard from Paul your story about how the three of you took out ten walkers on your own."

"Yeah, so, what's the big deal? If three roamers instead of four had gone after Mary we wouldn't be here right now," Jimmy stated casually as he stared at Sam.

"Well, maybe to the two of you killing ten...roamers did you call them? Why do you call them that?" He asked.

"The ones that don't stay in the cities, the ones who like to roam across the land looking for food; we call them roamers," Henry stated.

"Very clever, makes sense, too. I think I'll implement it among my men, as well," Sam said.

"Yeah, you do that," Jimmy said in a flat tone. "Now, what were you saying about a problem?"

"Oh, yeah, right, my problem. Well, you see, there's a small town about five miles from here that's full of walkers. All the living are either dead or gone. I want to clean the place out so we can take it over, but I lack the man power to do it. The few guards you saw are really the base of my security force. Most of the town's people are women and children... and the old, of course."

"Okay, so what do you want from us?" Henry asked.

"Why, I want you to go in with my men and clean the place out," Sam said. "As I was saying before, taking out ten roamers as you call them is pretty impressive around here and I need men who can handle themselves in a fight."

"No, thanks, no way, I'll pass. It sounds like suicide," Jimmy said as he held his hands in front of himself."

"I'm afraid I have to agree with him Jimmy. It sounds pretty reckless to me," Henry said from across the desk.

Sam leaned forward again and smiled.

"I don't think you gentlemen understand me. You will help me or your friend dies."

Henry and Jimmy turned and looked at each other, both hiding the shock of the threat aimed at them and Mary. They both knew what the other was thinking. All of a sudden the town had gone from salvation to desperation.

They were now trapped inside a town with no weapons and one of their own severely wounded. They didn't really have a choice in their decision to Sam.

Henry looked at Sam and smiled. "Well, since you put it that way, we're in. Sign us up."

Sam's smile grew wider as he looked at them both.

"I thought you'd change your minds if reasoned with properly. Why don't you get some rest and tonight we'll discuss my plan over dinner." Then he clicked his two-way radio twice and Paul opened the door to his office.

"Paul, see to it these men get a room for the night and some food," He told him, standing up to see Henry and Jimmy out.

Henry and Jimmy filed out of the room and were escorted outside where another cart was waiting for them.

As they were about to climb in the small vehicle, Jimmy was about to say something to Henry when he was stopped abruptly.

"Later," Henry muttered as they climbed into the cart.

Jimmy nodded, getting what his older friend meant.

The cart took off, driving down the perfectly manicured street, and soon pulled up to the building which housed their rooms.

As Henry watched the people on the street, he could see the fear in their eyes before they quickly looked away. He believed he was getting a small understanding of what was going on here.

The town wasn't just the resident's salvation from the hordes of walking corpses constantly attempting to gain access. Like Henry and Jimmy, the town could also be their prison.

# CHAPTER TEN

THE CART HAD stopped in front of a quaint, two-story, brick building with a sign on the left facade that declared: ROOMS FOR RENT-weekly or monthly.

Henry and Jimmy hopped out of the cart and walked up the stairs to the front door. Jimmy looked over his shoulder to see Paul heading off down the street again, weaving his way through the pedestrians.

"They don't seem too worried about us wandering away, do they?" Jimmy stated.

"Why would they, they've got Mary as insurance," Henry said seriously, pushing the door open and walking inside.

The foyer of the building was lit by the wan light seeping in through the curtains. Jimmy walked over to a small end table where a stack of mail sat. As he flipped through them, he noticed the last stamp date was about three months ago to the day.

"The mailman must be late," he said.

Henry only nodded while he surveyed the room some more. Then he heard footsteps coming closer, and a moment later a middle-aged woman with slightly graying hair walked into the foyer from a side door.

"Good afternoon, gentlemen, my name is Susan. I was told of your arrival and your rooms are ready. Follow me please." Without seeing if she was being followed, she turned and walked up a stairway hidden at the back of the foyer.

The two men followed her up the stairs, and in a moment were in a hallway lined with four doors on each side. She pointed to two doors which were partially open and then turned away to leave.

"Oh, I'll have food sent up in an hour or so. The shower works, by the way, although we're wanting for hot water." She pointed to the ceiling. "We have a water tower on the roof." Then she turned and walked away, and in seconds her footsteps receded down the stairs and silence reined again in the hallway.

Jimmy was about to say something when Henry held up his hand for him to stop.

"I know what you're going to say, but wait. Let's shower and eat and then we'll talk, we definitely have the time."

"Fine, it will be nice to take a shower," he agreed, and waving farewell, he stepped into his room and closed the door.

Henry stared at the closed door for a moment, thinking about everything that had happened to them in the past few days. Then he slipped into his room and closed the door.

*    *    *

Henry's eyes played over the room, taking it all in at a glance. The room looked like a hundred bed and breakfasts across the country.

He walked over to the one window at the end of the room and looked outside.

He watched the pedestrians of the town as they scurried to and fro.

Henry paid particular attention when he saw one of the security guards from the night before walking down the sidewalk. The man strolled with a gait that said don't mess with me, and Henry watched as the people on the sidewalk did everything but bow when the guard walked past them.

Further down the street, a woman was bent over what looked like a bag of laundry that had broken at the seam. As he watched, the guard came up behind her, kicked her out of his way, and then walked through the laundry, sending it flying all over the sidewalk.

The woman crawled back to the pile and quickly gathered the clothes in her arms and then hobbled down the street until she was out of sight.

Henry leaned away from the window and thought about what he'd just seen.

The guards seem to act like the people they protected were insignificant. That would explain the incident with the old man earlier in the day.

As Henry shrugged out of his filthy clothes, he decided he didn't like what he'd seen, but it wasn't his problem.

They'd do what the Boss of this town wanted and then they'd grab Mary and leave at the first possible opportunity.

The shower was fantastic and while Henry toweled off, he couldn't remember the last time he'd felt so clean. Even the towels were wonderful. They were so soft it was like the material sucked up the water on his skin instead of just pushing it around.

There was a knock at the door, and when he opened it, he discovered a small rolling cart with a tray of food on it. Retrieving the tray, he closed the door with his foot and set it down, then proceeded to get dressed again.

He noticed the closet in the room was open and upon exploring, he found it full of men's clothes. Various sizes filled the interior, from very small to sizes that would fit right in at a Big and Tall store.

Assuming it was all right, he found a shirt and pants that fit and put them on.

With a shower and clean clothes, he felt like he could take on every ghoul in the deadlands single handedly. Then he sat down and had himself a nice lunch of homemade baked bread and cheese, washing it down with a warm can of soda.

There was a silver knife on the tray and he decided to keep it. It wasn't a great weapon, but it was better than nothing, he thought, as he placed it inside his sock. The empty leather sheath on his hip gaped at him and he felt a twinge of loss without his panga.

When he was finished eating, he went to the door and walked across the hall to check on Jimmy.

On the second knock the door swung inward and Henry was greeted by the face of a clean Jimmy. Henry noticed he looked even younger than his nineteen years. His brown hair was still wet from his shower and he stepped away from the door to let Henry enter.

"Oh, man, that shower was great. I didn't want to get out," Jimmy said happily while he wiped water from his face with a towel. "What's up? Are you ready to talk yet?"

Henry nodded and went and sat on the bed. Looking around the room, he noticed Jimmy's closet was full of clothes, also, and an identical lunch tray sat on the side of the bed, almost all of the food gone.

"There's really not much to talk about," Henry said. "That bastard Sam has got us good. As long as Mary's immobile, he's got us by the balls. I say we do what he asks, but keep an eye on a way to turn the tables on him. Then, if the opportunity strikes, we grab Mary and run for it," Henry finished, playing with a throw rug on the floor with his boot. The hardwood floor was so smooth the rug would just slide back and forth as if it was on glass.

Jimmy nodded approval and said: "I still don't like being forced into doing something, especially when that something could get me killed."

"I agree with you, buddy, now put on some of those clothes from that closet over there and let's get out of here. I want to check out this town some more. Maybe we can figure out what's the deal with the way everybody acts around here."

While Jimmy put on new clothes, Henry filled him in on what he'd seen from his window earlier and when Jimmy was ready, the two of them left the room to go exploring.

When they reached the bottom of the stairs, they were stopped by Susan, who was waiting with her arms folded like a cross mother.

"And where do you think you're going?" She asked the two of them.

"Outside, why?" Jimmy asked.

"Because I have orders to keep you here until you're summoned for dinner by Sam," she said, as if that settled the matter.

"Look, lady, I don't give a damn about your orders, now step aside or I'll go through you," Henry said with a rumble in his voice that told her he was serious.

Susan knew she was no match for the two men so did as requested, and when the two men walked by her, she couldn't resist a parting quip.

"Sam shall hear of this, I assure you," she said.

With his back to her, Jimmy just raised his hand in a wave and the two of them stepped outside into the glare of the sun.

## CHAPTER ELEVEN

JIMMY AND HENRY walked down the stairs to the sidewalk and stopped for a minute, eyeing the landscape.

"So, which way do we go?" Jimmy asked, while he looked around.

People hurried by them as they went to their destinations, no one giving them the slightest bit of attention.

Henry watched a few and no one would make eye contact with him. He shrugged and pointed to the right.

"This way should be as good as any other," he said as he started walking.

Jimmy followed, the two men strolling down the street side by side.

Whenever they came upon another pedestrian, the person would immediately give way for the two men.

"This is really weird," Jimmy said in a low voice to Henry.

"Yeah, I know what you mean," Henry replied out of the side of his mouth.

The two men walked a few blocks until they came to a small, gray building with a dark, neon sign in the window.

Henry squinted in the glare of the sun at the sign.

"Murphy's Pub," Henry said. "You want to get a drink, Jimmy?" Henry asked with a smile.

"But I'm too young, they'll card me," Jimmy said disappointed.

Henry slapped him on the shoulder. "I highly doubt that will happen, Jimmy my boy. The rules have changed or haven't you noticed?"

Jimmy's face lightened as he realized what Henry meant and the two of them entered the bar.

The wan light coming through the dirty plate glass window in the front of the bar was the only illumination for the men to see by.

There were about ten small, round wooden tables clustered together on the floor and a long wooden counter was off to the right of the door.

Patrons were scattered around the room.

Henry and Jimmy went over to the bar and the bartender moved over to them.

The bartender was an older man of about sixty with thin, gray hair and about five days worth of stubble on his wrinkled chin.

"What'll it be boys?" He asked in a gruff voice.

"A couple of beers, I guess, what do you use for currency around here?" Henry asked as the barman pushed a couple of lukewarm beers at him.

"You boys are the Boss's new men, right?" He asked as if he already knew the answer.

Jimmy nodded. "Yeah, I guess we are."

"Then the drinks are on me. Security drinks for free around here." With a wink he shuffled away to attend to his other patrons.

Henry and Jimmy put their backs to the counter and surveyed the other people in the bar.

In the far corner there were four men who looked to Henry like security. They were playing cards and drinking what looked like whiskey.

Henry smiled to himself.

What did they think this was the Old West?

A few of the other tables had pairs of older men who kept their heads down while they nursed their drinks.

Then a woman came from the back room with a box in her hands. She walked over to the counter and set the box down heavily. The contents of the box rattled as the glass inside was jarred.

"Easy, ya damn cow, those are fragile," the bartender snapped at her.

"Sorry, Bob, my hands slipped," she said in a deferring tone.

Bob just grunted and pointed at the four men playing cards in the corner.

"Go make sure those boys are happy. And hop to it girl, I don't pay you to goof off."

Moving away from the bar, Henry heard her mumble, "You don't really pay me anyway."

Then she was moving across the floor to attend to the men.

Henry couldn't help but notice she had a slim figure with perky breasts. Her blonde hair was tied back, but Henry believed it would probably fall to the middle of her back if allowed to hang free.

Looking askance, he saw Jimmy had seen her, too, his eyes following her across the room like a wolf watching a stray sheep. The woman was talking to one of the four men, and as Henry and Jimmy watched, their voices went up a notch.

Then the man grabbed her by the arm and slapped her across the face.

The sound of flesh striking flesh echoed across the room and the woman fell back against the wall.

Regaining her balance, she stood up and grabbed a half-full mug of beer from a neighboring table and threw it into the man's face.

The other three men at the table started laughing at the man as he sputtered beer from his mouth, but Henry could see the wet man wasn't amused.

That's when soggy man stood up and closed on the woman, his arm going back to strike her again.

Before Henry could stop him, Jimmy was moving. Just before the wet man's arm would have connected with the woman's face, Jimmy stepped in and blocked the swing with his arm.

"Look, buddy, I don't know what you're so mad about, but that's no way to treat a lady."

The wet man turned and looked at Jimmy and in the blink of an eye had punched Jimmy in the stomach, then pushed him away.

"Fuck off, runt, if I want your opinion I'll beat it out of you," the wet man said to Jimmy as his buddies laughed harder at Jimmy's humiliation.

But Jimmy wasn't done yet. Regaining his balance, he moved in again. But the man was ready for him. Before Jimmy could throw his first punch, the other man had nailed Jimmy in the jaw.

Jimmy went flying backward to land on another table. Then he slipped off and fell to the ground. The other patrons were now making a hasty exit from the bar as the wet man walked over to Jimmy

The man was about to kick Jimmy in the ribs when Henry got in his way.

"All right, buddy, you've made your point. What do you say we end it?" Henry asked with his hands out in front of him.

The man just snickered. "Fuck you, old man. It's over when I say it's over."

Then he leaned his foot back to kick Jimmy.

Henry sighed, knowing what he had to do. While Henry was in no way a naturally violent man, he knew how to handle himself when necessary. Before the man could kick his friend, Henry pulled his arm back and sent a blow that connected with the man's jaw like a hammer to glass.

The man fell back into his buddies at the table as they roared with laughter. He righted himself and rubbed his jaw, hatred now in his eyes.

"You just made a big mistake, asshole," he said, running at Henry again.

The man ran at full speed with his head down so he could tackle Henry. But Henry sidestepped him, and as he went past, Henry brought his elbow down on the back of the wet man's neck. The guy went to the floor like a bull that had been shot in the head.

The man quickly got to his knees, shaking his head, and was in the process of standing again when Henry stepped in and sent a punch to the man's kidneys. The air went out of him in a whoosh as he bent over in pain.

That's when Henry sent an uppercut that sent the man's head snapping back, his body following.

The wet man landed on the table behind him, and as the table gave out under his weight, he crashed to the floor and lay still, with only a few small moans to indicate he was still alive.

Seeing their friend flat on the floor, the other three men stood up. But by then Jimmy had regained his footing and was next to Henry again.

"Now, fellas, we really don't have to do this. It's all a big misunderstanding," Henry said while he and Jimmy backed away from the three men.

When the men pulled their guns, Henry knew the situation had gone past the point of a simple bar fight.

He thought about the knife he had in his sock, but decided it was past the time it could be of use. That's when the sound of a shotgun being cocked filled the room and stopped the three men in their tracks.

Looking over his shoulder, Henry could see a silhouette framed in the barroom's door. The figure stepped inside a little more, and when the door closed behind the figure, Henry was able to make out the features of Sam. He had to admit the man looked imposing as he stood there with a twelve-gage in his hands.

"Someone want to tell me what the fuck is going on here?" He rumbled in his low voice.

"Nothing, Boss, we were just havin' some fun," one of the men said as they all made their weapons disappear.

Sam grunted and gestured to the unconscious man on the flattened table.

"Pick up this pile of shit and get the hell out of here," Sam ordered them in a tone that brooked no argument.

The three men went to their buddy and picked him up. Then they stumbled out of the bar and back into the light of day.

When the door slammed shut behind them, Sam relaxed a little and went to a table and sat down.

"Join me, won't you?" Sam asked, while leaning the shotgun on a chair next to him.

Jimmy and Henry looked at each other and then Jimmy shrugged. The two of them crossed the bar and sat down with Sam.

The blonde woman came over and started to clean their table.

"How's it going, Cindy?" Sam asked as he looked up at the girl's face. He could see the red mark where she'd been hit, but decided not to mention it.

"Fine, Boss, everything's fine. Should I get you some beers?" She asked as she turned to move away.

"Sure, honey that would be great," Sam said as he watched her walk away. Then he turned to Henry.

"I figure if I have you here now, we might as well talk about what I need you for," Sam said, picking up one of the mugs of beer Cindy was now placing on the table.

"Sure, why not, there's no time like the present," Henry said as he picked up the fresh beer in front of him and took a sip.

Jimmy wasn't paying attention, he only had eyes for Cindy.

Henry noticed and gave him a push in the arm so he'd pay attention.

"Oh, sorry," he said.

"That's fine, son. I remember what it's like to be young," Sam said, taking another drink from his glass.

Then he shared with Jimmy and Henry his plans to clean out the next town. His idea was nothing short of suicide. He thought he could just walk in there with a few guns and clean the whole town out in one fell swoop.

Henry sat quietly listening, and realized while he may have been a competent man, Sam had no real idea of what it was like fighting the walking dead in the trenches of a city or town.

Henry listened politely, already making up his mind that he and Jimmy would not be participating. But he knew he had to bide some time so Mary could get back on her feet.

When Sam was finished laying out his whole plan Henry nodded.

"Okay, sounds fine, but can I request a few days to get to know your men and to do a little reconnaissance of the town we're gonna go into?

Sam mulled it over for a few seconds and then nodded. "Sure, I think that can be arranged."

"What about our weapons?" Jimmy asked as he took a sip of his beer. He grimaced at the taste. He wasn't a big fan of bear, never had been.

"I'll see that they're returned to you, unless you would like to retrieve them yourselves. They're with my armorer. I'm sure by now he's cleaned and oiled them."

"That would be great," Henry said, finishing his beer. There weren't any napkins to be seen, so Henry used his shirt sleeve. "If that's it then we'll be going."

Sam gave them directions to the armorer's residence and the two men headed for the exit.

Just before they walked through the door, Sam called to them, standing up, as well.

"Hey, Henry," he called, and Henry turned around to look at him.

"Just because I'm giving you your weapons back doesn't mean I trust you," Sam said this with a face set in stone.

Henry looked him straight in the eyes from across the room and said: "Understood; and the same goes for us about you."

Then Henry and Jimmy stepped outside and the door closed, blocking them from Sam's view.

Sam sat down again and finished his beer, and when finished, he flashed Cindy a smile and left, too

In the now quiet bar, the old bartender waddled out from behind the counter and began to clean up the mess made by the fight so business could resume.

This was nothing knew to him. It was just another day in the new world.

# CHAPTER TWELVE

HENRY AND JIMMY walked down the sidewalk on their way to the armorer.

Looking up at the sky, Jimmy frowned at all the grey clouds floating over the town.

"It looks like rain and you know that's never good," Jimmy said, dodging an old woman who was in front of him.

"Yeah, we'll keep an eye on it and duck into a building if it starts raining," Henry said askance of him.

The two men followed Sam's directions and were soon standing in front of a small store with an American flag hanging in the window. The building was nondescript, so Henry searched for a sign of the building's function.

Not waiting, Jimmy walked up the few steps to the front door and was surprised when it opened.

"Not locked," he said. "Should we go inside?"

Henry nodded and followed his friend through the door.

The first thing Henry noticed upon stepping inside the building was the air in the room was filled with the smell of gun oil. The room was piled high with empty boxes that were once filled with ammunition. Henry noticed while walking around the small room, all the different caliber of rounds once contained in the boxes.

In front of Jimmy was a small counter. It had a piece on it that could be lifted up for access to the back room. On the middle of the counter was a small bell like you'd find in a hotel for a bellhop.

Jimmy glanced to Henry, but he just shrugged, so Jimmy slapped the bell two times.

After a minute and no one came out, Jimmy hit the bell again, louder this time.

The two men waited and then they heard a soft voice.

"All right, hold your horses, I'm coming," said the voice, which was soon followed by the sound of feet shuffling across the floor.

A small head appeared in the back doorway, a man in his eighties walking slowly to greet them.

"Hello there, my young friends, how can I help you today?"

"Are you the armorer?" Henry asked.

"Why, yes, I am. What can I do for you?"

"You're joking right? This old fossil is the gunsmith for this whole town," Jimmy spit, unimpressed.

"I may be old, son; but I know my craft. I served in WW2 and I know my way around a weapon like no one else you'll ever know. Now, if you're done insulting me, what do you want?"

"I'm sorry, sir, my friend sometimes talks before he thinks. My name's Henry and this is Jimmy. I believe you have our weapons. Sam sent us to retrieve them."

"Ah, the outsiders, yes, of course, come this way. I just finished cleaning them. I have to say they were in bad shape. You should take better care of them," he said, leading them to the back of the building.

Upon stepping into the back room, Henry's jaw dropped. All four walls were covered in every kind of weapon imaginable. There were pistols, rifles and shotguns. He even saw something that he was pretty sure was a bazooka.

"Wow," was all Jimmy could say.

"Ah, you like what you see, huh?" The old man cackled. "There's a lifetime worth of weapons here. Little did I know all those years ago it would be my firearms that would save our town from extinction," he said as he picked up Jimmy's shotgun and handed it to him.

"Here you go, my boy. All clean and ready for action."

"Thank you," Jimmy said as he took the weapon from the old man's frail hands.

"You're quite welcome. Now, go out front and get some ammunition. There should be a few boxes to the right of the counter," he instructed and turned back to his workbench.

Jimmy nodded and then ran out front, acting like a kid on Christmas morning.

"Good, now that we are alone, I wanted to talk with you privately," the old man said.

"Really, about what?" Henry asked, curious.

"That was me in the road earlier this morning. If it wasn't for you, I fear I probably wouldn't be standing here right now. I just wanted to say thank you."

"It's not a problem, happy to help," Henry smiled.

"Well still, I'm very grateful to you, so in appreciation I want you to take whatever you need off these walls," he said, waving his hand over his vast collection.

"Wow, ah, that's really great, thank you," Henry sputtered, not really knowing what to say.

"No my boy, thank you." he replied, while Henry got to work picking the guns he thought he and the others might need.

When he'd finished picking the weapons he could use, the old man (whom had identified himself as Thomas) showed Henry and Jimmy how to properly strip and clean their weapons. After the third time both men had gotten pretty good at it and Thomas had set them up with gun oil and cloth rags for future cleanings.

The two men were finishing up and packing their weapons when they heard screaming coming from outside.

They both looked at each other and then went to the door. Opening it, they quickly realized what was happening.

The rain had started falling in a downpour and some of the town's residents hadn't moved fast enough to escape the contaminated rain. As Henry watched, he could see at least fifteen people lying in different positions on the street and sidewalk.

As the two of them watched silently, the bodies began to twitch on the pavement. It wouldn't be long before they would be mobile and began to regain their feet.

A woman ran by with an umbrella, but she ran too close to one of the revived ghouls and was pulled down to the street kicking and screaming. Within a matter of seconds her throat had been ripped out, and blood ran red, mixing with the light-green rainwater covering the road.

She stopped moving, her blood slowing while the ghoul feasted on her flesh, tearing her skin from her body like he was unwrapping a present.

Then one of the newly born undead spotted Henry and Jimmy at the door and began stumbling towards them.

Henry slammed the door shut and turned the deadbolt.

"Shit, until the rain stops we're trapped," he said, looking around the room.

"We'll just wait for the rain to stop and then we'll blow the bastards to Hell," Jimmy said, cocking the shotgun.

Henry frowned, thinking about Mary.

"Don't worry, I'm sure she's fine," Jimmy said, having a pretty good idea what Henry was thinking about.

He was about to ask Jimmy how he could possibly know what he was thinking, when the door jumped in its frame.

"Damn it, they want in," Henry said.

"Don't worry, son, that door is made well. Unless they have a battering ram, they're not getting in."

Good to know," Jimmy said, plopping down onto the floor with his back to the door.

With the banging on the door continuing, the three men sat and waited for the rain to stop.

When it did, Henry knew there was going to be some messy work to do and as he checked his newly cleaned Glock, he knew he now had the tools to do it.

# CHAPTER THIRTEEN

TWENTY-FIVE MINUTES later the rain finally stopped, the clouds continuing their journey across the sky, leaving nothing but a dull drizzle.

Inside the Armory, the three men patiently sat and waited while the newly awakened ghouls pounded on the door.

Jimmy was looking out through the peephole in the front door and grimaced at the sight he was privileged to.

"Man, that sucks. All those people, dead." Then he grimaced. "Yuck, they sure do get ugly when they die," he said, pulling his eye away from the hole and stepping back. "It stopped raining and the sky's clear," he said, going to stand by Henry. "So, what's next?"

Henry was positioning his weapons on his body. He had a fourteen-inch panga strapped to his right hip. The long blade glistened in the light in the room before he slid it in its sheath. It wasn't the same make as the sixteen-inch blade he had taken from a soldier so many months ago, but it would serve his purpose well.

Including the Glock, he was now carrying a twelve-gauge shotgun similar to Jimmy's with two bandoliers full of extra shells criss-crossing his chest.

Jimmy picked up his like-new .38 Smith and Wesson and placed it back in its holster on his hip. He also had a spare .38 in a knapsack along with enough ammunition for both guns to keep him happy for a while. He was planning to give it to Mary so she'd have a weapon with a little more stopping power. Perhaps if she had used a similar weapon earlier, none of them would be in the mess they now found themselves in.

On his hip was strapped a six-inch hunting knife that would come in handy in a pinch, as well as his newly cleaned shotgun hanging from his back from a leather sling.

When they were as ready as they could be, they thanked the old man and got ready for a fight.

The old man had agreed to open the door, and would close it behind the two men once they had exited the building.

Jimmy took one more look through the peephole and then got ready to move.

"I see one deader in front of the door, the others are scattered around the street. I count at least fifteen or so. It's hard to see through that damn thing," he said, referring to the small peephole.

"That's okay, Jimmy, just remember, keep moving, they aren't as fast as us and that's our advantage. Ready?" Henry asked.

"No, but let's go anyway," Jimmy breathed as he psyched himself up.

Henry nodded to Thomas to open the door. "On the count of three, Thomas..." "One, two, three!" He yelled, with Thomas pulling the door open at the same time as Henry yelled three.

The newly risen dead man at the door was taken by surprise when the door flew inward and that was all the time Henry needed.

Stepping forward through the doorway, he put the shotgun no more than two feet from the pale-faced man's head and squeezed the trigger.

He was jarred from the kick of the weapon and so didn't notice the head disintegrate in a spray of blood and bone.

The headless body fell back and tumbled down the stairs where it remained, and Henry and Jimmy stepped over the corpse, their weapons searching for the next target.

With the shotgun reloaded the two men got ready to clean the streets.

Two zombies came at Henry from his right, and raising the shotgun again, he shot one point-blank in the face.

The slack-jawed countenance became a shredded mass of flesh and gore, the dead man wandering away blind. Henry ignored him. He was harmless now, and so concentrated on the next one coming at him.

The ghoul had once been a woman in her mid-fifties, but now she was an animal looking for meat. Henry turned and faced her and when she lunged at him with a guttural growl, he side-stepped her and cracked her skull open with the barrel of the shotgun.

She pitched forward to the ground in a heap of limp limbs, the back of her head oozing red from a shattered skull.

Henry turned to see who was next and realized he'd made himself a small amount of breathing room while the other ghouls slowly began moving towards him. He checked on his left to see how Jimmy was doing and was pleased to see the younger man was handling himself admirably.

After stepping over the corpse at the bottom of the stairs, Jimmy had moved left to stay out of Henry's kill zone.

He wasn't on the street for more than a second when a zombie who had once been an old man in his sixties lunged for him. Jimmy sidestepped the old man and then placed the .38 against the back of the graying head. As soon as the muzzle touched the thinning hair, he squeezed the trigger.

He was impressed with the small kick the gun had compared to his shotgun and as he turned away, he saw what was left of the old man's face as he fell to the pavement in need of a good plastic surgeon. The ghoul didn't move again.

Keeping in motion, he dodged another attacker who had come up on him from behind. When he pulled away from the ghoul, he felt his new shirt rip in the dead man's grip.

Turning quickly, he placed the .38 directly in front of the man's vacant left eye and squeezed the trigger yet again.

The eye disappeared like an exploded egg and the bullet plowed into the man's skull, then took a fist-size chunk of bone and brain matter with it as it exited its head. The brain spun to the ground, splattering on the pavement like someone had spilled a bowl of red jello, mixing with the rainwater still coating the street.

The body crumpled to the ground and was then forgotten.

Jimmy glanced over to his right and saw Henry watching him. Then he saw a ghoul come from behind a bunch of trashcans on the sidewalk, the dead man heading straight for Henry's back. There was no time to yell, so Jimmy raised his .38 and fired over Henry's shoulder, seeing the panic in his friend's face.

Just before the ghoul would have sunk his teeth into Henry's shoulder, the man's head snapped back and the body slumped to the ground.

Then Jimmy had to move on as other walking corpses began to come his way, attracted to the gunfire.


Henry watched Jimmy while he dispatched another zombie and then he felt his heart skip a beat when Jimmy turned his gun on him.

Before Henry could even ask him why, Jimmy was firing.

Henry felt the bullet zoom past his head. It was so close, if his head had moved more than an inch to the side it would have taken off his ear. Then he turned around as the dead man fell to the ground with a new hole in his forehead, and Henry realized Jimmy had just saved his life.

Before he could even say thanks, Jimmy was off to dispose of some more of the undead.

Other walkers were heading towards him and then he heard the sound of gunfire coming from down the street. Henry smiled, hoping it was help working their way toward them. Then three more foes came at him and he had no more time for thought.

Crushing the nose of the first ghoul when he punched it in the face, wanting to buy him some time, he back-stepped and raised his shotgun. From less than three feet away, he shot a second, female attacker in the chest. The feminine corpse fell to the street where she flopped around as she tried to regain her footing. That was fine with Henry, he just wanted to give himself some room for the other two foes coming his way. He idly noticed the woman's chest was a red mess of gore, her fractured ribs sticking up at odd angles, and he saw the plastic, deflated bags of silicone dribbling down her chest to mix with her blood. So much for the boob job she had invested in. At least she had made a curvaceous zombie. That is until Henry blew her chest into a hundred gobbets of flesh and bone.

Another foe came up on his right and wrapped his arms around him. Bending at the waist, he grabbed the exposed arm and sent the attacker flying over his back to land in front of him on the ground. He kicked the dead man in the face and then shot the first ghoul he'd punched in the face at point-blank range.

The body flew backwards where it then fell into the female ghoul with the giant wound in her chest. As the female ghoul crawled around, she gave Henry plenty of time to walk up to her and pull his new panga and see how it felt in battle.

With one good blow, he swiped at her neck.

Blood spurted six feet into the air when the panga severed the carotid artery in her throat.

Pulling the blade away, he marveled at how much blood there was.

Weren't these people supposed to be dead? And if so, then why was the heart still pumping? Then these thoughts became trivial and would have to put aside until later.

With half her neck sliced open, the female ghoul continued to crawl around, refusing to go down, so Henry raised the panga again, and this time severed her head from her shapely shoulders with one powerful blow. The head rolled away to land in the rain-slick gutter and her lipstick-red lips still moved, the eyes shifting back and forth like she was watching a tennis match.

Henry kicked the headless body to the ground, looking around for more targets.

Then the gunfire became louder and he saw Sam, Paul and two other security men come charging around the corner.

Sam took one look at Henry and Jimmy and all the dead bodies surrounding them and smiled.

"Well, I'll be damned. You two did this all by yourselves?" Sam asked, surveying the carnage.

Henry and Jimmy just stood silent, breathing heavily from their exertions. There was no reason to justify the question with an answer.

"Sorry, stupid question, of course you did. You see?" Sam said as he looked at his men behind him. "This is how you kill walkers. You men need to remember this when you go into battle with these two," he said, pointing to Henry and Jimmy.

"Is that all of them?" Henry asked Sam.

Sam nodded. "Yup. These are the last of the idiots who didn't seek shelter when the rain came. We took care of the rest on our way here."

"Good, then if we're done, me and Jimmy are going to check on our friend," Henry said, starting to walk up the street.

Jimmy followed and the two men walked side by side.

"I see you found your weapons," Sam called to their backs.

Henry stopped, turned around and looked at the man who was holding their friend hostage.

"And then some, thanks," he said matter of factly.

"This still doesn't change anything, you know that I hope," Sam said.

Henry nodded, his jaw tight. "Never crossed my mind. It was just something that had to be done."

"Fair enough," Sam said and turned to his men, needing to begin organizing body disposal.

Sensing Sam was finished with him, Henry turned and continued down the street, Jimmy at his side.

Mary was waiting and he was impatient to check in on her and make sure she was all right, especially after an outbreak happening so close to the clinic where she was resting.

# CHAPTER FOURTEEN

HENRY AND JIMMY weaved through the small streets of Pittsfield as they made their way back to see Mary.

The streets were a mess.

Bodies of the wounded and the dead alike were scattered everywhere. Henry watched a dog stroll by with a bloody, severed hand in its mouth. Wherever Henry and Jimmy looked, there were people moving about in a form of organized chaos.

Sticking to the middle of the street, the two went wide to avoid a headless body sprawled across what was once a vegetable cart, but was now nothing more than kindling for the fire.

Soft moans and harsh cries of pain were the sounds of the day as the wounded were helped out of the streets and to shelter.

Through it all walked Jimmy and Henry. They had done their part today in saving the small town. Let the old and the women address the wounded.

Henry was only concerned with Mary and that she was safe.

Turning a corner, Henry asked directions to the clinic from an old woman who was picking up litter from the gutter. She pointed down the street and sure enough, Henry recognized the building where they had left Mary earlier that day.

Walking the rest of the way easily, they made it to the building in minutes, but as old Doc Robinson was the only physician in town, he was overwhelmed with the wounded from the undead outbreak. People were everywhere, cradling wounds sustained from the revived ghouls.

Henry and Jimmy pushed their way into the building until they found Mary's room. The hall was filled with bodies, the sounds of people in pain echoing off the painted walls. Somewhere nearby, a baby cried fitfully.

Stepping inside, they were concerned when the bed had a woman and two children sitting on it, but no Mary. Before Henry could say anything Jimmy had slipped into the hallway where he tracked down a frazzled nurse.

"Hey, excuse me, where's my friend from this morning? She's not in her room," Jimmy said.

The nurse's face was filled with exhaustion and worry as she struggled to help those in need. To say she was overwhelmed would have been an understatement. She took a quick look in the room Jimmy pointed to, and when she saw Henry, her memory clicked and she smiled wanly.

"Oh, the young woman, the guard escorted her to the Boss's house to make room for all the wounded. When I saw her last she was awake and doing fine. Look, we're really busy, here, I gotta go," she said, pushing her way down the crowded hall and disappearing into another room.

Henry heard the exchange and slapped Jimmy on the back.

"Come on, let's get out of here, we'll check on her later when we see Sam for dinner," Henry told him, and then began pushing his way out of the building.

Once they had made it outside again, Henry breathed in the fresh air. After the packed hallways of the clinic, full of dirty bodies and wounded victims, it felt good to be outside again.

Once the two men had stepped down onto the street again, Jimmy shot Henry a laconic look.

"You think she's all right?

Henry shrugged slightly. "She should be. Whether she's with Sam or was here shouldn't really matter."

Jimmy nodded, agreeing with Henry's assumption. Besides it's not like they could do anything about it, as frustrating as that seemed.

"So, where to now, Boss? " Jimmy asked with a smile.

"Don't call me that," Henry said as he started walking.

"Come on, let's go back to our rooms. I'm hungry and could use another shower," he told Jimmy as he began moving towards their housing a few streets away.

Jimmy nodded, and with a jump to his step, followed Henry as the two men wound their way through the chaos in the street, both men barely paying attention.

✳    ✳    ✳

Mary awoke to the sound of screams.

Her head hurt terribly and as her vision slowly became clearer, she realized she was in a hospital room.

She felt a stab of pain from her arm when she tried to sit up, so she paused, then tried again, the gesture easier the second time.

How did she get here? Where were her friends?

She tried to recall the last thing she remembered before she'd passed out.

She had been fighting with a deader and it had been ready to rip her throat out. She had managed to jam her gun in its mouth. Then a flash of pain from her arm as the gun went off.

She vaguely recalled Henry and Jimmy standing over her... then nothing more.

Looking around the room, it was easy to piece together what had happened to her.

She had been shot and her friends had brought her here for help.

Wherever here was.

Voices floated in from hallway and she could see people rushing past in a state of confusion. Sliding off the bed on unsteady legs, her eyes scanned the room in more detail. Then her eyes spotted her clothes sitting on a small chair in the corner of the room. On unsteady legs, she walked over to the chair, and with much difficulty due to her arm, managed to get dressed.

She noticed idly that her shirt was different from the one she'd been wearing before, but paid it no mind. Once she was dressed, and feeling less vulnerable, she walked to the doorframe of her room and peeked into the hallway.

No one was paying her the slightest bit of attention and she slipped into the hall, her eyes only for the exit.

She hadn't made it more than halfway down the hallway when she felt a gentle but firm grip on her shoulder.

Thank God the hand wasn't on her injured side.

"Excuse me, miss, but I was instructed to escort you to the Boss's house as soon as you were able to move on your own. I guess that's now."

Mary turned to see a young man who looked to be around sixteen or seventeen years old. He had a kind face and gentle eyes. At least what Mary could see of it behind his long blonde hair. He was wearing a brown jumpsuit and had a rifle slung across his back.

Before Mary could answer him, a nurse went rushing by and struck Mary's bandaged arm. Mary let out a quick scream as pain shot up her arm. For a moment she felt dizzy, needles of pain flaring up and down her side.

After a moment the pain subsided enough for her to talk.

"Fine, just get me out of here," she said while the guard escorted her out of the building. Mary noticed how the people in the hallway would move aside and press their bodies tight against the wall so they could pass.

Mary watched the guard's face. To him the people moving out of the way seemed like the most normal thing in the world.

Within a matter of seconds they were at the exit to the street.

"Wait. What about my friends? Are they here? How can I find them?" She asked, confused.

"I'm sure the Boss will answer everything, miss," he said as he opened the front door and they stepped outside into the fresh air.

Mary's eyes were blasted by the bright sunlight, unaccustomed to the harsh glare after being indoors, and she closed her eyes and looked down, waiting for her eyes to adjust.

All around her there was chaos as people ran up and down the street.

If it wasn't for the guard helping her, she would never had been able to stand on the steps of the hospital with all the people flooding up and down the stairs in a continuous flow.

She watched curiously as the people would shrink away from them, and with heads down would quickly dash by. She was about to ask the guard what was wrong with everybody when she spotted a body in the street.

"What happened out here?" She asked the guard while he escorted her down the stairs to what looked like a golf cart.

"The rain came. Not everyone was able to find shelter quick enough so they turned into walkers. But don't worry, miss, we got them all," he said, sounding as if it was no big deal. It's a shame, though, I lost some good friends today."

She nodded, understanding only a little. She was still slightly out of it, so she followed him down the stairs where there was what looked like a golf cart waiting for them, a man sitting patiently behind the small steering wheel.

The guard motioned for her to get inside and he jumped onto the back.

Mary turned to look at her driver to say hello, but the man continued to look straight ahead, ignoring her.

She decided he didn't matter and looked ahead, as well. Maybe he was the strong, silent type.

With a slight jerk as it began to move, the cart surged forward and took off down the street at a moderate five miles an hour.

People would quickly move aside, the driver making no attempt to deviate from his course, the speed of the cart increasing

It was a harrowing ride for Mary and at any moment she expected them to run down some poor innocent pedestrian. But the frazzled people seemed used to the situation and always seemed to move out of the way in the knick of time.

After what seemed like an hour of narrowly missing people, but was actually only minutes, the cart pulled up in front of a beautiful, Victorian house on the edge of town.

Mary admired the beauty of the majestic home while the guard hopped off the cart and moved to stand next to her.

"Miss", he said, with his arm held out in a gesture for her hand.

Mary smiled and let the young man help her out of the cart. Then she was escorted up the long black cement driveway until they came to a stop in front of a grand front porch.

Beautiful wooden columns held up the porch's roof, carvings etched into the poles as if by a master craftsman. Mary studied the architecture, and was amazed by all the ornate carvings in the wood around the door and window frames.

The guard walked up the stairs and struck the door with the brass knocker, then waited for a reply.

Within moments, a small woman with graying hair who appeared to be in her late sixties opened the door and smiled up the guard and then over to Mary.

"Why, hello, son, what do we have here?" She asked.

"I've brought the Boss's guest from the clinic," he answered, matter of factly.

The old woman's smile grew wider.

"Ah, excellent. The Boss will be pleased. Bring her in." Then she stepped back inside to make room for her guests.

The guard turned to Mary and waved her on. Mary nodded, stepped through the doorway and into the grandest foyer she had ever seen.

The walls were hung with elegant paintings and almost all of the windows looked to be made of stained glass. The carpet was an elegant shade of burgundy and at the end of the foyer she saw a beautiful wooden staircase with beautiful carvings scattered amongst the rails.

Her reverie was broken by a chuckle from the old woman.

"Nice eh? Only the best for the Boss of this town, he saw to that," she said.

"What do you mean by that?" Mary asked

"Nothing, nothing, I've said too much already. Come on, dear, let's get you fixed up. I'm sure you're tired."

The exhaustion seemed to flood back into her as the old woman mentioned it and she nodded.

"I am feeling tired. I probably shouldn't even be out of bed yet. I was shot you see," she said, holding up her arm.

The old woman nodded and smiled at her. "I know, dear, we've been expecting you. Follow me and I'll show you to your room. You can rest there until the Boss comes back."

Then she waddled away with a quick glance over her shoulder to make sure Mary was with her.

"Do you know where my friends are?" Mary asked, following her up the winding wooden staircase to the second floor.

"Now don't you worry, dear, your friends will be here for dinner, as well as the Boss. You can see them then."

By now they had made it to the end of the hall. There were doors on both sides of the passageway and the old woman opened one near the end and waved Mary through, following behind her.

Mary did as requested and entered a spacious room with velvet drapes and matching bed linen.

Once in the room, she turned to look at the old woman.

"Now, you stay here and relax, dear, and I'll come and get you for dinner," the old woman said, stepping out of the room quickly.

Then the door closed and she was gone from sight. Before Mary could say or do anything, she heard a soft click from the door. She walked over to the door and tried the doorknob, but it was definitely locked.

"Great," she said, looking around the room again. It may have been beautiful, but a jail was a jail. No matter how you dressed it up.

Sighing heavily, she lay down on the bed and tried to figure out what she should do.

Her injury got the better of her, though, and within minutes she was fast asleep.

There would be time to think about escape later, like when she was reunited with her friends again.

# CHAPTER FIFTEEN

HENRY AND JIMMY made their way back to the boarding house in silence.

The walk was uneventful and within a matter of minutes they were once again standing inside the hallway leading to their rooms.

As the men each opened their doors to enter their rooms, Jimmy halted.

"Hey, Henry, after I get cleaned up I was thinking about going back to that bar again to see that girl. You know, the pretty blonde one, Cindy," Jimmy said, a little bashfully.

Henry smiled, watching his young friend blush. "Sure, Jimmy, just bring a weapon and watch your back."

Jimmy nodded. "Sure, I got it," and then with a farewell wave, he slipped inside his room.

Henry stood at the opening to his room a few moments after Jimmy's door closed with a soft click.

Ah, youth, he thought.

Emily's face floated into his thoughts and he grinned wistfully. He missed her more every day, but perhaps her dying when everything went to Hell wasn't really such a bad thing. He could never have seen her slogging around what was left of America fighting walking corpses, anyway. Hell, when he thought about it too much it threatened to drive him mad.

Snapping out of his reverie, he stepped into his room where he would finish off the leftovers of bread and cheese and then have a quick shower to wash off the blood and gore from the battle earlier. He had no particular order to his tasks, but he knew when he was through, he would then follow it all with a nap.

He smiled to himself as he thought of taking a nap, like it was just a normal day in his past life. He loved naps. Always had and probably always would.

Deciding he had delayed long enough, he began to strip off his filthy clothes, careful not to touch the small gobbets of flesh and patches of blood on them from all the ghouls he'd had to kill earlier. Then he went to the shower to wash away the morning.

\*     \*     \*

After Jimmy cleaned himself up and redressed, he strapped on his .38 and headed off to the bar where he hoped to see Cindy again.

Walking down the middle of the street, he noticed how the people would once again move out of his way.

How 'bout that, they think I'm with their security force, he thought to himself.

He continued walking until Murphy's Bar was once again in view, and after pausing at the door to make sure there was no one at his back, he opened it and walked inside.

The bar looked about the same as last time, although minus a few tables. The gloom suffused the room and he cautiously moved up to the counter and sat down on one of the stools.

Scanning the room for the second time, he did a quick count of the people he could see. There were eight or ten at the moment, a few occupants hidden in the back where the smoke and shadows did an excellent job of hiding them from view.

The bartender wandered over to him, and when he recognized Jimmy, his face creased into a deep frown.

"You again; look, I don't want any more trouble. I just finished cleaning this place up from the last time you were here," the old bartender grunted.

"Relax, pal, I just want a beer. And besides, what happened last time wasn't my fault." Jimmy said, trying to get more comfortable on his stool. "Your customers need to have better manners."

The bartender just grunted and slammed down a cracked glass with lukewarm beer in it; then shuffled away.

Jimmy picked up his beer and made a sour face when he took his first sip. "God, this tastes like piss," he said, placing the glass back onto the counter.

"Well, what did you expect? Without power there's no refrigeration," a voice said from the corner of his vision where he couldn't quite see.

Jimmy turned at the sound of the voice and was pleased to see it was Cindy.

He smiled at her and said: "Even if it was cold, I probably wouldn't like it. I'm not much of a beer fan."

"Oh, then what are you a fan of?" Cindy asked, moving up to the counter to stand next to him.

A small chill went up Jimmy's back at the closeness of her body to his. He didn't know why, but he felt an attraction to her from the first time he'd seen her.

Her hair was tied back again and the tight shirt she wore left nothing to the imagination. The jeans she wore were also skin tight and seemed more like they were painted on than that they were actually clothes. But despite this, Jimmy could see that her sexuality wasn't intentional. Looking at her, he thought she would probably look good in a potato sack.

Jimmy was snapped back to reality as she bent over and put her face in front of his.

"Hello, anyone in there?" She said, waving her hand in front of his nose.

"Uh, oh, sorry. I guess I wandered off there. What did you say?" Jimmy asked.

"I said, what else do you like?" She grinned, her eyes twinkling with amusement.

"Well, I like pretty girls," Jimmy said. It felt like his stomach had a thousand butterflies inside it, he felt so nervous.

"Oh, yeah? Any pretty girls specifically?" She asked with a playful smile across her lips.

Jimmy turned beet red as he looked at her. "Well, you, for one." Then he looked down, unable to keep eye contact with her. He was no wuss, but being this close to such a pretty girl was intimidating the hell out of him.

"That's sweet," she said. Then she put one of her fingers on the tip of his nose and tapped it once. "You're cute, too, and you don't act like these other pigs," she said, gesturing to the room to, signify the other men in the bar.

"Look, I finally get to leave here about ten. Why don't you come back and get me and we'll go for a walk or something," she suggested, looking into Jimmy's eyes.

Jimmy just nodded, and with a squeaky voice said: "That would be great."

"Hey, Cindy, get your ass in gear and wipe those tables down!" Bob the bartender yelled to her.

She put up her hand in a "gimme a second" wave and then said: "Yeah, yeah, I'm goin'," then with one last smile directed to Jimmy, went back to work.

Jimmy sat on his stool feeling on top of the world. He stayed that way for another fifteen minutes and was about to leave when he heard raised voices coming from the back of the room.

Turning, he saw three men seated at a table and two of them were in a heated argument about something.

The man who was facing him had an old Texan hat on and "Tex" wasn't pleased about something. The other man in the argument had his back to Jimmy. All he could see was the outline of his shoulders in the smoky haze of the bar, and his bald head as it reflected the oil lamps on the wall where the other men were sitting.

As Jimmy watched, Tex threw his playing card at Baldy and yelled at him some more. Jimmy heard the word "cheating" float over to him as Tex's voice went up in pitch.

What Tex couldn't see, but Jimmy could, was that Baldy's hand had slowly moved down under the table, where he had a pistol or revolver strapped to his leg. It was hard to tell in the gloom of the room.

As Tex continued to yell, the third man at the table slowly eased himself away, as if he could sense the trouble brewing and wanted to be far away when it came down.

Then before Jimmy or anyone else could have done anything to prevent it, Baldy pulled his weapon and shot Tex in the chest. Tex went flying backward in his chair, the momentum of the bullet throwing him against the wall.

A red spray covered the wall behind Tex, the exit wound splattering the dirty, wood paneling. Tex fell over to the floor where he remained still, dead before he hit the ground.

Chaos broke out in the bar a split second after the gun went off as everyone searched for the culprit, but Jimmy had seen everything and was immediately up and moving across the room toward Baldy.

Baldy had just regained his feet with the smoking gun still in his hand when Jimmy plowed into him.

The two of them fell to the floor, with Jimmy making sure to keep Baldy's weapon away from their bodies. Then he kicked his leg up into the man's crotch.

Baldy howled, his testicles now pushed up inside his body, and he shuddered in a spasm of pain. At the same time Jimmy ripped the man's gun from his hand and then jumped away, climbing to his feet.

But there was no rush, because for the moment Baldy was out of action, lying curled up on the floor.

One time when Jimmy had been about twelve or so, he and his friends had been playing on their bikes. They had taken some wood and had made ramps so they could jump over stuff, like the stunts they'd seen on TV with dirt bikes.

On one particular jump, Jimmy's tire had slipped off the ramp and his body had come down hard on the bike's main support bar between his legs. As his balls had connected with the cold metal of the bike, he had seen stars in his eyes and felt a pain that was almost impossible to describe. His breath had left him and he had fallen to the ground where he then had remained as still as possible until the pain subsided.

But ten minutes later, he had been back on his bike as if nothing had ever happened.

Jimmy stood over Baldy while order was restored to the bar. Old Bob had sent for security and within minutes two young men in coveralls came into the bar with rifles at the ready.

"Relax, guys, it's all under control," Jimmy said, stepping back and pointing at Baldy, who was just starting to get over the pain of his crushed testicles.

"This guy shot that guy in cold blood," Jimmy said, pointing at each man. His hand hovering in the air as he pointed at the dead man lying behind the table on the floor. The guards looked at Bob, who nodded in agreement.

The two guards slung their weapons over their shoulders and walked over and picked up Baldy. Within moments, Baldy was in a pair of handcuffs and was being escorted out of the bar.

"What's going to happen to him?" Jimmy asked, while the guards opened the door to leave.

"Don't you worry about it, pal," one of the guards said with a cold smile. "The Boss will know what to do with him. He usually takes care of murderers personally." Then the door closed on their backs and the three men were gone.

Jimmy looked around the room as the remains of the fight were cleaned up. Two men were picking up Tex and dragging the corpse toward the door where Bob the bartender was ready to open it for their passage outside. Cindy had retrieved a bucket of dirty water and was cleaning up the blood splattered on the wall and floor.

Jimmy decided now would be a good time to leave, so repositioning his gun belt on his hip, he set Baldy's weapon down on a nearby table (he absently noticed it was a .45 pistol) and left the bar.

He walked directly back to his room where he had decided he would stay until he was retrieved for dinner at Sam's house later that evening.

Luckily, the trip back to his room was wonderfully uneventful.

# CHAPTER SIXTEEN

HENRY AWOKE TO banging on his room door. He stumbled to his feet, and when he reached the door, he slowly opened it, wary for who may be on the other side. Though he doubted it was trouble, as trouble wouldn't take the time to knock.

"Yeah, what's wrong?"

"I've been sent to get you for dinner, sir, to the Boss's house," a young man of no more than seventeen said.

"Okay, give me a minute to get dressed and I'll be right out," Henry told him, shutting the door and going to retrieve some new clothes from the closet. While he was getting dressed, he heard faint knocking coming from what he assumed was Jimmy's room and then muffled voices.

Within five minutes Henry was dressed and ready to go. He put his .38 behind his back inside his pants waistband and then used his shirt to cover it from view.

Then he opened his door and stepped into the hallway.

Jimmy was just opening his door and smiled in a way of greeting when he saw Henry. The two men followed the guard outside where there was another golf cart waiting for them.

"Don't you guys use cars around here?" Jimmy asked the guard while they all climbed into the cart and it sped away down the street.

"Not inside the town limits. It wastes too much gas and once it's gone, it's gone for good," the guard said, avoiding an obstacle in the road.

"What about outside the town?" Henry asked.

"Well, yeah, then we do. Like when we go to other towns looking for supplies and stuff." The guard went quiet as if that explained it all.

Jimmy and Henry let it rest. That was enough information for now. Henry was distracted anyway when he saw the beautiful Victorian house they were pulling up to.

Henry's face brightened when he saw Mary standing on the porch, waiting for them. She waved to them and ran down the stairs, flying into Henry's arms before he had completely stepped out of the cart. Henry saw her bandaged shoulder and did his best to not hurt her.

"Oh, Henry, I was so worried about you, and you too, Jimmy," she said, placing a hand on Jimmy's shoulder.

"Us, too, it's good to see you're all right," Henry said, giving her another big hug.

She winced in pain from her wound and then quickly pulled away.

"Sorry, my arm still hurts. Come inside, wait to you see the amount of food they have for us," she said, starting up the stairs again with Henry's hand in hers.

Jimmy followed behind and in seconds they were all standing in the foyer. Henry and Jimmy looked around and took in the beautiful architecture.

"Wow, this place is nice," Jimmy said, as he wandered around the room and then stopped when he saw the dinner table through the doors leading into the next room.

An old woman seemed to appear out of the gloom surrounding the dinner table, and appeared to glide over to the companions, her long dress hiding her feet.

"Good evening, my name is Martha and I look after the Boss's affairs. If you'll follow me, I'll seat you for dinner. I've just received word that the Boss will be here in a matter of minutes."

Henry and Jimmy looked at Mary who nodded her approval and the three of them followed the old woman into the dining room, where they were each directed to sit in a specified chair.

Once everyone had been seated, Martha poured wine from what looked like an expensive vintage, although none of the companions were familiar with the finer points from the vineyard.

No sooner had the drinks been poured, then the master of the house and leader of the town walked into the room.

"Ah, good. I see that you're all here, excellent. Just let me get cleaned up and we'll eat and talk. I believe Jimmy has a few things to share with me, as well. About his second visit to Murphy's Bar, perhaps?" Then he walked off to wash and change.

Henry looked at Jimmy with questioning eyes and asked: "What's he talking about?"

Jimmy held up his hand to stop Henry from asking anything more. "You'll hear about it when I tell Sam, it's no big deal, really," he said.

Jimmy looked to Mary for help and she complied by changing the subject and asking Henry about what had happened since she'd passed out on the grassy plain in what seemed like weeks ago. Henry filled her in on most of what had happened, but was wary of what to say with Martha never too far from the table.

Then Sam entered the room, now wearing an ordinary plaid button down shirt and a pair of jeans.

He had on what looked to Henry to be a .357 Colt. The handle was polished so it reflected the candlelight in the room as Sam moved around the dining room and sat down at the head of the table.

Henry noticed there were two guards with rifles in hands standing in the hallway just outside the dining room. With a call from Sam, they would be in the room in a matter of moments, as Henry was sure Sam had planned it.

Sam noticed Henry's gaze and gave Henry a smile that carried no warmth in it.

"Just some insurance, my friend, nothing more, now, what do you say we eat?"

Sam looked to Martha, who nodded. Martha exited the room and within moments returned, leading three serving women who were carrying large bowls of stew.

The bowls were placed in front of the companions, the steam rising into the air to be lost in the darkness of the ceiling. Jimmy was the first to inquire about the meat floating in his bowl.

"That's deer and maybe some rabbit," Sam said, digging into his bowl. "We have good hunting not too far from town and have been able to bag a few animals from time to time. Since the contaminated rain began, the animals have learned to stay dry and their numbers are slowly coming back," he said, around a mouthful of stew.

The companions dug into their bowls and all agreed it was excellent. The stew was fragrant with the smell of garlic and onions. Large chunks of potatoes and carrots floated next to the meat, adding to the flavor. The meal was rounded off with a couple of loaves of fresh baked bread that was excellent to sop up the remaining gravy left in the bowls.

When everyone was finished, the dishes were cleared away and heaping bowls of canned peaches were brought in and placed on the dinner table.

Jimmy dug in with gusto and was the first to finish. He leaned back in his chair and reached under the table, inconspicuously unbuckling his pants to make room for his swollen belly.

Wow, he hadn't eaten like that in quite a while.

When the others had finished desert, and Martha had the helpers clear the dirty dishes away, she returned with two pots of piping, hot coffee. Then, with her job finished, she looked to Sam who nodded and waved her away.

Once she had left, Sam sat up in his chair, and removing a cigar from his shirt pocket, lit it and leaned back.

"Now that dinner's finished we can talk business," Sam said, looking at his new guests.

"What's going to happen to that guy from the bar?" Jimmy asked Sam.

Sam smiled, "First, why don't you tell me exactly what you saw there today."

Jimmy nodded and in quick short sentences, filled in Henry, Mary and Sam, who probably already knew what had gone down, about the shooting in the bar earlier that day. When he was done he sat back and waited.

Sam nodded. "That's what I heard, too. You did well today, Jimmy, you acted fast and took the man down."

"Yeah, but what happens to the guy now?" Jimmy asked again.

"Well, normally I would just have the man executed after we got to the bottom of it. I don't have any sympathy for murderers. As you know, there's not a lot of human beings left alive as it is, so we sure as shit can't go around killing each other." He took a long drag from his cigar and blew smoke across the table.

"I run an ordered town, here. Follow the rules and you'll do fine, but if you break my rules, well… let's just say, seems we're gonna do a recce of the neighboring town of Costington that I've got plans for the man other than a bullet in the head."

The three companions looked at each other, not understanding the meaning of Sam's last sentence.

Then Jimmy spoke up again.

"What's the deal with all this Boss shit that everyone calls you by?" Jimmy asked.

"Jesus, Jimmy, shut the hell up!" Henry hissed from across the table.

Sam only laughed at the young man, sat up, and placed his elbows on the table.

"That's okay, Henry, I don't mind the question. You see, Jimmy when everything went to shit a few months ago the police force around here were one of the first casualties. There was no one to lead the town and nobody seemed to want the job. So I took over as sheriff and mayor and whatever else needed to be done. I wasn't afraid to make a decision and whether it was the right one or the wrong one, I stood by it. The people around here respected that and after a couple of people jokingly called me Boss, well, the name just kind of stuck. I'm a fair man, Jimmy, but cross me and I'll cut your balls off as soon as look at you. That's what this town needs and I think I've done a pretty good job of taking care of it. The only thing is there aren't many grown men around. After Paul and a few other men, I've had to use boys no older than seventeen or so. That's where you men come in. You're experienced and know what to do when a walker is staring you in the face. That's why I need your help in taking over Costington. They have resources we sorely need here and until now I didn't have the manpower to go there. I think you two men would be enough to lead my security force into the town where we can wipe out every goddamn walker there."

His speech finished, Sam leaned back in his chair and blew more smoke across the dinner table.

Henry frowned and looked at his fellow companions. They nodded in confirmation of what they knew he was going to say.

"Well, Sam, I think this is a fool's errand and would prefer to just leave your town behind us. But as you've made abundantly clear, that isn't an option, so I guess we're in."

"Excellent," Sam said and leaned over and a retrieved a map of the local towns and surrounding area from a side table.

"Now here's what we'll do," he said through a smoke cloud from his cigar.

For the next hour and a half, Sam filled the companions in on his ideas on how to take the town, but first, in the morning, they would do a simple recce of the town and see what they had to deal with.

When dinner was over, Henry and Jimmy were escorted back to their rooms at the boarding house and Mary continued to stay in Sam's house where she could be watched. Sam knew she was the only leverage he had over the two warriors other than threatening their lives, and that would be counterproductive.

Henry and Jimmy had talked for a few minutes in the hallway outside their rooms, each discussing what the next day would bring, then they bid each other a goodnight and went into their rooms.

Once back in their separate rooms, Henry and Jimmy each lay down in their beds, and due to their full stomachs, it wasn't long before they drifted off to sleep.

Unfortunately for Henry, his sleep was filled with dreams of loved ones being ripped to shreds by ravenous zombies.

He tossed and turned until he woke in the middle of the night in a cold sweat.

There was a pitcher of water on his nightstand that been placed there when he had been at dinner and he now filled a glass and drank greedily from it.

When he was full, he lay back down on the bed and closed his eyes.

Sleep eluded him for a while, and then like it so often does, it crept up on him again. Before he realized it, he was fast asleep.

Thankfully, the rest of the night was peaceful.

## CHAPTER SEVENTEEN

THE NEXT MORNING brought the convoy rolling through the open gate of the barricade surrounding the town of Pittsfield.

The convoy consisted of two pickup trucks and an old bread delivery truck that had been modified as a mobile base.

Inside the bread truck were the extra weapons and ammunition that might be needed on their recce of the neighboring town of Costington. In the lead vehicle sat Henry and Jimmy. Sam was in the passenger seat and Paul was driving.

Henry noticed that the pickup trucks had been modified with steel pipes and canvas so that with the first fallen raindrop, a canvas sheet could be thrown over the back of the cab to protect anyone within from the deadly rain. Although at the moment, that particular threat was nonexistent, but was a possibility later in the day.

As the convoy drove through the gate, the sun was just rising on the horizon, where it cast an amber glow across the austere landscape on both sides of the highway.

The light also highlighted the light-green clouds that crackled with thunder as they floated across the otherwise clear blue sky.

Jimmy noticed the gray clouds and looked to Henry, who was also watching the sky warily.

"Think it might rain?" Jimmy asked him.

"Could be; just be ready if it does. I don't feel like putting a bullet in your head today if I can help it," Henry said with a wry smile.

Jimmy just frowned, finding the comment unamusing.

As the convoy rolled down the two lane road, they sometimes had to detour around old and abandoned cars spread out across the road at odd angles. The piles of metal were slowly starting to rust wherever the paint was scraped or scratched, and Henry figured within another few months they would be much, much worse.

The tires on the derelict vehicles were either flat or missing, scavenged by neighboring towns who knew there would be no more tires manufactured in America for a long time to come.

He silently wondered about the people who had been in those cars and what had happened to them. Had they been infected by the first rainstorm that was contaminated with bacteria? Or had they been attacked and ripped to pieces by roaming ghouls who had made them for lunch one afternoon.

While the convoy rolled past the rusting vehicles, he put those thoughts out of his mind and focused on the here and now. That kind of daydreaming could get you killed in the new America. All it took was one lapse in judgment and you could find yourself dead, or worse, you could find yourself walking around without a soul, dead, but still ambulatory.

Henry gazed out the front of the pickup as a dry wind blew some dust devils across the two-lane highway. He watched them until they hit the waist high grass that was now overgrown along the road, where they then dispersed, leaving no trace of their passage.

Sam turned in his seat and put his mouth near the small back window separating the back of the truck from the bed.

"We'll be there in about ten more minutes," he said with a slight grin.

Henry just nodded and stared off across the landscape, where there was nothing but grass and trees.

"What do you think we'll find there?" Jimmy asked him over the blowing wind as the truck drove down the middle of the highway at around 40 mph.

Henry just shrugged as he cast his eyes to Jimmy. "We'll find out when we get there, I suppose, but I'll tell you this…we're not gonna like what we find."

Then he turned to the front again and watched the road.

A little more than ten minutes later the first pickup, with Henry and Jimmy inside it, rolled to a soft stop at the edge of Costington; the other two vehicles pulling up behind them.

No more than five hundred feet away was the first building that signified the beginning of downtown. They had passed houses on their way, but they had been too spread out to pose much danger to them. All the homes had been abandoned, some fire blackened from past conflagrations. Some had animals living in them, Nature taking back what was rightfully hers, now that man was on the run.

As Henry and Jimmy hopped out of the cab, Henry could see a few bodies spread out across the road.

A murder of crows was busy picking at the remnants of dead flesh from the corpses, though all the soft, tender morsels were long gone.

Jimmy picked up a rock and threw it into their midst.

Their heads popped up at the bouncing rock and then they flew away, landing on the surrounding telephone wires, where they seemed to scold the convoy with their caws of annoyance.

Henry noticed the first building on the road into Costington was a VFW; the American flag still hanging from the white metal post in the front of the building.

The flag had faded over the past three months of inclement weather and it appeared to be torn around the edges from the constant abuse from the wind, the material slowly thinning. Henry thought there would be a time in the next few months when the flag would probably rip from its moorings, and then flutter down to land on the street where it would blow away to end up in the gutter.

That seemed to be a good analogy of America at the moment, he thought.

Then his eyes caught movement on the edge of his vision and he turned to see Sam leading a man in handcuffs from the bread truck.

"Hey, that's the guy from the bar yesterday," Jimmy said in a low voice to Henry while the man walked by them and was stopped at the front of the convoy.

"All right, Mike, here's the deal. I'm going to uncuff you and you're going to walk into that town."

"But what if I don't want to?" Mike said back, contemptuously.

"Then I put a bullet in your head right here and send someone else in," he said, giving the man a hard smile devoid of warmth.

Henry was starting to rue that smile when he saw it cross Sam's face.

Mike thought it over for a moment and decided he had nothing to lose.

Maybe when he was inside the town, he could make a break for it. Then he'd find his way out the other side of the town's limits and try for the next settlement.

The man nodded and Sam leaned forward and took off the man's handcuffs, then without any preamble, Sam shoved him forward.

"Go on, git, and if you try to run, I'll shoot you down like a dog. Just like you did to poor Roger yesterday."

With a shuffling of his feet, Mike started walking toward the town.

When he was closer to the first structures, he could see a lot of the buildings had seen fire and were now nothing more than blackened skeletons.

He walked under the crows and they cawed at him, as if they were condemning him for entering their sanctuary. In moments he was past them and was moving past the VFW. The flag snapped in the wind as the slight breeze pushed it across the pole.

The town looked empty and abandoned as he slowly shuffled up the middle of Main Street, Costington.

Above his head, a ripped banner flapped in the wind, proclaiming some summer celebration that would never happen. The road had parked cars lined up against the curb; their owners long gone and probably long dead.

When he was two more buildings into town, Sam called for him to stop. Then Paul jogged up to the VFW and pulled what looked like fireworks from his coveralls.

Lighting the pack of firecrackers, he threw them so they landed in the middle of the street. The fuse ran down and as Paul jogged back to the pickup, the firecrackers went off.

The loud popping sounded like gunfire as it echoed off the silent buildings.

Mike just stood there, wondering what the hell was going on, when suddenly he heard a moan coming from an alleyway to his right.

He turned to see two walkers shuffling out into the light of the street. Their bodies were desiccated and their faces were nothing more than skulls with bits of tattered flesh still sticking to the parched white bone.

As they shambled forward on what to Mike seemed like legs that couldn't possibly support motion, he started to back away.

That is until he heard the crashing of a trashcan and turned to see more walkers shambling out from whatever hiding places they had been using.

The fireworks had stopped now, but their mission had been successful. Every ghoul that was within earshot had heard the noise and was now investigating.

All they found was Mike.

As Mike turned in a circle, he found himself surrounded by the walking dead. There was nowhere to run.

He saw a small opening between what was once a man and a woman and went for it. Charging like a football player, he plowed through the desiccated couple, but he didn't make it more than ten feet before his legs became tangled by another walker and he pitched forward, straight into the pavement.

His nose was flattened when his face struck asphalt and blood poured from his nose to drip onto his shirt. With blood turning his shirt vermillion, he tried to get back to his feet, but it was too late.

Seconds after he struck the ground, the walkers surrounded him, and with hands like claws, they grabbed and ripped at his clothes and skin until they had him spread eagle on the street. His back felt hot when his skin touched the warm pavement and his shirt was ripped from his body; the asphalt beginning to heat up from the sun.

When the first nails and teeth sank into his flesh, he began to scream, but soon the pain grew in intensity, causing him to shriek instead.

Some walkers dove in and ripped a piece of flesh from his body, and then stumbled away with the tender morsel, while others dove in and continued to feed; unmindful of the other ghouls around them.

Within a matter of seconds his chest had been ripped open and the walkers were ripping him apart piece by piece, gobbets of meat flying in all directions, a massive pool of blood growing under the decimated body.

But still Mike was alive.

Through his pain he screamed to God to let him die, but the pain continued until he finally blacked out; which was just as well as the he wasn't able to feel it when his head was separated from his body.

In another few seconds his body was unrecognizable as once being human, the walkers gorging themselves on the raw meat.

Then, with most of the meat devoured, the zombies started to wander away back to their holes and hiding places.

A few spotted the three vehicles and started to move toward them, but it would be a few minutes before they reached the trucks, so no one in the convoy was panicking.


Through the entire ordeal of the slaughter of Mike, Henry and Jimmy stood on the pickup truck's bed and watched with wide eyes.

Jimmy's jaw was slack as the last of Mike's shrieks echoed off the buildings and floated away. They had lost sight of the man when the ghouls had surrounded him, and when Mike had fallen to the street Henry knew it was over for the poor bastard.

Jimmy knew the man was a murderer, but no man deserved to die like that.

"Christ, was that really fuckin' necessary?" Jimmy breathed, climbing down to the street, his face slightly pale. Though not a stranger to carnage and bloodshed, even Jimmy felt there was something off about such a barbaric execution.

"Yes, Jimmy. I'm afraid it was," Sam said. "First of all, you needed to see what we're up against, and second, that man murdered another man in cold blood. When we get back to Pittsfield, why don't you go ask Roger's wife if it was necessary."

"Point taken, but Jesus, a bullet in the head would've been more merciful," Jimmy mused.

"Perhaps, but I chose this and it's my goddamn town," Sam said, with a hardness to his voice that told Jimmy he was pushing his luck.

Henry heard the tone and hopped down next to Jimmy.

"Okay, Sam, we got it, you're probably right. Besides, what's done is done," Henry said, hoping to diffuse the situation.

Luckily, it seemed to work and Sam's eye's seemed to soften just a little. Then he turned away and directed his men to take out the walkers without using bullets, so as not to attract any more attention to their position.

In all, about twelve bodies were shambling in that drunken gait all who now survived knew so well. They left the town behind and moved towards the convoy to investigate the trucks and men. All stumbled down the middle of the road like blind men without their canes.

Henry pulled his panga, which he was now glad he'd brought, and together with the other men they got to work taking down the walkers.

Jimmy found a long metal pole lying in the truck's bed and he flicked it back and forth in his hands. At just over six feet, the pole would make a good long distance weapon against the walking corpses.

Sam had a twelve-inch Bowie knife that he expertly twisted in his hand, while he waited for the walkers to move closer.

Henry watched one of the young guards, studying his body movements. The boy kept tossing his knife back and forth from hand to hand nervously. Henry walked over to him and placed a hand on the boy's shoulder. The boy jumped from the touch, but relaxed when he saw who it was.

"What's your name, son?" Henry asked him in a soothing voice.

"Uh, Domenic, sir."

"Well, Domenic, pick which hand you want your knife in and leave it there. You don't want to end up dropping it at the wrong moment. Have you ever fought one of the dead before, son?"

"N...n...no, sir," he stammered, clearly nervous.

"Okay, well then, listen to me, because I've killed more deaders than I can count."

"Deaders?" Domenic asked.

"Just another name for a walker, son. Now listen, they're slow so as long as you keep moving they can't get a lock on you. But be careful, because if they do grab you, their grip can be damn hard to break. You hear me?" Henry asked, looking into the boy's eyes.

Domenic nodded, taking in all the information Henry was giving him; then it was time to fight, as the walkers were now only a few feet away.

"Look, kid, just stay by me and do what I do and you'll be fine, Okay?"

Domenic nodded, and was about to say something else when it became too late; the undead were now on top of them.

Sam waded into their midst with no fear and severed a head with his Bowie knife before anyone else. Henry watched as the man ripped the head off the corpse and then threw it at the face of another one. The skull of the severed head crushed the nose of another walker, but otherwise did little damage.

Henry watched as Jimmy impaled a ghoul in the mouth with the end of his pipe. The dead man struggled at the end like a puppet, until Jimmy twisted the pipe and the man fell to the ground. Then Jimmy brought the pipe down like a club and caved in the dead man's skull.

Blood and brains spread across the road as Jimmy slung the gore off the end and then went after another one.

Henry had his hands full for a few moments as well when two attackers went for him and Domenic. Henry had already taken his panga out, and when the first walker was within his blade's reach, he brought his knife down and severed the ghoul's hands at the wrist. The walking corpse was already pretty desiccated and only a minimal amount of blood spurted from the severed joints. It kicked its own hands in the street like a soccer ball as it stumbled toward him, barely noticing the missing limbs.

Henry kneeled down and swung his panga horizontally across the ground, taking out the ghoul's legs at the knees. The body dropped to the ground like a felled tree and then proceeded to crawl, but by then Henry had forgotten it as the ghoul was mostly harmless.

He turned to see Domenic and the boy wasn't faring so well.

Domenic's small, seven-inch knife didn't give him enough reach to do a lot of damage to the dead woman attacking him, and thanks to his inexperience, he was barely holding his own. The woman continually tried to grab him and it was only blind luck that was keeping Domenic safe. Then he slipped on one of the severed hands on the ground and fell hard onto his back, his head striking the pavement.

For a moment all he saw were stars, then his vision cleared and he looked up at the face of the woman's pale and slack-jawed face as she bent over to rip his throat out.

He became frozen in fright, and as he closed his eyes and waited for the inevitable, he suddenly heard a thwacking sound and then felt a small amount of liquid dripping onto his cheek.

He opened his eyes to see Henry's panga firmly imbedded in the dead woman's forehead. Almost casually, Henry pushed her off his blade with his foot for leverage, and as she tumbled to the ground in a heap of limbs, he held out a hand for Domenic to take.

"Come on, kid, its all right, killing deaders isn't for everyone."

Domenic smiled shyly and let Henry help him to his feet. Henry slapped him on the back and then went off to see who needed his help.

But when Henry looked around the open street, he could see the battle, or massacre, was over.

Jimmy had just finished off the last one and was even now pulling the pipe from the back of a ghoul's skull where he had imbedded it like a nail going through a piece of wood. When the pipe came free, he had to shake it to release the round, two-inch piece of skull that had become wedged into the hollow tip.

The piece of skull popped out and was followed by a wet plopping sound, brain matter falling to the ground behind him.

Jimmy made a disgusted face, rubbing the end of the pipe in the dirt to try to clean it.

"Shit, that's got to be one of the nastiest things I've seen lately," he said as he finished cleaning the pipe and walked back to the pickup.

On his way to the truck, a severed head got in his path, so he lined it up like a football and kicked it onto the shoulder of the road.

"And it's good… two points… and the crowd goes wild!" He said, jogging back to the truck with his hands in the air in celebration of his kick.

Henry shook his head at his friend's antics, hopping back into the pickup's rear bed. It was all so classic Jimmy.

Sam came up and stood beside the truck and placed his arms on the side rail.

"Well, what do you think?" he inquired, looking up into Henry's face.

"I think it might be doable after all. Just give me some time to work out the kinks and I'll get back to you later in the day. Also, I'd like to ask why we fought those walkers when we could have just driven away. What was the point?" Henry asked.

"The point," Sam said. "Is that my men need experience and I can't give them that hiding behind our barricade. I can't think of a more controlled exercise than what we just had. Can you?"

Henry shook his head. "No, I guess not. I just hate taking chances for no reason, is all."

Sam nodded also, agreeing with him. "I agree, but if my men can't deal with a few stragglers, they're useless to me."

Jimmy walked up to them and jumped into the bed. "Well, that was fun," he mused, dropping the pipe back onto the floor of the truck. "I especially liked it when the zombies came."

Sam was about to say something when Henry placed his hand on Sam's shoulder, shaking his head no. Sam smiled at Henry, understanding what he meant.

Sometimes with Jimmy, the best thing was to say nothing at all.

"All right, men, let's pack it up and head home!" Sam called out, getting the men to begin packing it up. The recce was over, it was time to leave.

It took only minutes for the convoy to load up and turn around. The sound of crunching rose up from the road as the convoy crushed miscellaneous bloody body parts under their wheels.

The convoy headed back to Pittsfield, with Henry pondering a few ideas to retake the town from the dead.

Behind them, the crows returned and began to feast on the fresh corpses, their cries following the convoy down the highway, chastising them for coming in the first place.

## CHAPTER EIGHTEEN

THE TRIP BACK to town was taken in relative silence, everyone digesting what they'd seen.

Henry was already formulating a plan that would have them taking back the town with minimal losses. He only had to work the finer points out with Jimmy before he would take his proposition to Sam.

The small convoy of three vehicles began climbing to the top of an incline in the road and upon reaching the top; the town of Pittsfield came into view.

From the smoke coming from the interior of the town it was easy to see there was a problem.

Henry leaned down to the back window of the truck to see Sam on his two-way radio. When he finished talking, Henry spoke up.

"I can see smoke. What's going on?" He inquired.

Sam's face was set like stone as he turned his face to the small opening.

"The damn library's on fire and there's people trapped inside. We have a fire department, it's small, mind you, just one truck, but it'll do the job. When we get inside the town I'll need your help. Our fire department is mostly volunteers."

Henry nodded yes. "Of course we'll help," he said, looking to Jimmy.

"Hell, yes," Jimmy said in agreement.

Sam smiled in thanks and turned forward again, telling the driver to pick up the pace.

His people needed him now.


Ten minutes later the convoy rolled through the makeshift gate and then continued on into the town.

Moments later, the pickup had to stop, due to the street being choked with people who were curious or there to help.

Henry jumped off the back of the truck and surveyed the fire.

The library was a quaint old wooden structure with two floors. The second story of the building was now burning, black smoke billowing into the sky where a light breeze would catch it, sending it across the town.

Sam was already in the thick of things as he shrugged into a yellow, fireman's jacket.

The fire truck had already pulled up and men were busy scrambling to unravel hoses from the old relic.

"Holy shit. That thing should be in a museum," Jimmy said, looking over the fire truck.

The fire truck had to be at least sixty years old with a big round container on the back that held hundreds of gallons of water.

Sam came up next to the two companions and smiled.

"I know what you're thinking, but it has its own pumps, and with the pressure for the hydrants off, I'd say that's pretty damn good," Sam said proudly.

Henry had to agree. With power off in every major city, many small town's had gone back to a simpler way of performing functions, such as washing clothes and gardening. Technology was only as good as the power to supply it.

Henry and Jimmy grabbed a hose, and with Sam in the lead, they dragged it to the front of the library.

Henry looked around and saw some of the men he'd seen at the bar the day before. This time instead of having drinks in their hands, they carried fire axes and buckets of water as they threw them on adjoining buildings to stop any sparks from spreading to the other structures.

"If we don't get this fire under control, we could lose the whole damn town!" Sam shouted over the roar of the water as it surged out of the hose nozzle.

It took the three men to hold it steady, the water pressure inside making the hose buck and kick like a giant snake. Luckily, the wind was blowing the spray away from the companions as they held the hose tight.

Then an old woman stumbled out of the front door of the library, coughing and gagging from breathing the acrid smoke.

A security guard ran up and helped her down the stairs, and after a few moments the guard ran up to Sam. It was hard for Henry to hear what the guard was saying, but in a moment he left and Sam turned his head to look over his shoulder at Henry.

"He said the old lady says there's at least ten more people inside; some of them children. But the front hall ceiling collapsed and there's no way to get to them."

"What about a fire escape on the back of the building?" Henry asked, yelling over the noise.

Sam shook his head no. "A lot of these old buildings aren't up to code. Before everything fell apart a few months ago, we were in the process of upgrading. But after everything that's happened it didn't seem like a priority!" He shouted back.

Henry just nodded. With the world the way it was now, just staying alive was a full time job.

Sam sprayed the water at the front of the library. The waterfall of water slowly pushing the fire back. To Henry it looked like the fire was under control and would be out shortly.

That's when he got a better look at the color of the water coming out of the fire hose. With all the chaos, he hadn't even thought to check, but with thing's now growing under control, he could see the water was tinted a light-green.

He tapped Sam on the back and yelled: "Where did the water in the fire truck's tank come from?"

Sam shifted his weight and sent the spray to the other end of the building. The fire was out and men were starting to clean up and shoo people away. Sam was spraying the façade of he building now just to be safe.

"I'm not sure, why?" He replied.

"Well, if that's contaminated water then were killing the people trapped inside the library!" He yelled, but then lowered his voice when Sam turned the valve on the hose and shut off its flow.

With the water dripping slowly from the nozzle, Sam threw it to the ground like it had burned him.

"You don't mean…" He trailed off, not wanting to admit it, even though he already knew what Henry was going to say.

"Yeah, I'm afraid so. If any of the people inside were saturated with water then they're probably walkers by now."

"Oh shit, that sucks. We killed them trying to save them," Jimmy added, a mournful look on is face.

Paul heard the conversation and walked over to the three men.

"You had no choice, even if you knew, Boss. That damn fire could have spread to the whole town. Who knows how many would have died then," Paul said, reassuringly.

"Don't you think I fucking know that?" Sam snapped back, then stopped and caught himself. Taking a deep breath, he turned to Paul and placed a hand on his shoulder.

"Sorry about that. I shouldn't have snapped at you. But Jesus, we're losing people so damn fast that within another six months the damn town will be deserted," Sam said.

"Perhaps, but you can't think like that. If you give up, then you might as well just eat a bullet now and save yourself some suffering," Henry said from behind him.

Sam seemed to ponder that for a moment. Then his jaw set firm and his eyes twinkled just a little.

"Damn it, you're right. I'm not ready to die yet and neither are my men. Am I right men?" He shouted this over the small group of volunteers who were in the area and had heard the exchange between Sam and Henry.

A small roar of shouts and yells went up as the men cheered their leader. Then when the voices had died down, Sam stood on the bumper of the fire truck.

"All right, we know what we have to do. If some of the people in the library have turned into walkers then we have to go in there and destroy them. They're not our friends and family anymore. Now they're abominations, and if we don't kill them then you better bet your ass they'll try to kill us. Are you with me?" He shouted loudly while pumping his arms in the air.

Cheers went up as the men showed their support for their leader.

Henry and Jimmy stood at the edges of the group of men and watched the show.

"Well, you've got to admit the man knows how to get people motivated," Jimmy said through the side of his mouth.

Henry nodded in agreement. "Yeah, well, what choice do they have? It's kill or be killed."

Jimmy was about to add something more when he stopped at Sam's approach.

"Pretty nice speech," Henry stated.

"Yeah, well, it had to be said. The men need it every now and then. Look, you don't have to help, but you and your friend here are pretty handy with your weapons and I could use some help inside the library. What do you say?"

"I say you release Mary and take us at our word that we'll help you with Costington and you've got a deal," Henry said, seriously.

Sam just stood there and looked at the two of them as he considered Henry's proposition. Then to Henry's surprise, Sam grinned, the smile going to his eyes, as well.

"All right, I think I can trust the two of you to honor your promises. After what I've seen since you came to my town, I believe you're both honorable men. Deal," Sam said, holding out his hand for Henry to shake.

Henry grasped the man's hand.

He could feel the power in that handshake, and wondered if Sam had wanted to, if he could have crushed his hand.

But then his hand was released as Sam turned to Jimmy, shaking his hand as well. When he released Jimmy's hand, Jimmy was clearly in a little mild pain and he waved his hand up and down like he was trying to shake water off it.

"Damn, that's a firm grip," he gasped, flexing his fingers.

"Oh, quit crying, you're fine," Henry said with a subtle smile across his lips.

Then the three men walked over to the front of the library where they joined up with a few volunteers and guards.

"All right, I want you, you, and you, to go inside the library with me and these two men," Sam said, gesturing to Henry and Jimmy. "These two know how to handle themselves and if they tell you to do something, you better damn well do it. Do I make myself clear?" Sam asked the surrounding men.

After hearing grunts of agreement, Sam nodded. "Good, then let's get armed and see what's inside?"

There was a flutter of activity while men went off to retrieve their weapons from the pickup trucks. The sound of rifles and revolvers being cocked and checked filled the street as weapons were readied for the dirty job of cleaning out the library.

Sam looked to Henry and Jimmy as the big man pulled his weapon from its holster.

"You two ready for this?" He asked, pulling back the hammer on his Colt.

"Ready as we'll ever be. Right, Jimmy?" Henry asked, askance of Jimmy.

"Damn straight. Let's go kill some deaders," Jimmy said, pumping himself up for action.

Sam quirked the side of his mouth in a subtle grin at Jimmy's name for the walkers, then he nodded in approval, the three of them, followed by three guards, starting up the wet stairs of the library.

Hopefully there would be survivors. Alive and well, preferably.

But if not, then unfortunately, it's nothing a bullet to the head won't fix.

# CHAPTER NINETEEN

HENRY WAS THE first one through the library's front door, his shotgun leading the way. The point of the barrel left a scratch on the beautifully, oak-stained, wooden door as it opened to the side.

No one cared.

The first floor of the library was a large room split off into different sections for fiction, drama, mystery and the like, with a large mahogany desk set squarely in the middle.

The ashes from the fire covered the front desk and every available surface like a blanket of black and gray snow. The air inside the room smelled like burnt, wet wood. Hundreds of books everywhere were destroyed by water damage as the water had found its way down from the second floor.

Henry stepped around a steady drip where a knot of wood had dislodged in the ceiling panels, allowing the water to pass through. The others followed suit and within minutes the six men were clustered inside the room.

The gloom was omnipresent, the men scanning the room for survivors.

"Everyone must have gotten out of here okay when the fire started," Sam suggested from Henry's side.

Henry just nodded, moving deeper into the room, his feet squishing on scattered remnants of books spread out on the floor like a soggy, paper carpet.

Then they heard the floorboards creak above their heads and everyone stopped in their tracks.

"Do you think that's just stuff settling after the fire?" Jimmy asked no one in particular.

Then another thump, sounding like something had been knocked over, filled the silent room from above.

Henry turned to look at Sam, waiting for his approval to move on. With a silent nod, Sam pointed to the stairs leading to the second floor.

Pumping his shotgun and placing a reassuring hand on his panga, Henry moved across the room. The shadows were deeper by the stairs, the windows covered with tint to protect the books from damaging sunlight.

Henry was about to place his foot on the first step of the stairwell when a walker lunged from the shadows with both hands raised to kill.

Henry jumped back from the dead man's manic charge and then smacked the ghoul in the face with the stock of his weapon. The ghoul hesitated for a moment, but didn't fall.

Jimmy moved in and kicked the dead man in the balls, slowing him further. Then Henry pulled his panga free of its sheath in one fluid motion.

The fighting was in close quarters due to the shelves of books, so Henry took the panga and thrust it at the man.

The metal blade slipped into the walking corpse's mouth and pinned the man's tongue to the roof of his mouth. With a slight twist, Henry pulled the knife out and a waterfall of vermilion cascaded down the stairs.

Jimmy had his .38 ready now and placed two bullets into the man's pale face. In the midst of spraying blood and brains, the ghoul fell over to land on the first few steps, laying still with the exception of a few death twitches.

Without hesitating, Sam leaned down and pulled the corpse off the stairs for easier passage, dragging the body by its shirt collar.

With Henry on point, the six of them climbed the stairs. After only moments, Henry reached the top and scanned his surroundings with the others following right behind him.

The ripe air could be cut with a knife and the men raised neckerchiefs or put rags over their mouths to dull the smell of burning meat. The massive bookshelves were spread across the floor and from above would have looked like a maze.

Henry turned to Sam. "We should split up. We don't want anything getting past us. Two teams, three each," Henry suggested.

Sam nodded. "Sounds good. You take Fred here and I'll take the other two," he said, stepping to the side for his men to gather around him.

"All right, you check left and I'll go right," Henry stated and then with a nod to Jimmy he turned off and disappeared behind a bookshelf with encyclopedias stacked to the ceiling, Jimmy and Fred close behind.

Sam waited for them to leave and then turned and went off to the back of the library with his two men close behind him.

The hunt was far from over.

*   *   *

Fred was about twenty-five years old, with a skinny body and a head that was too large for his small frame. Jimmy turned to look at him and couldn't help but think of those artists at the beach or a town fair, who would paint your picture with the head larger than the body.

Jimmy playfully punched Fred in the shoulder.

"Relax, man, we're professionals," Jimmy smiled, turning a corner of a book shelf and walking smack dab into a walker.

Jimmy jumped back, pushing Fred into the bookshelf behind him. For the moment, Jimmy was alone, separated from the others. Henry was on the other side of the bookshelf, while Fred was struggling with being buried under a pile of books behind him.

Jimmy brought up his weapon, but in the tight aisles, he caught it on the binding of a very large book about evolution. By the time he'd freed it, the zombie had pounced onto him and forced him to the floor.

The dead woman's mouth, of what had once been the librarian, tried to sink her teeth into his neck as he struggled under the dead weight of her body. His weapon and arm were trapped under him at an odd angle and he didn't have enough leverage to pull it free.

His left hand grasped a leather bound book on his left side, and acting quickly, Jimmy picked it up and thrust the book into the woman's mouth.

Instead of sinking her teeth into the soft flesh of his neck, the dead librarian had to settle for leather.

With those teeth out of action for a few precious heartbeats, Jimmy was now able to get his hand under her chin and push her head back and up.

Then a police Glock came through a side shelf where the books had fallen, and stopped at the side of her head. With a gentle squeeze of the trigger, the dead woman's right ear and most of her cheek disappeared, coating the adjacent shelves with blood and brain matter.

The body slumped onto Jimmy and remained still.

"A little help here?" Jimmy asked from under the dead weight of the now fully dead corpse.

Fred grabbed an arm of the body, and with a few good heaves, pulled her off enough for Jimmy to climb out and regain his footing.

Jimmy looked at Fred with a mixture of disappointment and hate.

"Where the fuck were you man? That bitch could have killed me?" Jimmy snapped at the man as he wiped some brain matter that had fallen onto his shirt.

Fred stood there with his mouth open, not quite knowing what to say.

"Forget it, man, just forget it," Jimmy said in a disgusted tone and then turned to move down the cramped aisle.

"Thanks, Henry, you saved my ass, again," Jimmy said, rounding the bookshelf and catching up to Henry.

"No problem, you can repay the favor later when there's something trying to bite my ass," Henry said with a grin.

"Deal," Jimmy agreed with a disdainful look over his shoulder at Fred. Then the three of them moved deeper into the labyrinth of bookshelves, Jimmy now being more cautious after his close call with death.

Sam heard the noise of Jimmy struggling with the librarian, but knew he was too far away to be much help.

Besides, he had his own problems at the moment.

Stepping into a room to his right, his heart broke when he realized it was where all the children's books were kept.

With his Colt leading the way, he stepped into a charnel house of blackened wood and burned meat.

From the damage in the room, it was easy to see this was where most of the blaze had been concentrated, a few melted candles scattered across the floor hinting at the possible cause of the fire. While smoke continued to drift from the water-logged ruins, his eyes scanned the room for movement.

He noticed a table in the corner, and when he moved closer, he saw two, small, unmoving bodies curled up into balls under it.

Both of the tiny corpse's eyes were open in death, their faces contorted in pain.

Sam crossed himself, saying a silent prayer for the two lost souls to find Heaven, and then his breath lodged in his throat when the pupils of the two bodies swiveled in their sockets, the heads moving slightly, blackened flesh falling from their necks like flakes of chipping paint.

"Oh my Lord," Sam gasped as the two children crawled out from under their hiding spot. The sound of creaking leather filled the room, their burnt skin shifting on their bones. The guards behind Sam each backed up a step, both too shocked to do anything more than stare.

Slowly, with mouths hanging slack, white teeth popping out against their charred faces, the two newly risen ghouls approached Sam.

At first he didn't move, too shocked to do more than stare at the small monstrosities. No matter how many times he witnessed a walker, it still mystified him. These were dead human beings, somehow still functioning. And the fact they were children only made the pill that harder to swallow.

Swallowing a knot in his throat, he realized he needed to do something. If not, the two ghouls would escape to cause trouble and possibly kill others.

With infinite slowness, he raised his Colt to waist level, which was eye level with the first dead child. Milky white eyes gazed back at him, teeth gnashing at empty air as they struggled to cross the room and reach him.

With a tear sliding down his cheek, he bit his lower lip and sent a lead slug into each child's brain.

The bodies were thrown across the room like rag dolls, the force of the powerful rounds literally blowing their heads into a dozen pieces. The small forms dropped to the floor and remained still, a deep-red scarlet spilling from the jagged wounds to mix with the Dr. Seuss and Pied Piper books strewn across the floor.

"Jesus Christ, those were kids," one of the guards said from behind him.

"Yeah, but there's nothing we can do for them now. The question is… where are the mothers of these kids?" Sam asked, not expecting an answer.

Turning back around, he started to leave the room when he heard a scratching coming from the far wall.

"Both of you, stay sharp," Sam hissed, slowly creeping across the room, his ears tracking the sound he'd just heard.

His feet crunched on the debris scattered across the floor as he carefully picked his way across the room. His foot landed on The Cat in the Hat, the slick, wet cover of the book almost sending him flying onto his back before he caught his balance.

He turned to see if his men had seen him, but they had barely noticed, as they too, scanned the room for signs of life, or death, as the case may be.

His pride intact, Sam started off again, and within moments was standing at a closet door at the end of the room.

A six foot bookshelf had fallen onto it and had protected the door from the brunt of the fire and heat. After first slipping on a pair of leather, water-proof gloves to protect himself, he began pushing and pulling on the wet, soggy books lining the shelves so he could move the heavy piece of furniture out of the way.

After a few minutes of work, his task was done and the shelves were bare. Taking extra care to stay away from any puddles on the floor, he pushed his large frame against the shelf, and after a few seconds, levered it away from the door.

Then he stood back and took a breath, the rank air in the room making him want to gag.

"All right, boys, I'm gonna see what's inside," he said, wiping soot from his gloves onto his pants.

"Good luck, Boss," one of the guards said, reassuringly.

"Yeah, thanks. You just be ready for whatever happens next," Sam ordered as he stepped back up to the closet door.

The scratching sound was louder now that the shelf had been removed.

"Hello, anyone in there? Are you okay?" Sam asked the door, hoping for a response.

Nothing came to his ears but more scratching. "Shit, I hate this part," he said.

Slowly, he reached up with his large hand and grasped the doorknob of the closet.

Turning the knob, he gently pulled the door open, the debris on the floor moving to leave a clean spot as the door dragged along the wooden floor.

The door wasn't open more than a few inches when a small arm reached out into the room. The arm was as black as night, the charred skin flaking off to show the pink and red of muscle and sinew beneath.

As hard a man as he was, the sight made Sam jump back for a moment, taken off guard.

Then the door swung open more and a small child of no more than eight or nine stumbled into the room. Or at least it was once a small child.

The only reason to assume this was because of the size of the blackened body.

What was left of the face hung in dark ribbons, the white of bone peeking through. One eye was missing, and as the small walker staggered into the room, its nose fell off and was crushed under its own small feet with a crunching sound.

One of the guards saw this and had to turn and vomit, his lunch splashing across the floor to his right, where it mixed with the black soup already on the floor.

The child ghoul's clothes were practically nonexistent as it tried to decide who to attack first.

Sam stared in horror, deducing that the child must have been on fire when it had run into the closet to hide and was then trapped by the falling bookshelf.

His heart felt like it was ripped out of his chest as he thought of this innocent child suffering like that. He wondered if it had been on fire before or after it had been zombified.

He hoped after, assuming there probably wouldn't have been pain.

The small ghoul had decided on the puking guard for a target and had started toward him when Sam walked up to it and placed his Colt against the charred temple.

Without hesitation, he pulled the trigger, sending bone and brain matter spraying across the room. The body pitched to the side and landed lightly due to its weight. With half its head now missing it did not move again.

With a weight in his heart after having to put three children down in almost as many minutes, Sam left the room, at the moment not really caring if his guards were with him or not.

He hadn't made it more than a few steps out of the room when he was assaulted by two women ghouls.

The female walkers were no more than five and a half feet tall each, and they each grabbed an arm and tried to pull Sam to the floor.

With a yell, Sam brought his arms together, the two women colliding in front of him. Their heads connected with a dull thump and Sam pushed them away.

The bodies flew into a bookshelf, knocking it down; where they then became buried under an avalanche of books.

Sam heard noise behind him and turned to see his guards come rushing through the door from the children's room.

"Oh shit, that's Miss Mahoney. She lives on my block," one of the guards said.

"Is she all right?" He asked.

"No, she's not all right. She's fuckin' dead!" Sam shouted at the ignorant man.

"Now get the hell over here and take them out. Or do I have to kill every goddamn one by myself?" Sam yelled at the two men.

"Yes, sir, Boss, I got this," said the guard on the right. Sam was pretty sure his name was Steven or something that began with an S.

The guard brought up his rifle, and after checking to see the safety was off, lined up one of the women in his sights.

The ghouls, however, weren't waiting patiently to be slaughtered and were already on the move again. After a few clumsy attempts at standing, the two dead women managed to regain their footing and started toward the guard.

Sam waited to the side for the guard to shoot, but after a few tense heartbeats, he realized the kid had froze up.

"You," Sam said to the other guard. "Shoot those bitches before they kill your buddy."

The guard nodded and raised his rifle. At least this man was able to keep a clear head.

With a buck of the rifle, the guard fired across the room at the approaching walkers. The bullet struck the left woman in her right breast, a spray of blood shooting from her chest.

"The head man, shoot her in the head!" Sam yelled to the guard.

The man quickly adjusted his aim and fired again. This time his shot was true and it plowed into the woman's right eye. The back of her skull exploded as the ghoul fell to the floor; this time dead for good.

The other dead woman hadn't slowed in the least as she continued toward the guard. At the last second, the guard snapped out of his stupor and realized the danger he was in. The woman charged into him, pushing his rifle against him so the barrel was pointing straight up at the ceiling.

The woman leaned in to take a bite out of the guard's left cheek, but at that precise second, the guard squeezed the trigger of his rifle in panic.

The bullet went straight up, passing through the woman's jaw from underneath and then plowing straight up into through her head.

The top of her skull exploded upward like a Jack-in-the-box. Bits of skull and brain matter spun in the air to rain down on the frightened guard while he stood in place. He hadn't realized yet that he had just killed his first walker.

"Well I'll be a son of a bitch. That was the luckiest thing I've ever seen," Sam said, walking over to the guard.

The corpse of the woman was still leaning against him and Sam grabbed it by the blue dress it was wearing and tossed it to the side.

"You should be dead right now. You know that, don't you, son?" Sam asked the guard.

The man just nodded weakly as bits of brain and blood slid down his cheek.

Sam slapped him on the back. "Well screw it, a kill is a kill. Come on; let's go see how the others are doing."

After a moment to get themselves squared away, the three men went off in search of the other half of their group.

# CHAPTER TWENTY

HENRY HEARD THE muffled shouts of Sam and his men, so he turned to Jimmy and quietly asked: "Think they're all right?"

Jimmy shrugged. "Don't know, want to go check?"

"Nah, Sam's a big boy. He can take care of himself."

Jimmy was ready with a comeback to that when he stopped and cocked his head to the right.

"What is it, you hear somethin'," Henry asked quietly, again. He didn't know if it was because they were on a recce of the building or just because it was beaten into him since he was a child, but he couldn't help keeping his voice down inside a library.

Jimmy held up his finger in the classic, give me a second. He listened for another moment and then gestured to the left with the business end of his .38, off behind a set of bookshelves.

Henry turned to follow his pointing finger, and after a moment of hearing nothing but his beating heart in his ears, a soft slurping sound made itself known.

As he watched the bookcase, he was able to see subtle movement through the gaps on the shelves, where the books were stacked halfheartedly.

It was a ghoul. It had to be.

Nodding to Jimmy, he used hand signals to tell Jimmy to circle around to the left, so as to flank the walker behind the bookcase. Then he pointed to himself and waved his hand to the front, telling Jimmy he was going to come at whatever was there from the front of the bookcase, and thereby the two of them could catch the ghoul in the middle.

Jimmy nodded and crept off down the aisle. Henry then turned to Fred and pointed to the floor directly in front of the man. Stay put, his sign language told Fred.

Fred nodded and did as he was told while Henry slowly crept to the front of the bookcase.

Creeping closer, the slurping sound grew louder and Henry swallowed the saliva building in his mouth in expectation of what he would find on the other side of that bookcase.

With his shotgun leading the way, Henry made it to the end of the aisle and slowly poked his head around the wooden end cap.

For just a second he hesitated. He'd thought he was immune to the sights of gore and horror after months of fighting the undead, but what he saw at the end of the four foot aisle was enough to make even the toughest man feel bile growing in his throat.

Spread out on the floor, with her chest ripped open, was a woman who couldn't have been a day over twenty-five. Straddled on top of her like a cowboy riding a horse was a small child of no more than five years of age.

Henry took a step closer, his boot crackling as he crushed a piece of debris. The child's head snapped up and turned to look at Henry.

Its small blue-white eyes seemed to burn into Henry's soul as they flared with malevolence and its skin had taken on a pale-blue and gray color, depending on what part you were looking at.

Henry was so taken aback; he actually took two steps backward before he caught himself. Then, straightening his shoulders, he renewed his resolve and stepped into the aisle.

As he moved closer, he could see the child had been busy. The woman's chest had been ripped open and blood and entrails littered the floor around her.

Henry noticed some of her shirt looked singed, probably from the fire.

Evidently, with the rush to escape, the child had been sprayed with the contaminated hose water and had then attacked its mother as the woman had tried to get her child to safety.

The irony was too sickening to even think about, so Henry pushed it from his conscious mind. There was only going to be one end to this sad little story and it involved a bullet to the head.

Pumping his shotgun, Henry stepped toward the dead child. The child looked up at Henry, blood dripping from its chin, and hissed at him.

Jimmy was now at the other end of the aisle, and with his jaw hanging open, he walked up to the mother and child.

The child was now off its mother and had started to crawl toward Henry, leaving a bloody trail behind it, like a sick parody of a snail.

Jimmy watched the child crawling closer to Henry and he waited for his friend to blow the little ghoul straight to Hell, but he just stood there.

"Come on, man, what the hell are you waiting for?" Jimmy snapped.

"Nothing, it's just...Jesus, Jimmy, it's a goddamn kid," Henry breathed as he stared at the little body slowly moving toward him.

"It was a kid. Now it's just another deader that needs to be killed. Now, if you're not gonna do it, get out of the way and I will," Jimmy said, his jaw taut as he raised his .38.

"Okay, relax. I'll do it. It's just..."

"I know, man, it sucks, but it has to be done," Jimmy said quietly.

Henry nodded and then let out a long sigh.

The tiny ghoul was about to reach up and grab Henry's pant leg when Henry took a step back and placed the shotgun just above the top of its head.

The blast from the shotgun blew through the small head and the little body was slammed to the floor like it had been stepped on by a giant boot. The ferocity of the blast made the head literally disappear, the floor beneath becoming pockmarked with buckshot and skull fragments.

Henry just stood there, in a state of mild shock. He'd killed zombie children before and it had never hit him as hard as this one did.

Maybe he was burnt out.

Jimmy stepped over the small corpse, careful not to place his boots in the river of blood, and placed his hand on Henry's shoulder.

"You had to do it, man. There wasn't any choice."

Henry looked down at the small corpse and then turned away, walking back out to the main thoroughfare that bisected the library.

Jimmy took one more fleeting look at the two bodies, mother and son, and then followed.

Fred looked up as the two men reappeared and let out the breath he'd been holding.

When Henry and Jimmy headed off deeper into the library, he'd started off after them, but had then stopped, remembering Henry's order to stay put.

Before the world had gone to Hell, Fred was about to graduate high school and was probably going to work in his father's local hardware store.

He had a pretty girlfriend and an old car that he loved to tinker with. Things were going fine. And then the deadly rains came and shattered any hopes and dreams he had for a normal life.

Now he was walking around a burnt-out library looking for the walking dead with a couple of bonafide zombie hunters.

How could his life get any worse?

Stepping around a pile of moist books spread across the floor, he stopped when he heard a creaking sound.

He called out to the others, but they didn't hear him. Listening intently, he tried to pinpoint where the sound had come from when the creaking sound began again, this time coming from above him.

He glanced up at the ceiling and noticed water droplets collecting on the thin ceiling panels. He was about to call out to Henry and Jimmy again, when the ceiling cracked open down the middle, directly above his head, and a deluge of water poured down onto him, splashing him like had entered a small waterfall.

Sputtering and coughing, he cursed life.

Great, now on top of everything else, he was soaking wet.

Walking out of the path of the now trickling waterfall, he stomped his boots.

He was about to start yelling at the others to help him when all of a sudden his vision began to blur. Placing his hands to his eyes, he rubbed them, wondering if the water was messing with his eyesight. But after a moment he realized it was his eyes themselves that were malfunctioning.

Then a wave of nausea flooded through him and he started to feel weak. Through blurry eyes he looked for a place to sit down and rest, not comprehending what was happening to him.

Then, like a light switch being turned off, he fainted and slumped to the floor.

His body made a small splash when it landed in the green-tinted puddles spread out around his boots.

His eyes fluttered for a moment and then closed forever.


At the sound of the collapsing ceiling, Henry and Jimmy turned with weapons ready to fire.

Upon seeing Fred drenched in water, Jimmy immediately moved to help him, but was stopped short by Henry's firm grip on his arm.

"Wait, damn you, if that water's contaminated then he's already dead! And you will be too if that shit gets on you, as well!"

"But we've got to help him!" Jimmy yelled, ripping his arm from Henry's grip.

"No! It's too late, look!" Henry yelled back, trying to get Jimmy to see reason.

Jimmy hesitated for another moment and watched Fred lay on the floor. After only a minute and change had passed, Fred began to stir on the ground, life returning to previously dead limbs.

"Look, he's okay!" Jimmy said with a smile across his face.

"Wait, Jimmy, give it another second," Henry warned him calmly. He'd seen this a thousand times and knew in a matter of moments Jimmy would realize the boy was gone and then do the right thing.

Fred was now sitting up. Much like a puppet on a string, he awkwardly regained his footing. He looked around the library, acting like he was seeing the room for the first time. Then he turned and looked at Jimmy and Henry.

"Hey, man, you okay? You scared the shit out of me," Jimmy said, taking a step toward Fred.

Fred just looked at Jimmy with a vacant stare, like Jimmy wasn't really there.

Then Fred raised his rifle and awkwardly pointed it at Henry and Jimmy.

In death his hands had locked onto it and only now did Fred realize it was in his grasp, although with his limited intelligence, he didn't comprehend how to use it.

Henry saw the rifle come up and dodged for cover.

"Jimmy, move now; before you get shot!" He shouted to him while he dived behind a pile of hardcover books stacked on the floor.

For a moment Jimmy just stood there, not believing what he was seeing.

Then Henry yelled to him again and broke him from his stupor.

"Jimmy! Move your ass...Now!"

Jimmy seemed to shake the cobwebs clear and then jumped to the other side of the thoroughfare, behind an old desk buried under a mound of books.

"Holy shit. Do you think he knows how to use it?" Jimmy called from across the room.

"Don't know and I'm not taking any chances," Henry hissed from behind the stack of books.

Then Fred's finger involuntarily squeezed the trigger to his rifle, sending a bullet across the room toward Henry.

The bullet struck the wall no more than five inches from Henry's head and he was peppered with tiny splinters from the shattered wood trim.

"Jesus, did you see that!" Henry yelled, ducking lower behind his makeshift barricade.

"Yeah, you all right?" Jimmy called.

"Fine, bastard lucky, though, I'll tell you that. We need to take this bastard down, now, before one of his shots finds one of us!"

No sooner had the words left his mouth then another bullet flew across the room, this time lodging about three feet above Henry.

Absently, Henry wondered why this newly risen walker was picking on him.

Shoot at Jimmy for a while! He thought selfishly.

Just then the sound of heavy footfalls could be heard coming toward them.

A second later Sam came charging around the corner of the large room, and with his Colt drawn, sighted Fred's head in his crosshairs and squeezed off two rounds in quick succession.

The .357 rounds struck Fred's head directly in the middle of his face, the double onslaught of bullets exploding the new ghoul's head like a rotten egg.

The exposed neck shot blood six feet into the air like a red fountain until the reservoir went dry and became a trickle. The body stood immobile, minus a head, and then its hand squeezed the trigger one final time in its final death throes.

Luckily, the bullets went high and were lost in the infinite stacks of books lining the shelves above Henry and Jimmy.

The body collapsed to the floor in a disheveled heap, blood pooling onto the stained, hardwood floor where it was then diluted from the water still remaining.

Henry poked his head up and relaxed when he saw it was Sam, followed by his two security guards.

"Everything all right?" Sam asked, stepping over the corpse to stand closer to Henry.

"It is now. I can't believe a deader got the drop on me," Henry said, a little embarrassed.

"Yeah, no shit. That's all we need, deaders that know how to shoot back," Jimmy said, picking himself up from behind the desk.

"Well, I think that was a fluke, Jimmy," Henry said, looking at Sam. "Any more deaders in the building? Henry asked.

Sam shook his head no. "I'm pretty sure he was the last," Sam said, pointing casually to Fred.

"Sorry about your man," Jimmy offered, looking down at the headless body of Fred.

"Thanks but there will be time to mourn the dead later. Come on, let's get out of here and let the cleanup crew get to work," Sam said, turning to leave.

Then he paused and turned to his guards.

"You two get that rifle… and take his boots, too. And whatever you do, don't splash any water on you or you'll wind up in a hole next to him," Sam ordered them, gesturing with his Colt at the body of Fred.

Henry and Jimmy followed Sam out of the building while the two guards got to work retrieving the dead man's belongings. Henry watched for a moment as he walked by them and then they were lost from sight when he turned a corner.

The boots made sense.

It's not like if you needed a pair of shoes you could just go down to the local mega mart and pick up a new pair. No, those days were over.

Within half a minute the group of men had arrived at the main doors to the library again.

Throwing the doors wide open, Henry and Jimmy squinted, the bright light of the afternoon sun blinding their eyes for a moment, the fresh air tasting good in their mouths.

Looking down and waiting for their eyes to adjust, the two companions walked down the library's stone steps.

A small work crew wearing white overalls, gloves, and masks over their faces, charged up the stairs and into the library, the grim job of clearing the dead now ahead of them.

"Shit, why didn't we get coveralls like that to protect us? Maybe if we had, Fred would still be with us," Jimmy said, watching the white-clothed men entering the building.

The sun felt good on Henry's face. The library seemed to suck time like a black hole and he was surprised to find only about a half an hour had passed since they had gone inside. It seemed like much longer.

"That's a good point, Jimmy, but it's too late now, so just leave it, will you, please?" Henry pleaded.

Jimmy was about to answer when he was distracted by Sam approaching.

He turned and watched the big man walking over to him and Henry, the Boss of the town now finished with giving orders to his men about what he needed of them and how best to start the cleanup.

Sam was only a few feet away when his mouth opened to say something, but an alarm bell began ringing from across the town, in the direction of the front gate.

"What the hell is that?" Jimmy asked, looking around for any signs of a problem.

"That's the alarm we jury rigged at the main gate. If that bell's ringing then there's something wrong."

"Never a dull minute, huh, Sam?" Henry asked with a grin.

"Shit, not since you showed up," Sam snapped back, playfully.

"Hey, I resemble that remark," Jimmy said jokingly.

"I've got to get to the gate. You two coming?" Sam asked.

Henry looked at Jimmy who just shrugged and mumbled: "Sure, what the hell."

Then the three men hopped onto a security cart and Sam hit the tiny gas pedal.

They maneuvered through the streets, Henry wondering what the hell could be possibly wrong now.

The he realized even if he had known, he probably wouldn't have liked the answer.

# CHAPTER TWENTY-ONE

WITH A SLIGHT screeching of brakes, the golf cart pulled up to the barricade surrounding the small town of Pittsfield, just to the right of the closed gate.

Sam was the first out of his seat, and within a heartbeat, was climbing the aluminum ladder leading to the walkway spanning the inside of the wall.

"What's up? I heard the alarm," Sam said when he reached the top.

The guard on duty was a young man in his early twenties, with shaggy brown hair and a few pimples left over from puberty. Sam remembered his name was Tommy. He had personally picked him to be part of the security of the town despite the fact he usually left such matters to Paul, his second-in-command.

"Well, Boss, see for yourself," Tommy said, waving his arm across the land on the other side of the barricade.

Sam turned and gazed out over the vista of the empty highway and open grassy plains. He just stared and watched in horror at the sight that greeted him over the wall.

"Oh my God," he whispered.

By now Henry and Jimmy had climbed the ladder and joined Sam on the thick wooden plank. Jimmy was on the plank first, and with a loud gulp slipping from his mouth, he also stared out across the plain with Sam at his side.

Wondering what was so interesting, Henry moved to the edge and followed their gaze and promptly stopped cold as he looked out on the grassy plain, as well.

When Henry had arrived at the town of Pittsfield just a few days ago, the rolling plains had been deserted. Now there had to be at least fifty walkers scattered across the land.

Henry studied the closest ones to the wall, breathing through his mouth as the smell of death drifted up to him on the wind.

Some of them looked to be original ghouls, from the first days the contaminated rains had fallen.

It was easy to spot these from the others; their bodies were more desiccated from the ravages of time. These ghouls were usually nothing but skin and bones. Their eyes were always sunk into the sockets and the skin over their mouths always drawn tight to expose the teeth and gums. And of course the smell was the worst. With the soft tissue decaying and then becoming the home to thousands of maggots and beetles, the insects would quickly infest the rotting bodies.

The other walkers spread out around the grassy plain and the highway looked to be anywhere from three months old to no more than days.

It was hard to tell as Henry was just guessing.

Watching the walking dead shuffling around the plains like blind men and women, he noticed the clothes some were wearing. He saw a policemen's uniform and a soldier's green fatigues. He saw what looked like a nurse and off in the corner was a big brute of a man with a leather jacket and tattoos covering his arms. A biker maybe?

Henry watched as a female ghoul with more than half her leg missing tried to make her way across the plain. She would move no more than a foot or two and would then lose her balance and fall to the grass. Then in a second or two would push herself to her feet again, and after another foot, would fall again. This continued until Henry got tired of watching and turned away. He couldn't help but think the dead woman deserved an "A" for perseverance, though.

Directly below the barricade some of the walkers were uselessly trying to climb the rugged wall. No sooner would they make headway then their uncooperative limbs would slip and they'd tumble back down to the ground; sometimes crushing another ghoul in the process.

Henry watched the remnants of a little league baseball team trying to climb the wall, only to fail again and again.

"Holy shit, when did this happen?" Jimmy asked askance of Henry, his mouth hanging open in awe. The moans of the dead were clear now that they were on the wall, the wailing rising and lowering in pitch like an off-key opera group.

"A little after you returned from your reconnaissance of Costington and went to help with the library fire," Tommy said. "There was no one to help; all you guys were fighting the fire. They can't get in, so I figured what's the rush?"

"What's the rush? You stupid bastard!" Sam yelled, slapping Tommy on the back of the head. "The minute you saw the first one you should have been on the two-way reporting this. Now they're everywhere. How the hell do you think we're gonna be able to leave the town now?"

Tommy just stood there, too intimidated to answer.

"Can't you just shoot them all? There's not that many," Jimmy suggested.

Sam shook his head. "No can do, Jimmy, we only have so much ammunition and once it's gone we're down to bows and arrows. This many would severely drain my stockpiles. Head shots are the only way to take them out and I don't have any sharpshooters. We'd waste a lot of ammo trying to take out over fifty walkers. That's one of the reasons I need what's in Costington. They have a gun store and there should be a shitload of ammo in there. That is, if it hasn't been looted."

"What about a back door. Didn't you make an exit on the other side of town in case of an emergency?" Henry inquired of Sam.

"Of course I did. I'm not an idiot," Sam snapped at Henry. Then seeing the look in Henry's eyes at being spoken to in that tone, Sam dialed it back a bit. He was afraid of no man, but Henry had earned his respect. Hell, even the kid, Jimmy, was a hell of a fighter.

"I mean, yeah, we did, but if we used that way it would take more than half a day to try to circle around to this side by way of back roads. That's a waste of gas and resources that I don't have much of," Sam said in a more conversational tone.

Henry nodded, taking it all in, then an idea struck him.

"Look, these roamers are probably from Richmond. If there's no more food there then it would make sense that they would have to spread out more."

"When you say no more food, you mean people, right?" Sam asked quietly.

"Yeah, Sam, I do. It probably means that you're one of the only towns left for miles. And if the roamers know you're here, well then, this…" Henry waved over the wall at the animated corpses on the plains. "Is only the beginning."

Almost like it was planned, a ghoul fell from the wall just before it had made it to the top, its body bouncing off the jagged pieces of the barricade to land on top of a zombie high-school band player. With a crash of cymbals, the two bodies sprawled on the trampled grass.

The ruckus solidifying Henry's point of the shit to come.


The ride back into the town proper was sullen, everyone taking in what was happening around them.

They were now under siege by the undead. The worst thing was that no matter what happened, there would be no reinforcements.

All they had were themselves to rely on.

Henry thought back to about a month ago when Mary, Jimmy and himself were trapped inside a small convenient store on the outskirts of Washington, D.C.

There were at least thirty roamers screaming for their blood and Henry would have sworn it was going to be the end of them.

But they had pulled a fast one and had made it out of their alive, leaving a few more corpses to rot in the street.

This time was no different; he just had to come up with a plan.

The small golf cart pulled up to Henry and Jimmy's boarding house to let them off.

"I'll have one of my men come and get you in about an hour. We'll have a meal and go over a plan of action," Sam said from the driver's seat of the cab.

Henry nodded and turned to walk up the small stairs in front of the building, Jimmy by his side.

"Sounds fine, see you then," Henry said over his shoulder to Sam.

"Oh, and Henry, while we were gone I had some things returned to you. They should be up in your rooms by now," Sam said with a sly grin. Then he hit the gas and the little vehicle shot off down the street.

Jimmy's eyebrows rose, asking the question, "What's that about?"

Henry just shrugged. "I guess we'll see in a minute."

Moments later the two men each entered their rooms to cleanup and change. Staring at the freshly made bed, Henry was pleasantly surprised to see his old knapsack that had been confiscated when he'd entered the town.

He checked through the contents and was pleased to see everything was there, although in a different order than he could remember packing them.

A smile came to his lips when he found a small wallet size picture of Emily.

He still remembered the day he'd taken it. She'd been sitting in their backyard on a swing he'd built for her, and as the sun shone down on her, he remembered how beautiful she'd looked. He'd gone into the house to retrieve his camera, and after taking the picture, the two of them had sat together and talked until late in the day. Then they'd gone into the house and had dinner.

It had been a simple thing people had done every day. God, how he missed those times, now.

Taking his 9mm Glock out of the bag, he set it down on the bed, then sat down next to it.

He'd had the weapon since everything had first fallen apart and he hated to admit it, but he had formed a bond with it. Sighing, he stood up again and began to unbutton his shirt.

Stripping off his clothes, he jumped into the shower and washed the grime from the morning away, thankful to get the smell of wet, burnt wood, and smoke out of his hair and skin.

Stepping out, he looked at his frame in the mirror. He'd dropped a few pounds in the last three months. But what did he expect? He'd been living hard and on the run, never staying in one place for very long.

Where there used to be a little flab there was now only hard muscle. He had known before everything went to Hell he needed to get into shape, but like a lot of people he kept putting it off. Who would've known that all it would take to get into shape would be an apocalypse? That the rise of the dead would make him slim and trim?

He ran his hand over his chin, feeling the rough stubble. He decided against shaving. He'd do it later if he had a chance.

Shrugging into a new set of clothes from the infinite vastness of the room's closet, he laced up his boots and strapped his weapons back onto his torso. First he secured the panga and Glock on his hip, then slid the .38 under his shirt. He left the shotgun in his room, knowing he couldn't go around loaded for bear, at least when all he was doing was going to Sam's for dinner.

Then he entered the hallway to check on Jimmy.

The door opened silently with the first knock Henry placed on the door. Not trusting why the door was unlocked, Henry drew his Glock from its holster and edged silently into the room.

Jimmy was nowhere to be seen. Ears open to catch any stray sounds; Henry scanned the room for anything unusual. Jimmy's clothes were scattered on the floor and on the bed was his returned backpack.

Henry heard footsteps from his side and turned with the Glock leading the way toward the danger.

Instead of seeing a bloodthirsty ghoul or an unruly security guard, all Henry got for his trouble was a naked Jimmy strolling out of the bathroom.

Jimmy took one look at Henry with his weapon out and went into combat mode, moving to the bed to retrieve his .38.

"Whoa, sorry, Jimmy. Your door was open and I didn't know if everything was safe," he said, averting his eyes away from Jimmy's wang.

"What? Oh, shit, sorry, I must have forgotten to push it closed all the way," Jimmy said, calming down and wrapping a towel around his lower half, to Henry's obvious relief.

"What's up?" Jimmy inquired, using another towel to wipe his hair dry.

"Nothing, I just came to get you so we could go to Sam's. I didn't think you'd still be in the shower this long. What were you doing in there?"

Henry thought about his last question and quickly changed his mind.

"Ah, you know what? Forget it, I don't want to know," Henry finished.

Jimmy just smiled and then dropped his towels and shrugged into his clothes. He had decided to stick with what he was wearing. He liked the way the pants fit and the shirt was cool. The odor of wet smoke didn't bother him as much as Henry.

Henry noticed this and spoke up.

"Come on, Jimmy, that shirt has blood on it, at least change the shirt, for Christ sakes."

Jimmy looked down at his chest, and sure enough, there were multiple blood drops and small bits of gore on the material. With a small shrug, he decided Henry was right and took off the shirt, tossed it into the corner, and went to the closet to retrieve another.

Brushing his hair back with his hand like a comb, he strapped on the holster for his .38, and then with the shotgun on his shoulder, smiled at Henry.

"Okay, I'm ready to go."

"What's the shotgun for?" Henry asked. "I left mine in my room."

"Simple, with all those roamers outside the wall I'm gonna make damn sure I'm ready for anything," he said and accented his statement by pumping the weapon.

Henry smiled at this. "Fine, whatever. Just don't be surprised if Sam makes you check it at his front door."

"I'll take my chances. So, come on, are we going or what?" Jimmy asked, impatiently.

"Yeah, let's go. And don't forget to close your door this time," Henry scolded, stepping into the hallway.

"Yes, Dad," Jimmy quipped back, but did as requested.

"Don't call me that, Jimmy, ever again," Henry said, clearly annoyed.

"Yeah, yeah, fine, old man," he said sarcastically, and when Henry glanced at him, he grinned widely.

Deciding to let it go, Henry moved down the hallway, Jimmy right behind him, grinning the entire time. In less than a minute the two men were standing outside again.

Henry watched the people as they passed by him. Watching their faces, he could almost feel the tension in the air.

They knew they were in trouble, but were helpless to do anything about it. All their hopes were placed in Sam and his men to keep them safe.

While Henry and Jimmy waited for their ride to Sam's place, he came to the realization that these people's lives had inadvertently fallen into his hands, as well.

All he could do is hope he was up to the challenge

\* \* \*

A quarter mile or so away from where Henry and Jimmy were waiting for their ride, twenty roamers slowly worked their way through a small gap in the rear wall at the back of the town.

The workers hadn't finished it yet, thinking that because it was located in the woods, it wouldn't matter.

Unfortunately, with the exodus of ghouls from the state capital flooding across the land, it was just a matter of time before it was found, and through an unlucky quirk of fate, one of the undead had stumbled upon it.

The walker slipped through the gap and entered the town, the other ghouls in the area following it, until the wooded area was empty once again.

The undead were slowly massing outside the makeshift barricade of the town on the highway, but no one was guarding the rear, assuming it was safe from an undead presence because of its solitude. If it hadn't been for hindsight to build the barricade in the first place, the town would have been overrun and all the residents killed long ago.

Still, the walking dead filed into the back streets, and once the twenty were inside the walls, the gap became invisible again to casual scrutiny.

So, while the residents went about their afternoon business, the score of walking dead slowly shambled into town.

They knew there was fresh meat ahead…and they were hungry.

# CHAPTER TWENTY-TWO

MARY WANDERED AROUND Sam's house, trying to keep occupied.

Earlier that morning, Sam and his men had left the town to show Henry and Jimmy the neighboring town of Costington.

The men leaving her to stay home like a good woman.

No, that was wrong, she knew Henry and Jimmy valued her by their side, but she just wasn't up to it, her bullet wound still fresh.

In another day or so she'd be back to peak performance, she knew.

But that didn't solve her boredom now.

With nothing else to do, she had taken a nap, read from Sam's vast collection of books (she'd been told Sam inherited them with the house), had a light brunch, and was now exploring more of the house.

The architecture was stunning, with the carved wooden moldings and oak doors. Considering how most people lived nowadays, Sam was doing all right for himself.

As the hours passed by, she found herself becoming anxious for her friends to return.

When the fire had broken out at the library, she had been told by a houseboy that Sam and her friends had returned and were helping with the fire. When that little crisis had ended, she had then found out from Martha that Sam was on his way back to the house.

Now, as Mary waited for the men to return, she found herself in a small study.

As her eyes scanned the room, it was clear to her the room was still being used.

There were papers scattered on the desk and butts from a few burned-up cigars sitting in a marble ashtray on the right hand corner of the desktop.

She walked around the desk, her eye catching a picture of a beautiful, black woman sitting in a six by five picture frame.

She had an ebony complexion, strong white teeth and her eyes shone with a sparkle of happiness that seemed to jump right off the picture.

Mary couldn't help herself, and as if drawn to it, reached down and picked up the picture so she could see it better in the wan light coming in through the double windows at her back.

"Beautiful, wasn't she?" A low voice said from the doorway of the study.

Mary looked up with a look of a child who had been caught in the cookie jar before dinner.

"Oh, I'm sorry, I hope it's all right I was in here. I didn't mean to snoop," Mary said, placing the picture back on the desk.

"No, that's fine, Mary. Besides, even if you were snooping, there's nothing to find." Sam smiled only a little, almost as if it was forced. "No, I'm afraid what you see is what you get with me," he said, walking into the room and picking up the picture himself. His eyes filled with emotion and his jaw softened as he gazed down at the woman in the photo.

"Who was she?" Mary asked; wanting to change the subject from her being in a place she probably shouldn't have been in.

"She was my wife," Sam said with a longing that only another widower could understand. "She died when the rains first came. Before anyone really knew what the hell was going on."

"What was her name?" Mary asked quietly.

"Sharona," he said, gently placing the picture back on the desk with a sigh.

Then, shaking his melancholy like a bear shrugging water from its fur after a swim, he looked at Mary and smiled again.

"Enough of the past, it's the future we have to worry about now, or more precisely, the present," he said, in a booming voice. "Your friends will be here soon. Some shit has gone down that you'll likely be interested in and you're welcome to sit with us."

Then he turned and stepped into the hallway, calling for Martha.

When the old woman arrived, he informed her he would need a table setup for five for lunch in about an hour. Then with the old woman shuffling off to see to the meal, Sam turned back to Mary.

"You should be pleased to know I've come to an agreement with your friends," he said, from across the room.

"Oh, what about?" Mary asked simply.

"About whether or not you're my prisoner," he said with a grin.

"Oh, really, and what was the result of this agreement?"

"The result, my dear, is that you are no longer under duress to stay here. I've gotten to know your friends in the time we've spent together and I believe they're honorable men. So I've given them their weapons back and agreed not to use you against them for their cooperation," he said, pleased with himself.

Mary nodded approval. "That's great. So where do we go from here?"

"That will all be worked out when your friends arrive for lunch. Until then, if you'll excuse me, I'm going to get cleaned up."

With a subtle nod as a farewell, he backed up and turned down the hallway. Within a few long legged strides, he was at the end of the hall where he then disappeared behind a door leading to another stairwell.

Mary stood in the study for another moment, and then with another casual glance at the photo, she too, left the room to go wait on the porch for her friends.

*       *       *

Mary waited on the porch for her fellow companions, watching the few people passing by as they went about their daily chores.

She jumped when she heard a gunshot in the distance, wondering where it came from.

An elderly couple hobbled by on ancient legs. As the couple passed the porch where Mary was, the old woman casually turned her head to look up at Mary.

Mary raised her hand in greeting, but all she received in return was a scowl.

Then the geriatric couple was beyond her.

Mary wondered about that scowl. Evidently, everyone in town wasn't pleased with the way Sam ran things.

Another gunshot sounded in the distance, causing Mary to lose focus on her thoughts.

Her hand absently went down to her waist where her .22 should have been. She felt naked without it and swore under her breath. She'd have to talk to Sam about returning her weapon to her if what he said about their arrangement changing was true.

Another twenty minutes went by with nothing more exciting than an occasional echo of a gunshot bouncing off the town's buildings.

Then she spotted one of the golf carts the security in town was so fond of. As the vehicle grew closer, a smile spread across her face when she realized Henry and Jimmy were the passengers.

When the cart was only moments away, she ran down the front stairs. Henry exited the cart and was nearly blown over as Mary ran into his arms.

"Hey, guys, I've missed you. I've been so damn bored here I can't even tell you," Mary said, releasing Henry and then going over to Jimmy and giving him a hug, as well.

"So, when are we leaving?" She asked, brushing an errant hair from her face.

"Honey, I wish I knew," Henry said in a subdued voice. "Hasn't anyone told you what's going on?" Henry asked.

"Going on, about what?" She asked clearly not understanding.

"Oh, man, what the hell have you been doing all day while we've been running all over this friggin town?" Jimmy asked; the annoyance in his voice clearly noticeable to Mary.

"For your information, I've been stuck here. Held hostage, despite the fancy trappings, and not by choice," she snapped at Jimmy.

Jimmy was about to give her a rebuttal when Henry stopped the argument.

"All right, you two, enough, please. Mary, the wall around this town is surrounded by roamers. For the moment we're trapped here. At least until we can think of a way to clear them out," Henry said grimly,

"Oh, wow, I didn't know. No one said anything. Do the townspeople know?" She asked.

"Probably, although everyone seems to be keeping it to themselves," Jimmy said, repositioning his shotgun on his shoulder.

"That's what we're here for. To try and get a plan together with Sam on how to deal with all them," Henry said, turning to look at the guard on the cart.

"Thanks for the lift," Henry said, starting to walk up the porch stairs.

"Sure, no problem, just doing my job," the guard said as he stretched his feet to the side of the cart. "I'll be here when you come out, too."

"Okay, fine, see you then," Henry said over his shoulder. He had chatted lightly with the guard on the way over and found he liked the man.

Then he was stepping into the foyer of the grand house again with Jimmy and Mary by his side.

"Hey, Mary, I've got something for you," Jimmy said while he looked at her with a smile.

"Oh, yeah, what?" She asked, still not over what he'd said outside on the street.

"This," he said, and pulled another .38 from the back of his pants and handed it to Mary. "This should be better then that pea shooter you've been using. With this, they stay down when you shoot them." He smiled, proud of himself.

"Well, I'll be, when the hell did you sneak that on? I was watching you get dressed and never saw it," Henry asked, surprised.

"It's all in the hands, old man," Jimmy said, waving his hands in the air like a magician.

Just then, Sam walked down the stairs across from the foyer.

"Ah, good, you've arrived. I'm starving. What do you say we go and eat and talk shop at the same time?" He asked the small group in front of him.

"Sure, Sam, that's fine," Henry said for the three of them.

Then, amid the light of oil lanterns, the four of them went into the dining room for some food and hopefully to formulate a plan of action that would take care of their undead problem.

\*　　\*　　\*

Near the rear of the town, where nobody went, the walkers that had gained access through the gap in the wall slowly came closer to the heart of the town.

Their noses flicked with the scent of live prey and off in the distance they perceived movement as the town's people scurried to and fro on errands.

As fast as their decaying legs would work, they shuffled and stumbled down the back streets.

If they could tell time they would've know that within a mere ten minutes they would be feeding, their hunger finally fulfilled; their patience rewarded.

But the dead didn't tell time. So they kept walking, the patience of death urging them on.

## Chapter Twenty-three

THE THREE COMPANIONS gathered around the dinner table, and with a gesture from Sam, they sat down. No sooner had they sat then Martha came out with a tray of cooked meat.

Without hesitation, Sam drove his fork into a steaming piece and motioned for the others to do the same.

Henry took a piece of what he guessed was either rabbit or squirrel, both of which he'd eaten on his trek across America. He looked at Jimmy across the table who was chewing happily on the moist, red meat.

"So, do you have any ideas on how to clear the walkers away from the walls?" Henry asked over a mouthful of food.

Sam shook his head. "No, not really, I just wish old Thomas had a few grenades laying around or some plastic explosive," he said, pouring himself a glass of what looked like wine, but could have been cranberry juice. "That would take care of those bastards, blow them straight to Hell," Sam finished.

Mary lifted her head up from her plate when she heard Sam mention plastic explosives.

"What about dynamite, would that work?" She asked laconically while nibbling on a small piece of meat. The taste was a bit gamy for her palate, but she had learned quickly to always eat when there was food in front of her. After all, you might not know when or where your next meal might be.

Sam's eyes lit up with hope. "Dynamite! Do you know where to get some?" He asked, clearly excited.

"Why, yes, I do," she looked to Henry. "Henry, do you remember that construction van we passed on our way here?" She asked politely.

Jimmy threw his fork down onto his plate, the metal clinking as it settled.

"Son-of-a-bitch, the van! It had dynamite in it! We could use that," Jimmy said, clearly getting excited, as well.

"Whoa now, everybody slow down. I know what you're thinking, but that stuff was old. One bump too many on the way back here would blow us to kingdom come and back. It's way to risky," Henry stated.

"I'll say what's risky in my own town, thank you," Sam said, standing up.

"Mary, could show me on a map where you saw this van?" Sam asked.

"Sure, I guess. Do you have one with highways and streets and stuff?" She asked.

"I'm sure we do. Hot damn!" He slapped his hands together. "I knew there'd be a way!" He exclaimed, clearly excited to get the plan in gear.

Then before Henry could say anything more to change his mind, gunshots were heard coming from the street directly outside the house, followed by screams of pain and terror.

"What the fuck is going on out there!" Sam yelled at the room.

Martha came running into the dining room, terror clearly on her face.

"Boss, the walkers are in the town!" She yelled. "Oh my God, we're all doomed!"

Then she turned and fled the room.

Sam reached behind him where he'd hung his Colt on the back of his chair and pulled the weapon from its holster.

"Shit, how the hell did that happen?" He snapped, checking his weapon. Satisfied it was ready; he turned to leave the room and only stopped when he noticed the companions weren't following.

"You folks coming, or what?" Sam asked, clearly telling them to come with him, despite the question.

Henry sighed. "Come on, boys and girls, let's go join the party," he said as he stood up and backed away from the table.

"Hell, yeah, that's why I brought ol' Betty here with me," Jimmy said, while he stroked his shotgun.

"What about me? Do I get to play?" Mary asked.

Henry looked at her and smiled. "Normally the answer would be yes, but you know you're not up to peak performance yet. Tell you what, stay on the porch and watch our backs, okay?"

"Okay, that's fair," she said as she lifted her new .38. Luckily, her shooting arm was fine, as her left was the damaged one.

The group then followed Sam out into the foyer and to the front door.

"Hey, Mary, watch the kick on that. It's a little bigger than your .22," Jimmy said when they'd stopped at the door.

"Okay, thanks, Jimmy," she said, getting ready for Sam to pull the front door open.

The door swung open and the foyer was washed in sunlight, the sounds of suffering death flooding into the room.

\*    \*    \*

A few minutes ago.

While the guard watched Henry and his two friends walk up the stairs, eyeing the swaying hips of the brunette for a second longer than he need to, he stretched out his legs and closed his eyes.

This was the life.

All he had to do was drive around a couple of the Boss's guests, and while they were inside, he figured he'd grab himself a few winks.

His side of the street was relatively peaceful for the moment, so he closed his eyes, enjoying the down time, a smile coming to his lips.

Most of the pedestrians would go around him anyway. They always gave the guards a wide birth; respect, plain and simple…and a touch of fear.

The guard drifted off into a peaceful daydream where he was the Boss of the town and all the women wanted him to pick them to have sex with.

The smile grew a little larger as he let his imagination go wild.

In fact, he was so wrapped up in his own fantasy; he didn't notice the scuffing of bare feet on asphalt or the sound of dry, dead skin when it rubbed together.

His nose began to pick up an odd odor, like when the corpses would lay dead outside the walls before the cleanup crew could get to them to burn them, when a shadow crossed over his face, blocking out the sun.

At first he tried to ignore it, thinking it was just his imagination, but then the odor washed over him, stronger than before and he knew something was off.

Slowly opening his eyes, he froze in panic.

Not more than three inches from his face was a zombie!

He had never seen one this close before, and even in his state of shock, his eyes transferred the data sent to it.

The humanoid shape's face was a rotting pile of flesh, except where the white of bone peeked through. The nose was gone, long rotted off, and while he stared at it, a few maggots slid out of the nose canal to fall onto his lap.

A small squeak left his lips and he tried to scream, but his frozen vocal cords wouldn't allow it.

The zombie just stared at him, and though only a matter of seconds had gone by, it seemed like infinity more to the guard.

A small part of his mind where hope lived wondered if he was going to be all right.

His heart started to slow down and he was just about to try and run when the walker's mouth opened wide and its teeth clamped down on the guard's nose.

Cartilage snapped; the ghoul's teeth ripping the nose from his face.

He tried to scream but the blood poured into his mouth and back down into his sinus cavity, thereby choking off any hope of a scream other than a gurgling, bubbling sound.

The guard jumped to his feet, and amid the haze of pain suffusing his body, grabbed his rifle sitting on the seat next to him. But he never got the chance to aim.

Before he had fully stood up, two more walkers attacked him from behind, pushing him to the ground. Their teeth found exposed areas on his neck and arms and greedily ripped the flesh away, tearing at it as the skin stretched like scarlet elastics until it would snap off in a spray of red droplets.

One ghoul, in its zeal to feed, ripped into the guard's carotid artery, sending a spray of blood into the air until the man's heart pumped his life giving plasma onto the warm pavement.

The street now looked like it was painted red, the puddle growing in size to congeal around the tires of the golf cart. The walkers continued to feed on the now dead guard, ripping into his chest and pulling out the tender organs within.

Their faces were now stained a dark vermilion from the blood and gore of their victim, oblivious to anything other than the food in front of them.

Then one of the walker's heads blew apart when a bullet struck it between the eyes.

The others barely noticed, continuing to feed. Around them, the other ghouls had found their own prey as the hapless townspeople were pulled to the ground, where they were summarily torn apart and eaten.

Paul Williams lined up another rotting head in his gun sights and pulled the trigger, satisfied when he saw another corpse go down.

All around him was chaos as the townspeople ran from the walkers. Paul frowned; didn't the fools know if they just stood and fought they could dispose of this outbreak in no time?

Then he had no time to think when a trio of walkers turned his way and lunged for him.

He avoided one and struck the second with the butt of his rifle, but he already knew he was going to be too late to stop the third from getting him.

*   *   *

The three companions and Sam stood absolutely still for a few tense seconds, taking the visceral tableaux in.

Where only moments ago there had been a quiet little street, now it was a killing field. Walkers seemed to be everywhere, the shrieking townspeople running for their lives.

Henry watched the guard's body being torn apart by ghouls at the bottom of the porch steps.

A dead man in a stained and bloody blue suit had a hold of the guard's intestines, and as Henry watched in disgust, the walker pulled the red, greasy rope from the guard's stomach and began to walk away, chewing happily. The intestine just kept pouring out of the exposed stomach like it would go on forever, but then the dead man bit a piece of intestine on the wrong side of its hands and the rope fell to the street, looking like a long piece of thick rope spread out across the pavement.

As people rushed to escape the carnage, the thin red line of intestine was ground into the street until it was nothing more than a red stain cooking in the sun.

Then, like a light switch being flicked on, the three companions and Sam went into action.

Jimmy was the first into the fray and took the porch steps three at a time.

He'd spotted a lone ghoul that had a young woman cornered against a dumpster off the beaten path of the street.

Raising his shotgun, he knew if he tried a long distance shot he'd probably end up hitting the woman with the blast as much as the walker, so he sprinted as fast as he could to her aid.

There were other walking dead spread out across the street and Jimmy counted at least twelve before he focused his attention forward, nearing his prey.

Coming up from behind, he raised the butt of the shotgun to hopefully knock the ghoul's head clean off its shoulders, but instead his foot slipped on a piece of brain matter lying in the street and he lost his balance.

Instead of a controlled swing at the zombie, Jimmy's feet went out from under him and he plowed straight into it, knocking the walking corpse to the street, with him right behind it, his shotgun skittering away down the sidewalk.

For a few heartbeats, Jimmy was dazed. Then he shrugged it off and pulled himself back to his feet.

The woman had already bolted from the area the second the ghoul had fallen away from her and all Jimmy got a look at was her back while she dashed down the street, turned a corner, and was gone from sight.

"Your welcome!" Jimmy called to her, but it didn't really matter.

He spun around to see the ghoul on its feet, too, and before Jimmy could bring his shotgun up, the zombie lunged for him.

Jimmy immediately brought his arms up in front of him to keep the ghoul at bay, his arms sinking into the decayed flesh of its chest where its shirt had ripped open.

The walker's mouth kept snapping at him to try to take a bite out of his face, reminding Jimmy of a chicken pecking seed from a barnyard floor.

The corpse's fetid breath blew onto his face and he gagged from the smell of death and decay, the miasma making him want to vomit.

With the rotting face no more than ten inches from his own, he had a perfect view of the deterioration this particular human had suffered in the afterlife.

Pieces of skin hung from the face and the lips were pulled back tight, exposing stained and blackened teeth. The teeth were chipped from countless feedings of chewing on bare bone, the dried blood covering the spaces between each tooth.

He could see the ghoul's tongue lying in its mouth, reminding him of a dead slug he'd found under a piece of wood one time when he was a kid.

He grimaced, another blast of its vomit-inducing breath hitting him in the face

"Hey, ugly, how about flossing next time?" Jimmy quipped.

Then he reached down with one of his arms, his other one now doing double duty to fend off the corpse, and pulled his .38 free.

Bringing it up, he placed the muzzle under the zombie's chin and squeezed the trigger.

The top of the skull shot straight up, and rained down on the street behind it as the body fell away from Jimmy to land heavily on the asphalt.

Before the corpse had fully settled to the ground, Jimmy was already moving away, searching for another target. Spying one across the street, he turned to run, but pulled himself short when he realized Henry was already on it.

He turned, looked down the street and saw an old woman who had fallen down, a fat walker ready to pounce on her.

He stopped moving and brought the .38 up. The shot was a little far for his skill level, but if he didn't try then the old woman would end up as zombie-chow.

Relaxing his breathing, he placed the ghoul's head in his sights and stroked the trigger, letting the gun pull itself up from the recoil.

Down the street, the fat walker's shoulder blew apart, spraying the old woman with blood and gore.

She started screaming, turning to see what was standing over her, too terrified to move.

Jimmy lined up the obese ghoul again and this time sent a bullet straight into the back of its head. The face disappeared and bits and pieces splashed over the old woman, baptizing her in blood and gore.

The old woman looked down and saw one of the walker's eyeballs lying across her chest, still enclosed in its eyelid.

As she stared in horror, she saw it blink at her.

That was enough to break her from her fright. Pulling herself to her feet, she ran away down the street, oblivious of everything around her, her arms waving in the air until she disappeared into a neighboring building.

Satisfied with himself, Jimmy moved off to find more targets.


Henry watched Jimmy sprint across the street, happy to let him do the running. He decided to take out the ones closer to the porch, such as the one who had just eaten half the guard.

He stepped down onto the street and placed two fingers to his lips, then he blew, sending a high-pitched whistle across the area.

Like a dog whistle, the sound had every ghoul not in the process of feeding turn his way. As one, they started towards him, moving at a decent clip, despite their decay.

"Oh shit," Henry breathed to himself, wondering if that was such a great idea, after all. The Glock was in his hand, the weapon feeling good in his grip, like an old friend

The group of walkers moved closer and he decided the time for internal debate was over, so he raised the Glock to chest level.

Stroking the trigger twice, he shot the first one in the neck, nothing more happening than a puff of dust floating off on the wind as the bullet went through dried skin. The second bullet, however, was a little higher as the muzzle climb had brought the barrel up just a notch. This bullet entered the ghoul's face at chin level, blowing off half its face. But it still wasn't down; evidently enough of its brain was still intact to keep it moving forward.

Cursing himself about wasting three bullets on a single deader, he lined up the weapon one more time and put a lead slug through its forehead.

With a spraying of red and grey brain matter, the corpse pitched backward to the street, the others behind it just stepping over the prone body to get at the prey in front of them.

"Damn," Henry muttered. How many were left? He thought.

Spinning quickly, he fired at an attacker on his right. The bullet tore loose a stinking gobbet of dead meat from the ghoul's torso, not slowing the dead man down in the least.

Henry swore under his breath, the Glock he was using just wasn't doing the job today, so placing it back in its holster; he reached around to his back and pulled the .38 free.

Flicking the safety off, he lined up the head of the ghoul he'd been shooting, and fired one last time. He was satisfied when a hole appeared in its forehead.

The corpse dropped to the ground while he lined up the others, picking them off like targets at a carnival.

One had gotten past his guard and as he turned to fire, he realized he wasn't going to be in time to stop it from reaching him. He was already formulating a battle plan in his mind, how to keep those deadly teeth away from his flesh, when the ghoul's head exploded in front of him.

Turning around, he saw Mary standing above him on the porch in a classic shooter's stance, with legs spread apart and her gun at chest height.

She smiled as he turned to look up at her. "What, can't I have some fun, too?"

Then she rubbed her shoulder. "Jimmy's right, this gun does have a kick."

"You okay?" Henry asked from street level.

"Yeah, I'm fine. I don't think I tore my stitches. Is that all of them?"

Henry nodded yes. "I think so, just those few over there with Sam. And by the looks of things, he should be done in a minute. Where's Jimmy?"

"Right here," Jimmy said, jogging up behind him. "Just checking the side streets for any more, it looks like they stayed together as a group."

"Yeah, the question is though, how'd they get in here in the first place?" Henry mused.

"Well, we can figure that out later," Jimmy said. "For now, what do you say we enjoy the show?" He suggested and turned to watch Sam mop up the last few walkers.

The three turned and watched Sam while he waded into the fray with a knife in one hand and his Colt in the other.

*     *     *

Paul put up his hands to keep the last ghoul from biting him, the two of them falling to the street together. He felt a sharp pain in his back when his shoulder blade connected with the asphalt, momentarily stunning him.

Then he shook his vision clear and concentrated on staying alive.

The walker on top of him was a big one and hadn't lost a lot of body mass since turning into one of the walking dead.

With one hand under the dead man's chin, Paul frantically tried to bring his rifle up, but it was trapped between their two shifting bodies. He could taste bile in his throat, the redolence of decay filling his sinus cavity.

The superior weight of the walker was slowly overwhelming him and as the breath of the dead man washed over him again, he braced himself for the inevitable.

Then he heard a familiar gunshot, recognizing Sam's Colt.

The desiccated head exploded onto him, blood and brains dripping onto his face.

Closing his eyes and mouth, he panicked for a second, wondering if any of the fluids were his.

Then he felt the ghoul's weight lifted from him as Sam picked it up and heaved it to the side.

Opening his eyes wide, he saw Sam leaning over him, a big grin on his usually serious face.

"What, did you think I'd let my second in charge get eaten?" He asked.

Paul just blinked.

Sam lifted him to his feet and helped him wipe his face clean.

Just as his vision cleared, Paul saw a female ghoul coming up from behind them and pushed Sam aside. Paul sent a roundhouse punch that had the dead woman spitting teeth, her head rocking to the side.

Paul pulled his hand back, shaking it with pain. Wow, he thought, that hurt. It's not like in the movies!

But Paul's punch was enough to give Sam that split second he needed to come around and place the Colt no more than a few inches from the woman's cracked and pale face.

Squeezing the trigger, he was splashed with blood spray. The bullet tore into the face, demolishing half of the head as the bullet exited out the back of the dead woman's skull.

Powder burns burned the woman's hair and skin, the smell making Sam turn away for a moment, bringing his arm up to cover his nose.

The dead woman wobbled for a moment, as if unable to decide if she was truly dead or not. Then the decision was taken from her. Paul fired his now retrieved rifle into what was left of the ghoul's head and the rest of the skull disappeared, the now headless corpse slumping to the street, looking like a sack of potatoes falling off the back of a pickup truck.

Sam turned to Paul and nodded thanks.

Paul grinned back, then raised his rifle and blew away another walker in their area.

Turning, Sam fired two more rounds into what was once a homemaker. The first bullet ripping her clavicle apart, her head sagging awkwardly to the side. Then the second bullet placed a neat hole in her forehead and she dropped to the street to remain still. Some of the blue and yellow hair curlers in her hair popped out to roll into the gutter.

Sam moved around the street and placed bullets where needed until all the remaining walkers were down but one.

The ghoul slowly wobbled over to Sam with one leg twisted at an unnatural angle behind it. Sam calmly raised his Colt and squeezed the trigger.

Click!

The firing pin struck an empty cylinder.

"Shit!" Sam grunted, he hadn't kept track of his bullets and now he was out.

The walker shambled closer and Sam saw Paul raise his rifle to take it out.

"No wait!" Sam called. "I want this one," he said, reaching for the knife on his hip.

The small knife was no more than six inches in length, used more for cutting his food than in battle. But he knew it would do the job nicely.

Sam turned and started running at the shambling form, and when he was only a few feet away, he brought his right foot up in a half-ass karate kick that still did its job, pushing the ghoul onto its back in the street where its arms were spread out like Jesus on the cross.

Sam jumped onto its chest before the walker could do anything, and then plunged the knife deep into its right eye socket.

The knife slid into the socket like it was made for it and only slowed when the hilt of the blade scraped bone.

The zombie flailed for a moment under Sam until he twisted the knife in the socket and sliced the ghoul's brains to pulp. The body twitched feebly for a second and then the arms dropped back to the street and lay still.

Sam climbed off the corpse and took a second to clean his blade on its filthy clothes before sliding it back into its leather sheath. He would sterilize it later.

He looked around the area and was pleased to see that was the last of them.

Turning, he saw Henry and the others standing on the porch watching him.

Wiping sweat from his forehead, he walked over to them.

"Did you enjoy the show?" He asked, breathing a little heavier than usual from his exertions.

"Very much, I especially like the part where you judo kicked the deader," Henry said, having fun ribbing him a little.

"Well, the show's over, now." He looked for his second-in-command. "Paul!" He yelled as the man ran up beside him.

"Yes, sir," Paul said.

"I want to know how the fuck those goddamn walkers got into my town, and I want to know yesterday. You read me!" He snapped, clearly pissed off.

"Yes, sir, Boss, I'll get right on it," Paul said quickly and then ran off to gather some men so he could investigate.

Another guard was standing behind Sam, clearly trying to stay invisible when Sam turned around and looked at the man.

"You. I want you to supervise cleaning this shit up," he said, waving his hand across the street. "I want all these corpses disposed of ASAP. Grab any people you need to help. If they don't listen then you tell me about it. You hear me?"

The guard nodded emphatically, reminding Henry of those toy dogs you'd see in people's cars on the dashboard. Then, he too, ran off to gather helpers to clean the street of corpses.

With a sigh Sam turned and looked up at the three companions on the porch.

"Well, now that that's over, what do you say we finish eating?" He grinned and started up his stairs and was soon lost from sight after he entered the shadows of his house's foyer.

The three companions stared at each other for a moment, then Jimmy shrugged, following Sam up the stairs.

Henry held out his hand to Mary. "After you, my dear," he said, following her.

"Why, thank you, kind sir," she said, moving up the stairs.

When Henry was through the doorway, he began to push the door closed, just catching an echo of a gunshot coming from the direction of the front gate.

He hoped those guards were staying alert, because if they weren't, then it would just be a matter of time before the entire town would be overrun and the residents slaughtered …the three companions with them.

Then he closed the door and went to join the others to finish their interrupted meal.

# CHAPTER TWENTY-FOUR

EVERYONE WENT BACK inside and sat down at the dinner table again; if a little more subdued than before.

After finishing the meal, Martha brought out a desert of fruit preserves and yellow cake.

The four of them wrapped up the plan on how to retrieve the dynamite from the construction van the next day and then Henry and Jimmy got up to leave.

Sam walked them to the door followed by Mary who waved to them.

The two men walked down the stairs and started walking down the street, back to their boarding house. The golf cart was covered in blood and gore so the two agreed walking would be best.

The street was devoid of the bodies that were there only a short hour ago. There was nothing left to mark their existence other than a few red stains scattered across the pavement.

Those too would be washed away at the next rainfall.

The two men strolled down the street, the pedestrians moving aside. Then they turned a corner and Jimmy spotted Murphy's bar.

"Hey, Henry, I think I'll go get a drink. I'll see you tonight, all right?" He asked politely, although both men knew he would do what he wanted.

"Sure, Jimmy, just watch your ass, okay?" Henry asked of him.

"Yeah, sure, you got it," he smiled back.

Then he ran across the street and ducked into the bar.


Henry watched him go and smiled to himself. He knew why Jimmy was going to the bar; to see that girl. Good for him, he was young and could use some release.

For Henry, the open wound that was his wife's death was still sore. He sighed to himself and started walking back to his room alone.

Maybe he'd take a nap when he got back.

That put him in better spirits and without even realizing it he started whistling a familiar tune to himself. He whistled all the way back to his room where he then promptly washed up and took a long nap.


Jimmy stepped into the gloom of the bar and scanned the room for people. His alertness went down a notch when he realized the bar was empty.

He walked over to the counter and sat down when he heard a crash of glass coming from the back room.

Then Cindy came running out while yelling over her shoulder into the back room.

"No, I won't do it, that's disgusting," she said, clearly upset.

"Get back here and do what I say!" A rough voiced yelled back.

Then she saw Jimmy and ran over to him, standing near him.

That's when the old bartender came out and saw him, and with a frown, he walked closer.

"Oh, it's you, what do you want, we're closed," he snapped at Jimmy.

"No, we're not, don't listen to him!" Cindy yelled back.

"Well, for starters, what the hell is going on in here?" Jimmy asked.

"None of your damn business, now get out of here!" The old man yelled, pointing to the door.

"I'll tell you, he wants me to do stuff to him, gross stuff. You're my uncle for God's sake!" She yelled, her eyes filled with contempt.

"Is that true? I'll ask you one last time. Just what the hell is going on around here?" Jimmy asked.

"None of your fucking business. Now get the hell out of here before I call security," the old man snapped.

Jimmy placed his shotgun on the counter. "Yeah, well, I'm making it my business."

The old man looked at Jimmy and then his eyes glanced down at the shotgun. He shifted slightly, his eyes leading the way, as if he was going to reach for his rifle under the countertop.

Jimmy spotted his eyes and shook his head no.

"I wouldn't if I were you. I've killed more deaders then you have hair on your ass, and I don't mind adding one old man to that list."

The man looked at Jimmy, weighing his options. Though the kid in front of him looked to be no older than nineteen or twenty, there was a hardness to his visage that said he wasn't joking.

Finally, the old man backed down.

"Fine, take her. I didn't want her anyway. I was doing her a favor. I'm leaving and when I get back you better not be here," he said to Cindy, disappearing into the back room. A moment later an outer door slamming filtered into the bar and then everything went quiet.

Cindy walked around the bar and poured Jimmy a beer. Then she walked back and sat down next to him.

"Wow, what the hell was that about?" Jimmy asked, relaxing a little; although he made sure to keep the exits in clear view.

"He's my uncle. He took me in when my parents died. In exchange for room and board I work here. But then he started trying to get me to do stuff to him. You know...sex stuff."

Jimmy's eyebrows went up, but otherwise he remained silent.

So Cindy continued, this time starting from the beginning.

"When the rains first came my parents died. I was just back from college and didn't really have any friends here, so my uncle volunteered to let me stay with him. It wasn't that bad until about a month ago when he started trying to get me to do stuff with him. Now don't get me wrong, I've been with boys. But it's been with boys I like, not him, that's gross," she said, with her eyes downcast.

Jimmy just nodded, not really having an answer to her story.

"Now, what am I going to do? I mean, yeah, he was gross, but at least I had a place to live," she said, a single tear running down her cheek.

"Well, you could come with us when we leave here," Jimmy suggested.

"Really, you'd take me with you?" She asked, hope in her eyes.

"Well, sure, but you have to know it's dangerous out there. Sometimes we have to shoot to survive. Do you know how to shoot?" He asked her.

"Yeah, a little. I mean, I used to go hunting with my dad. I'm pretty good with a hunting rifle."

"Perfect. Why don't you grab your stuff and you can stay with me and Henry at the boarding house," Jimmy suggested.

"Okay, that'd be great, thanks," she said, leaning over and hugging Jimmy.

Jimmy just sat there, too shy to do anything. Then she pulled back and stood up.

"I'll be right back, there's not much to get." Then she disappeared into the back room while Jimmy sat and drank his warm beer.

Five minutes later, just as Jimmy polished off his beer, Cindy came back into the bar with a backpack on her shoulders.

"This is it. Anything of value I had the old bastard took long ago," she said with a scowl, setting the pack down on a table.

Jimmy walked around to the inside counter and retrieved the rifle the old man had stashed there.

"What about this?" He said, gently tossing it to Cindy. "Can you use this?"

Cindy caught it and held it up for a moment, and then she slid the top open to check for a shell. Satisfied, she pulled down and slid the chamber closed.

"Sure, this is a lot like my daddy's rifle, why?"

"Because it's yours now, call it severance pay," he said, walking back to stand by her.

She stopped messing with the rifle and looked up at Jimmy.

"I don't know how to thank you, really," she said. Then she leaned over and gently kissed Jimmy on the lips.

Jimmy turned beet red as he looked down at his boots.

"Wow, that's a start, thanks," he mumbled, his cheeks blushing more.

She leaned a little closer so that her lips brushed his ear.

"Play your cards right and there's more where that came from," she whispered into his ear.

Jimmy looked at her with a sparkle in his eyes. "Really?" He squeaked.

She nodded yes.

Then Jimmy regained his composure a little and turned toward the door.

"Come on, we should go before that asshole uncle of yours returns," Jimmy suggested.

She nodded and shrugged into her pack. Then she followed Jimmy out the door to hopefully a brand new life.

The two of them stepped out into the light of the afternoon and started moving down the sidewalk. After walking for only a few feet, she reached down and cupped his free hand with hers.

Jimmy turned his head to look at her and was pleased to see her smiling.

Smiling back, he felt like he was the luckiest man alive as the two of them went back to the boarding house for a long earned rest.

Off in the distance, the echo of gunshots continued to grow as more walking dead assailed themselves against the barricade.

# CHAPTER TWENTY-FIVE

HENRY WAS TOSSING and turning in his bed, a nightmare coming into resolution as the day finally caught up to him.

In his dream, he was walking along an open, grassy plain.

Off in the distance, he could see a cemetery shrouded in mist. He walked closer and could immediately tell the cemetery was in disrepair. Tombstones and markers for the dead were turned over and broken; some no more than rubble.

He slowly walked along the grave markers and read the names.

Here lies Scott Peters, friend, companion, but too slow to avoid a zombie.

Another read: Emily Watson, loving wife, RIP. There was even one that said:

Here lies Blackie, man's best friend to the end, etched into the stone.

He continued walking and reading, soon losing count of all the friends and family he'd lost since the rains came. He paused by a giant stone statue of an angel, wondering whose ego would be so big as to want such a large memorial.

Then he continued walking, lost in his own thoughts until he heard a muffled, digging sound, like when a dog tries to bury a bone and his paws just go crazy as he throws the dirt behind him.

He quickly turned around, looking for the source of the sound, but to no avail.

Then, moving a little deeper into the cemetery, he noticed an open grave. But this grave looked wrong, as if something had crawled up from below and pulled itself free.

His hand instinctually went to his hip where his weapons should be, but there was nothing there. He was defenseless against whatever was out there in the mist.

He had nothing but his hands and wits to protect him.

Warily moving through the soft earth, he came upon an open plain. Sitting in the middle of the area were four poles.

He moved closer, his eyes taking in the shadowy figures that were attached to the poles.

Their heads were hidden under thick black cloaks as he slowly continued forward. He felt drawn to this spot, despite the obvious danger.

He moved closer, the figures becoming clearer to him.

Four human shapes were tied to the poles, and as a cold wind blew across the plain, their cloaks fell away from their heads, showing the hollow faces of skulls beneath.

Where the eyes should have been there was nothing but blackness.

One of them opened its mouth to scream and Henry could see nothing but a bottomless void. The scream it let out was enough to chill his very soul; but still he was drawn to them.

Walking out onto the plain. he stopped when he was no more than six feet away from the quartet of death.

A piece of dust or dirt from the cemetery grounds caught on the wind and blew into his eye. Blinking to clear it, he became distracted and when looking back to the poles, he noticed one of the figures was gone.

With the hairs standing on the back of his neck, he scanned the area, but there was no sign of the cloaked figure.

Trying to see every which way at once, he continually moved his head as he spun in a circle. He didn't know why, but something told him he didn't want to be touched by the shrouded figure.

He stopped turning and watched the other three warily, not realizing the fourth had come up from behind him as if from midair.

He felt the presence suddenly, some preternatural sixth sense forewarning him of the danger, but as he turned around, it was all ready too late. The figure sent a skeletal hand straight into Henry's chest, where it wrapped around his beating heart.

With his breath frozen in his lungs, he watched as the figure pulled his still beating heart out of his body and held it out to him.

"Take it and be one of us," a soft voice hissed, sounding like glass crushed between two stones.

He slowly shook his head and started to back away, wondering why he was still alive with his heart still beating in the figure's skeletal hand.

Then he fell over, but instead of landing on the soft green turf, he fell another six feet.

He looked up and realized he was in a grave. His tombstone was sitting at the front of his grave and as he lay there, familiar faces leaned over and looked down on him.

Jimmy, Mary and Sam looked down on his cold lifeless body. He screamed at them that this was a mistake, he wasn't dead! But no one heard him.

With a tear in her eye, Mary picked up a handful of dirt and threw it onto him, the others following suit until he was covered with a thin film of moist soil.

Then he saw Scott, a friend from months ago, lift a shovel full of dirt, and before he threw it on him, he leaned down and whispered to Henry.

"Don't worry; it's not that bad being dead," he grinned, letting the pile of dirt fall from the shovel.

Then he repeated the process until Henry could barely see through all the earth covering him, suffocating him with its earthy smell.

He tried to yell one more time just as Scott let drop one final shovelful of dirt. The soil slipped into his mouth and he tried to spit it out, only to have it slide down his throat and choked him, causing him to gasp for his next breath.

Then the blackness overwhelmed him and he screamed.

His screaming allowed more dirt to fall into his mouth and throat and he began coughing, slowly suffocating.

He screamed until he was hoarse, but no one answered his pleas.

Then he woke up with his face buried straight down in the pillow of his bed.

Pulling his face away, he breathed in clean air and sat up. His body was covered in sweat and he realized he'd had a doozy of a nightmare, the images all ready beginning to slip away.

He stood up and checked the windup alarm clock on his nightstand. 12:01 a.m., it read. Wow, he had slept the rest of the day away and most of the night.

Standing up and stretching, he decided he needed to get outside and get some fresh air, the room now seeming far too claustrophobic to him.

He decided he'd take a shower and then go for a walk, and hopefully that would chase the cobwebs from his mind and the feeling of dread he suddenly felt.

*   *   *

Jimmy had talked with Cindy for hours after they had gone to his room. He'd gotten them some dinner, and after they'd eaten, they talked some more. He liked her, they just seemed to click. Sure, she was beautiful, but as he grew to know her, and found out what she wanted out of her life, her hopes and dreams, he found himself becoming drawn to her both sexually as well as intellectually.

After they'd finished talking, their dinner plates empty and discarded in the corner of the room, they'd lain down for a nap and had fallen asleep in each other's arms.

Later that night, Jimmy had been pulled from sleep to her soft fingers caressing him. He was soon awake, and the two of them had made at first, passionate love, and then a round of tender love. But by the third time he was spent, even his youthful reserves exhausted.

The two of them had then curled up in each other's arms and slept the peace of total satisfaction.

Both of them content to be near the other.

*   *   *

Henry stepped out into the crisp night air and began a lazy walk down the sidewalk.

The street was bare of life as he wandered where his feet took him, no particular destination in mind.

His hands reached down to make sure his weapons were positioned properly. Though he was only going for a walk, he made sure he was ready for anything. With a horde of the undead outside the fragile, homemade walls of the town, he wanted to make sure he was prepared for whatever might happen.

He had his .38 behind his back, and his Glock strapped to his hip, the weapon snug in its holster. He carried his shotgun over his shoulder on a sling.

Riding his other thigh was his own panga, the sixteen inches of metal a comforting weight on his body as he strolled down the street. He had left the other, twelve inch panga from Thomas in his room and planned on giving it back to the amorer when he had a chance. Now that he had his original panga back, he felt a part of him was now whole.

Passing a parking lot, he slowed his pace. His eyes caught the reflection of a large, thirty-two seat yellow school bus sitting silently in the empty lot. The words PITTSFIELD SCHOOLS were stenciled in black on the side. An idea came to him. If that bus could be strengthened, armored perhaps, it would make a fine war machine.

Placing the thought to the back of his mind, he continued onward, enjoying the peaceful night air.

He was already two blocks away from the boarding house when he heard some kind of a disturbance coming from a nearby alleyway. Drawing his Glock, he crept up to the alley's entrance and looked down into the gloom and shadows.

There were two of the town's security guards beating up a man.

When the clouds shifted overhead and splashed the alley with a dim light, Henry could see the beleaguered man had to be at least sixty.

Stepping into the middle of the alley, Henry called down to the men.

"Hey, what's going on down there? Do you guys need some help?"

One of the guards stopped hitting the old man and turned to look at Henry.

"No, we don't need any help. Fuck off; it's past curfew; get home or you're next," the man said, as he strained to see Henry in the dark.

"Look, pal, I don't answer to you and I want to know why you're beating up that guy," Henry hissed at the man, already figuring there was going to be trouble.

The second guard backed off the old man and turned to Henry, as well, the old man slumping to the ground and falling over, whimpering softly.

"What're you deaf? This is your last warning. Beat it or you're next."

Henry moved a little closer. "Look, fellas, I'm not going anywhere. Now, why don't you two leave the old guy alone and we'll forget any of this happened."

The two guards looked at each other and smiled in the dark. Then they moved towards Henry, each of them spreading out to take Henry in the middle.

Henry saw this and started to back up.

"Look, guys, trust me, you don't want to do this," Henry said politely as they grew closer.

The two men stayed silent and continued to move forward, coming to a halt when they were within reach of him.

Henry debated just shooting the two men dead and explaining it to Sam later, but decided that might bring him more trouble than he'd want. So he brought up his hands and got ready for a fight. As long as the guard's weapons stayed holstered, so would his.

The two guards came at him one at a time, barely covering themselves. They were used to the sheep of the town and would never have expected someone to put up a fight and defy them. They were about to learn a valuable lesson, however.

Henry couldn't see them well in the dark, so he just decided to call them Right Guard and Left Guard in his head, quickly preparing for Right Guard to attack.

Right Guard dove in and tried to grab Henry's arm, and was greeted with a solid punch to the face. The man flew back against the wall with a grunt of pain, and then Left Guard swung at Henry's exposed face.

At the last second, Henry dodged away and sent his left fist into Left Guard's belly. With a whoosh of expelled breath, the man doubled over. Henry then kneed the man in the face and sent his head flying back until the guard's back struck the alley wall.

Clouds floated across the sky, what little illumination there was fading, the darkness returning like a living thing.

Now fighting nothing more than shadows, Henry went on the attack. Walking up to Right Guard, he started swinging, his blows continually sinking into flesh.

His opponent would make grunting sounds with each blow that landed and Henry backed off a little, not wanting to kill the man.

Left Guard struck Henry in his side and Henry saw sparks in his eyes, the pain flooding through him.

With a snarl and a curse Henry turned to the man and blocked his next attempt to strike him. Then he sent an uppercut into Left Guard's chin that rocked the man back. His head struck the alley wall and the man fell to the ground, on the edge of being unconscious.

Right Guard saw his buddy fall and began to panic. That's when he drew his weapon from its holster.

The revolver gleamed in the dim light from the night sky and Henry knew this fight just went up a notch on the danger meter.

Moving quicker than the guard could see, Henry drew his panga and sliced it across the guard's arm, cutting a two inch gash into the flesh. The guard dropped his weapon and used his other arm to staunch the flow of blood.

Breathing heavily, Henry wiped the blade on his sleeve and stepped closer to the guard, the fight obviously out of him.

"Be thankful I didn't take your arm clean off, now get the hell out of here before you bleed to death!" Henry snapped, stepping away from the man to give him a clear path of escape. The man stood on shaky legs and then ran down the alley to disappear into the changing shadows of the street.

Henry then turned to the other guard who was shaking his head, more than likely now having a concussion, and took one tentative step towards him. The guard shrank back in fear, clearly having enough for one night.

"Go on, get out of here. Go check out your friend. Make sure he gets to Doc Robinson."

The man scurried out of the alley and was gone from sight. Henry pulled his Glock and waited for a moment to make sure neither of the guards was going to double back for a little revenge, but after five minutes had come and gone, he decided they were gone for good.

Holstering his Glock, he turned and helped the old man to his feet. After a moment the old man got his balance and smiled in the dim light of the alley.

"Thank you, son, I think they would have killed me if you hadn't intervened, he said gratefully.

"Your welcome. What the hell was that all about anyway? Why were they beating you?" Henry asked.

"Ah, quite simple really, you see, I was out after curfew," the man said, thinking that explained everything.

"Curfew, that's why they beat you? Does Sam know about this? Does it happen often?" Henry asked, curious about the man's dilemma.

"Whoa, son, slow down. No, the Boss doesn't know. There's a lot he doesn't know about. His guards, some of them, anyway, are greedy men who take advantage of the fact they're in power. Funny isn't it? The more the world changes, the more it stays the same." Then the man coughed up blood, spitting it onto the alley floor.

"Well, I'd better get home, my wife is surely worried," the old man said, turning to

leave. Then he paused and turned back to Henry. "Thank you again, good sir. If I can't repay you for your help tonight, surely God will some day." He smiled with a set of broken teeth, thanks to the guards. Then he hobbled out of the alley and was gone from view.

Henry stood there for a moment, pondering what had occurred. Then he slowly crept out of the alley, and once satisfied it was clear, he headed back to his room at the boarding house.

His walk had proven a little more eventful than he'd expected and now he was looking forward to lying back down and continuing the night in a hopefully dreamless sleep.


Twenty minutes later, he was back in his bed and was rewarded with a restful night sleep all the way through till morning.

Not even the echoing gunshots from the barricade when more walkers were shot off the wall disturbed his slumber.

# CHAPTER TWENTY-SIX

THE NEXT MORNING the town was a beehive of activity with the first stage of the plan to liberate the town from the undead horde beginning.

After a meager breakfast of bread and cheese, Henry and Jimmy had met up with Sam at the barricade's front gate.

Sitting at the gate, idling quietly were two pickup trucks.

Jimmy would take one and another would be driven by a young guard named Billy; with another guard named George riding shotgun with him. Jimmy would meet his backup man later, but for now he had to say some goodbyes.

Mary and Henry were standing together, trying to talk Jimmy out of going.

"I don't like this, Jimmy," Henry frowned. "It's too dangerous, this isn't our fight."

"Look, I want to do it. It'll be a piece of cake," Jimmy said casually, trying to hide his nervousness. "Plus, only one of us knows exactly where the dynamite is," he stated, tossing his weapons into the cab of the truck. "You just make sure you keep that gate clear for me when I get back."

"Don't worry, we'll be ready, you just call us when you're close and we'll start cleaning house. Good luck," Henry said, holding his hand out for Jimmy to shake.

Jimmy looked at the hand in front of him and smiled. Then took it and shook.

"Thanks, I hope I don't need it," he said with a wry grin. Then he turned and looked at Mary.

She jumped into his arms and hugged him. "You better come back in one piece. I need someone to argue with," she said wistfully. Then she kissed him on the cheek and stepped back.

"Will you two cut it out? I'll be fine. Now get out of here so I can go," Jimmy said, climbing into the driver's seat.

Jimmy looked over a few heads at the back of the gate and saw Cindy watching. He waved to her. She waved back, blew him a kiss and her lips mouthed the words good luck.

Jimmy nodded and then turned away.

Another guard hopped into the passenger side of the truck and Jimmy turned to see a young man, at least a year younger than him, next to him.

"Hi, my name's William, but people call me Will," he said, holding out his hand.

Jimmy took it and they shook. "Hey, Will. I'm Jimmy, nice to meet you. You ready for this?" He asked.

"Yes, sir, ready when you are," the young man said, placing his rifle across his lap for easy access.

Jimmy picked up the two-way radio on the seat and pressed the call button.

"All right, Sam, we're ready down here. Just open the gate and we'll go, over." Jimmy said.

"10-4, Jimmy, just give us a second to clear some of the walkers away from the gate. The minute you leave, we're gonna have some shit to deal with, over." Sam's voice said as it crackled back through the radio.

"Okay, Sam, ready when you are, over," Jimmy replied and then placed the radio down and looked at his new partner.

"What happens now?" Will asked; the nervousness clearly in his voice.

"Now we wait," Jimmy said, leaning his head back against the rear glass of the truck and closing his eyes.

The plan was relatively simple. A few guards would go ten feet or so to either side of the gate and then hang over as bait to draw the walkers away from the opening. Then, when they had distracted as many ghouls as possible, the gate would be opened and the two trucks would shoot through it and, hopefully, freedom.

Henry and Mary climbed up the ladder to be with Sam and help coordinate.

The guards moved across the wooden plank and then leaned over as far as they could go, with another guard as backup in case they slipped.

Only a few feet below the hanging men, the undead massed as food was tantalizingly dangled over their heads.

"Look, its working! Some of them are moving away!" Sam yelled, excited at the results.

Henry just nodded. The walking dead were unpredictable and he knew not to take anything for granted. Still, things appeared to be moving along well.

When enough walkers had been cleared away from the gate for the pickups, Sam gave the word to open the gate. Then he called down to Jimmy.

"All right, son, the gate's opening now, there's still a few stragglers, so be careful," Sam said over the radio.

Jimmy's voice came back loud and clear.

"We hear you, Sam, Let's get this done, over and out."

From on top of the wall, Henry watched the gate open and the pickups shoot out of the barricade.

"There they go," he said. Then he had bigger problems when twenty-five walkers poured into the hole left by the trucks passing.

The gate closed slowly as the walking corpses poured into the town, more than enough gaining access inside the walls. With a dull thud, the gate slammed shut, crushing one ghoul in two when it didn't move fast enough to get out of the way of the dropping gate. The bottom half of its body was laying outside the wall and its upper part was now trying to crawl into the town as the bifurcated corpse dragged itself across the dirty asphalt, intestines and organs falling out behind it to steam in the street under the warm sun.

The other walkers moved with purpose, finally seeing their prey in front of them.

Then five guards walked out from the side of the gate opening and opened up with rifles and shotguns.

Henry, Sam and Mary, along with the few guards on the wall, began shooting into the crowd of walkers. The barrage of bullets cut the undead horde to pieces in seconds, body parts falling to the ground amid blood and gore.

One ghoul was systematically cut to pieces as each bullet seemed to blow away a limb until the corpse was nothing more than a torso with a head. Then a stray round found its forehead and the zombie was put out of its misery.

Henry kept up the barrage until his Glock clicked dry, then he placed it back in its holster and pulled his shotgun from his back, where it hung on a sling.

Pumping the weapon, he started indiscriminately firing into the undead crowd.

The walkers were massed so close together that every blast from the shotgun found a target.

With the smell of burnt meat and blood filling the area around the gate, Sam climbed down to survey their handiwork.

As he walked through the shattered remains of the bodies, he would shoot one in the head every so often, slowly making his way to the end of the carnage.

Just before he stepped out, a hand reached out and grabbed his boot. For just a moment, a chill went up his spine, and then he shook it off and calmly placed his Colt to the forehead of the ghoul. With its teeth gnashing at empty air, he squeezed the trigger, ending the walker's life once and for all.

The smoke from all the weapon discharges filled the area until a light draft of wind caught it, causing the smoke to disperse.

Reaching the end of the bodies, Sam turned and looked back at the carnage his men had wrought. There were still some twitching in the middle of the mass of corpses, but they were harmless.

Henry walked up beside him, his shotgun casually leaning against his shoulder.

"We need to get this shit cleaned up before Jimmy and your men get back," Henry said softly, surveying the grotesque scene.

"Yeah, you're right." He called to his guards. "All right, men, get the cleanup crew in here, now, we need to get this mess out of here and get ready for the trucks to return!" He yelled out, his men jumping to action.

There was a shuffling from the crowd as people went about the nasty business of cleaning up the bodies. Guards stood watch to make sure none of the cleanup crew was attacked by any ghoul they thought wasn't quite dead.

With a few well placed bullets, all the corpses were soon down for good and the cleanup began in earnest.

For now the idea was to just haul the corpses to the top of the wall and throw them back over to the grassy plain below. Later, if possible, they could burn the bodies in one large funeral pyre.

The work went slowly, but in an hour or so most of the mess would be gone, leaving the asphalt stained a dark maroon.

Then all Henry and the others had to do was sit, wait, and hope Jimmy and the other truck would make it back in one piece.

*   *   *

Jimmy revved the engine, watching the gate slowly moving open. Looking in his rearview mirror, he spotted Billy in the pickup behind him.

Billy saw Jimmy's eyes in the rearview mirror looking back to him and smiled, putting his thumb in the air.

Jimmy waved back and then got ready to move.

The gate was three feet off the ground and Jimmy could see at least twenty pairs of legs moving around the gate while it rose.

Then, just before the gate was open enough to clear the top of the pickup, Jimmy floored it, timing it so that the top of the pickup missed the bottom lip of the gate by inches.

His pickup flew out onto the highway with Billy following, knocking walkers to the sides like they were paper dolls. Jimmy had to immediately take evasive action or the amount of bodies would swamp the vehicle.

He swerved to the right to avoid a group of walking corpses and ended up putting the grille of the pickup straight into what was once a middle-aged housewife, curlers and all.

The truck hit her so fast it cut her in two, the bottom half of her falling under the pickup where she was ripped to shreds beneath the undercarriage

The upper part of her was clinging to the grille and wouldn't let go.

Jimmy tried a few swerves but the undead housewife held tight.

Forgetting her for the moment, he plowed through another pair of ghouls, the front bumper catching one and sending it flying ten feet into the dirt on the side of the road.

Then the road was free of bodies, so he slowed the truck, continuing down the highway at a leisurely forty mph.

He checked his rearview and was pleased to see Billy right on his ass.

Jimmy watched Billy hit his wipers as he tried to clear the blood and brains that had found its way onto his windshield.

Jimmy looked forward again and stared into the undead, pale face of the housewife. Evidently she had held on and now had climbed up over the hood, what was left of her insides spilling over the front of the pickup where they dangled in the wind.

"Will, take that dead bitch out, will ya?" Jimmy asked calmly as he tried to see the road around the half of ghoul.

Will nodded and leaned out of the pickup's window with his rifle leading the way.

The man lined up the head and squeezed the trigger, the rifle shot sounding loud inside the cab.

Part of the housewife's head flew off and fell to the road where it spun for a moment and then lay still; but still she held on.

"Shit, you're persistent, aren't you?" Jimmy mumbled under his breath.

"Try, again, Will, and this time don't miss, huh? I'm tired of looking at this ugly bitch!" He yelled to be heard over the whistling wind.

Will nodded and lined up his rifle again. When he thought he had a shot, he fired the weapon. This time the housewife's head disintegrated and the torso fell to the hood of the pickup with a slam.

"All right! Nice shot, Will. Now get your ass back inside here!" Jimmy called to him.

A second later, Will had climbed back inside and sat down again.

"What are you gonna do about that?" Will asked, pointing to the headless corpse now lying on the hood. Blood was seeping out to coat the hood a dull maroon color.

"Watch and learn," he said.

First he put his hand out the window to signal Billy to back off his ass. Once that was done and he knew he was clear from behind, he hit the brakes hard and quick.

The pickup slammed to a halt for one brief second before Jimmy hit the gas pedal again.

The force of the stop allowed the torso to go flying in front of the pickup, where it rolled on the road and then came to a stop, now nothing more than a bloody piece of meat.

Jimmy didn't even bother trying to avoid the half body, the pickup going over the corpse like a speed bump.

Then he continued down the highway, all his problems solved.

Behind him, a few crows had already landed on the headless torso, their beaks digging into the red meat.

Their caws followed the two pickups down the highway.

## CHAPTER TWENTY-SEVEN

HENRY WATCHED PAUL sight another ghoul with his rifle.

Bam! Half the head of the walker blew apart as it dropped to the trampled grass outside the barricade.

"Nice shot," Henry offered.

"Thanks," Paul said in return and then placed his eye back to his rifle's gun sight for another shot.

This had been going on since Jimmy had left the town on what Henry thought of as a fool's errand.

All he could do was hope and pray his friend returned in one piece.

He looked out onto the once empty plain, now covered with the walking dead.

More walkers had continued to arrive and now there had to be hundreds outside the ramshackle barricade.

He looked up at the sound of heavy footfalls on the wooden plank beside him. Turning, he saw Sam walking up to him, his face set in a tight grimace.

"I just came from Thomas," he said, stopping next to Henry.

"And?" Henry prompted him.

"And, we're low on ammunition. These walkers are going to have to wait until we raid Costington for supplies. I know for a fact they have a gun store at the end of town. We need that ammunition if we're going to make it through this."

Henry thought for a moment and then nodded.

"You know, if they come back with the dynamite I think we could accomplish both goals at the same time," Henry said, modifying his original plan in his mind.

"Yeah, how?" Sam coaxed him.

But Henry just shook his head. "Later, when they get back. If they don't make it, my ideas don't mean shit."

Paul took another shot, blowing what was once a construction worker back to Hell.

Smiling, he looked at the two men. "It's just too damn easy."

"Yeah, well, go easy on the ammo, Paul. Don't shoot unless they're on the wall," Sam ordered his second-in-command.

Paul nodded affirmative and then turned back to watch the writhing bodies below.

"Man, I hope they get back soon. If not then we're totally fucked," Paul said, under his breath, but still loud enough for the other two men to hear.

Henry turned to look at him and said: "Brother, you don't know the half of it."

\*     \*     \*

Jimmy slowed the pickup at the top of a gentle slope on the highway. Below the incline was what they had driven all the way out here for.

"There it is," Jimmy stated to Will. "That's the van."

Billy pulled his pickup next to Jimmy's on the highway, the windows side by side.

Jimmy pointed down the hill at the van.

"There it is," he repeated for Billy.

"Well, what are we waiting for?" Billy said, then put his pickup in drive and headed off. Jimmy followed and in minutes both pickups were sitting on the side of the road with their doors open.

"So how are we going to do this?" Billy asked, the four men standing in a rough circle.

"Look, Henry told me that shit is unstable and I believe him. So what do you say we split the load between the two of us? That way the odds are better that at least one of us makes it back in one piece."

Will looked at Jimmy, his eyes wide. "What do you mean; 'in one piece'?" He asked.

"Simple, that shit is sensitive," Jimmy told him. "You hit one too many speed bumps and BOOM!" Jimmy said, putting his hands together and throwing them out into the air like an explosion.

"Oh shit, no one said anything about that," Billy said, backing away from Jimmy, with George following.

"Yeah, so what are you gonna do? If you go back empty handed what do you think Sam will do to you?" Jimmy said.

Billy stood quiet for a few seconds, weighing his options. Then his shoulders slumped, giving in.

"All right, fine, you win. We'll do it your way," Billy snapped.

Jimmy smiled at him. "Great, glad you're on board again. Oh and you might want to remember that this isn't even my goddamn home we're trying to save and I'm here helping," Jimmy snapped back.

Billy's face grew red with anger as he stared at Jimmy. He was reaching for his weapon when Jimmy pulled his .38 from its holster and aimed it at Billy's chest.

"Are we going to have a problem here? 'Cause we can settle it right fucking now," Jimmy snarled at Billy.

Billy stared at the end of Jimmy's weapon and decided this was a fight he wouldn't win.

Slowly lowering his hands, Billy smiled politely. "No, no problem. I'm good."

Jimmy looked into the man's eyes and smiled, then slowly holstered his weapon.

"All right then, let's get to work. Will, get the doors to the van and we'll start loading the dynamite," Jimmy said, deciding to stay back and keep an eye on Billy, just in case the man was harboring a grudge.

Will nodded, walking over to the van. Reaching out, he wrapped his hand around the left door.

Then the door shot outward, knocking Will to the dirt with a muffled grunt.

A ghoul jumped out and landed on top of the hapless guard, the dead man's teeth going for his throat.

Will screamed in panic, fighting to keep those teeth from ripping into him.

"Help me! For God's sake, please help me!" He screamed to the other men.

Billy and George just stood there, too frightened to move.

The dead man had decided Will's throat was out of reach and had shifted his attention to his exposed arm instead. Bright crimson flowed down Will's arm to pool on his shirt while he struggled to push the dead man off him.

Suddenly the weight on his chest lessened.

Jimmy had grabbed the man by the scruff of his suit collar, pulling him off Will.

Using his own body weight, Jimmy pulled his arms back and tossed the ghoul to the side, pulling his .38 from its holster in one smooth move.

The pale-faced man rolled onto his knees and snarled at him.

Jimmy calmly placed the barrel of the gun no more than inches from the ghoul's face and squeezed the trigger.

The head was thrown back as if punched, the force of the bullet pushing the body to the dirt. The body hit so hard it bounced once before laying still, a small hole now in the front of the corpse's forehead, a larger one on the back of its skull.

The dirt quickly soaked up the blood and gore oozing out of the damaged head and Jimmy turned away from it to check on Will.

Will was on his feet now, if a little unsteady, while Jimmy watched him.

Jimmy turned to Billy and George. "Well, guys, don't just stand there, help the man out," he snapped.

The men broke from their stupor and ran over to Will, helping him to the pickup, where they gave him a water bottle and placed a rag over his wound.

Jimmy followed them and stood by Will.

"It's not so bad Will, look at the bright side," he smiled casually.

"Bright side, what the hell could that be?" He squeaked when Billy put pressure on his wound.

"Well, if this was a movie that bite would mean that you're gonna become a zombie, too."

Will stopped squeaking for a moment, thinking about it. Then he cried out in pain again as Billy wrapped his wound. His arm had a one inch bite taken out of it from where the ghoul had bitten into the flesh. Nothing old Doc Robinson couldn't fix when they got back to town.

Jimmy turned and walked back to the prone corpse, now lying quietly in the dirt in its eternal rest.

The body was wearing what was once a one thousand dollar business suit. Gold rings adorned its hands. Jimmy wondered if he checked, would there be a fat wallet in the corpse's pants, full of maxed-out credit cards and season tickets to the next Cubs game.

He prodded the body with his boot; didn't matter, anyway.

The corpse made a gargling noise and Jimmy jumped back and pulled his weapon again.

What the hell? He'd shot it in the head! It should be dead!

Watching it for a moment, he realized it was nothing more than gasses escaping from the corpse while it decomposed, and had been decomposing since it had turned.

Walking back to the body, he kicked it in the stomach.

"Goddamn deader," he mumbled, embarrassed he'd jumped like a rookie.

Then he walked back to the others. Will was sitting in the cab of the pickup, sweat dripping from his brow.

"You gonna be all right?" Jimmy asked, watching him.

Will nodded yes and then closed his eyes.

Jimmy turned away and looked at the two remaining men.

"Okay, now where were we? Billy, help me split the dynamite up, half in each truck," Jimmy said, taking charge of the situation.

"George, stay sharp and keep watch. I don't want any more surprises."

"Okay," George said, hopping up into the bed of a pickup to get a better view of the area.

Billy joined Jimmy and the two men went to the van.

The van was now empty of any threats, and with a look of trepidation, the two men used the utmost care to begin dividing the case of explosives.

*　　*　　*

It was slow going, Jimmy and Billy carefully laying the sticks in the back of each pickup. The sweat kept dripping into Jimmy's eyes as he walked back and forth between the van and the pickup, the tension so thick you could almost see it.

After two long hours of moving the dynamite one stick at a time, the two men were finished.

Leaning back against the truck's rear bed, the two men drank from a water bottle and watched the insects pick at the corpse in the expensive suit. One particular ant was lifting small pieces of brain in its pincers, and would then scurry away to its ant hole, not more than five feet away.

The circle of life, Jimmy thought. One creature's death is another creature's sustenance.

"Let's give it another few minutes and then what do you say we head back," Jimmy suggested to Billy.

Billy nodded, then spit out a mouthful of water. "Yeah, sure, sounds good."

Whatever altercation had happened between Jimmy and Billy was in the past, the two men bonding over the simple fact death was a heartbeat away.

Jimmy looked over his shoulder at Will. The young man was in the passenger seat sleeping. Jimmy didn't mind. Let him rest up, he'd need him at full strength when they got back to the gate.

He frowned, thinking about it. That wasn't going to be fun.

Twisting the cap back on the water bottle, he tossed it into the back of the pickup.

Billy, sensing it was time to go, started over to his pickup while George climbed down from the bed of the truck and slid into the passenger seat of the vehicle.

"Now remember, Billy. Drive slowly, and for God's sake, watch the bumps," Jimmy said, jumping into the driver's seat of his pickup. Billy gave him a thumbs up in reply.

Will opened his eyes and looked askance at Jimmy. "We going?"

"Yup, you okay?" Jimmy inquired.

"Yeah, I'm cool. I'll be ready when you need me."

"Good," Jimmy said, patting him on his shoulder. "That's all I can ask."

Jimmy started the engine and put the pickup in drive. Checking his mirror out of habit, he pulled onto the road and headed back to town at a leisurely twenty mph.

Slow was good, he thought, looking in his rearview mirror at the small wooden box sitting in the bed behind him.

The two pickups drove off and were soon over the incline of the deserted highway, the engine noise lost in the wind.

Behind them on the ground where the corpse still lay, the ants continued their arduous task of picking the body clean.

# CHAPTER TWENTY-EIGHT

HENRY HAD BEEN busy since Jimmy had left.

He'd been wracking his brain for a way to get Jimmy and Billy back inside the barricade without letting every living corpse in Virginia inside with him.

And to make matters worse, there had to be over three hundred walkers milling outside in the plains surrounding the town.

Once the walkers knew there was food to be had inside the walls, they were relentless.

Paul had lost count how many he'd shot trying to climb the barricade and had only stopped when Sam had reminded him of the depleted ammunition supply. After that, he and the other guards had resorted to using spears and blades.

Sam had passed on that similar threats were being halted on other parts of the barricade surrounding the town, as well.

Unfortunately, most of the ghouls were congregating around the gate, the walking dead sensing this was an easy passage to the town.

The gap in the back wall had been sealed thanks to the diligent work of some of Sam's men.

Now all Henry had to do was get Jimmy back inside in one piece.

Not surprising it had been Mary who had come up with an idea.

A few months ago, when Henry, Mary and Jimmy had first come together, they had used Molotov cocktails to fight off the walking dead.

Now, that same idea would be used to get Jimmy returned to them safely.

For more than an hour Sam had been with his men, supervising the filling of wine bottles from Murphy's Pub with gas, using what was left of their meager stores of gasoline. After mixing the gas with soap detergent, it would make a crude form of napalm that would stick to whatever it came in contact with.

Sam had returned with two crates full of the deadly concoctions. The containers all had little, red and white rags sticking out from their tops, small colorful wicks waiting to be lit.

Henry had the men carry the crates up to the planks overlooking the gate as that's where they'd be needed most.

Then with the bottles secured, he went back to the arduous task of waiting for Jimmy to return.

*　　*　　*

A little more than an hour later, the two-way radio crackled on the plank near his feet.

"I said is anyone receiving me, over," Jimmy's voice said amidst a blast of static, the distance too great for proper reception.

Henry quickly picked up the radio and called back.

"I read you, Jimmy, this is Henry, over."

"Henry? All right, that's good. Listen, I've got the dynamite and Billy and me are about an hour away. What's it like there, you okay?" The line was quiet for a moment and then Henry heard a quick "over," Jimmy finishing his sentence.

"Yeah, Jimmy, we're fine, a lot more roamers are here than when you left, but we've got a plan to get you back inside, over."

"Good, I'll call when we're closer, over and out," Jimmy said, cutting off.

"See you soon, out," Henry finished, placing the radio back down.

Looking down to ground level, he saw Sam directing some of his men on what to do when the pickups returned.

"Hey, Sam, Jimmy just called me! He's about an hour out and he's got the dynamite. Your men ready for this?" Henry inquired.

"Shit, I sure as hell hope so. This'll be their first time in the thick of it, though. I've already made it clear if I see anyone cut and run I'll personally put a bullet in their head," Sam said with a grim look in his eyes. Henry had no doubt the man would follow through on his promise if given the chance by a cowardly guard.

Henry nodded. "Okay then, you know the plan. Your men should be in position no later than a half hour from now. Okay?" Henry asked.

Sam nodded. "You know, Henry, when all this shit is done maybe we could have a talk about you and your friends staying here with us. We could use a man of your experience on our security team," Sam proposed.

Henry smiled back. "Let's worry about the here and now for the time being, okay? Then we'll worry about later…if we're still alive."

Sam looked up at Henry and nodded, agreeing with the man, then he turned away, going back to his men.

There was a lot to do and very little time to do it.

Paul's rifle cracked and another ghoul fell from the wall, the echo of the shot drifting across the plains, where it was lost amidst the moans and howls of the living dead.

\* \* \*

Jimmy slowed the pickup truck at the top of the gentle rise on the empty highway leading to the small town of Pittsfield, Billy pulling up along side him.

The gate was no more than ten minutes away by vehicle and Jimmy figured now would be a good a time as any to take a break and call back to Henry, signaling him they had arrived.

It had been a tension filled ride back to town, expecting every bump in the road to be the one to set off the delicate dynamite.

But over an hour later they had made it; and in one piece.

Jimmy glanced through the passenger window of his pickup, past Will, into the other pickup truck idling quietly next to him. The sweat showed in dusty grooves on Billy's face, attesting to the fact how scared he'd been on the return drive back to town.

George just sat quietly, as if he'd already accepted the fate his God chose to throw at him.

Their trip back was mostly uneventful. A few times they had to avoid some roamers who were on the highway, but nothing that a little defensive driving couldn't fix.

If Jimmy had done what he'd wanted, he would have plowed over and ground every stinking, rotting pile of pus into the pavement. But that wasn't an option with the sensitive payload he was carrying.

Although one time, Will, who was feeling better, took the butt of his rifle, and as Jimmy slowly drove by a walker, Will swung the rifle like a bat for all he was worth.

The butt of the rifle had hit the ghoul's head with a crack and the corpse had gone down like a ton of bricks, twitching feebly in Jimmy's rearview mirror, until the road had dipped, the body lost from sight.

But now they were through with their journey and the last leg was only moments away

Jimmy smiled across the vehicles to Billy. "You ready for the hard part?" Jimmy asked the man.

"Hard part, what the hell are you talking about?" Billy asked, his voice going up a notch, whether from delayed puberty or nervousness, Jimmy didn't know.

"Shit, getting the stuff was the easy part," Jimmy told him. "Now we have to jockey our way back through the gate, avoid all the roamers and keep from blowing ourselves up all at the same time."

Billy just looked at Jimmy for a few heartbeats, then he turned to George, who just shrugged.

What would happen, would happen, George's shrug said.

Billy looked down at his lap and sighed.

"Fuck, this sucks," he whispered.

Jimmy saw his lips move and picked up the gist of what he'd said.

"I hear that," he agreed and then picked up the two-way radio and called Henry.

"Hey, Henry, it's Jimmy, we're back, over."

Henry answered almost immediately.

"Hey, Jimmy, it's good to hear your voice. We're almost ready for you, over." Henry's disembodied voice floated through the radio's speaker.

"Cool, what's the plan? Jimmy asked.

"You'll see, let's just say it won't be hard to miss. What's your ETA? Over."

"We'll be there in ten minutes, over," Jimmy replied, putting the pickup in drive.

"Good, we'll be ready, see you then, over and out," Henry's voice said, the radio going silent once more.

Jimmy placed the radio on the seat between Will and himself.

"You ready for this, Will?" He asked the young man.

Will rubbed his wound with his other hand. "Hell, yeah, let's get this over with so I can see Doc Robinson about this bite. I don't want to take any chances I might turn into a walker."

Jimmy smiled at that, thinking how silly it sounded. But then, if someone had told him America would be taken over by the living dead a few short months ago, he would have laughed and called them idiots.

The two pickups drove off down the highway, their exhaust echoing off the shoulder of the road.

Above them in the sky, the afternoon sun shone down on them, reflecting off both of the pickup's roofs, from above looking like nothing more than two insignificant specks, moving across a jagged concrete line across the land.

# CHAPTER TWENTY-NINE

FOR THE TWENTIETH time in the last ten minutes, Henry reached down to check his Glock.

He knew it was there, but just touching it gave his mind a second of peace.

He was counting the seconds until the pickups showed themselves on the crest of the highway.

Then things were going to get interesting.

Looking across the wooden plank running along the barricade, he counted more than twenty men. All were armed with various ordnance, from hunting rifles to .45s. One old codger had what looked like an elephant gun; the front of the barrel looking more like a trumpet than a weapon.

These were all the men Sam could spare. All across the barricade the wall was manned by people from the town.

Men and women alike were pitching in to keep the walkers at bay long enough for Sam and his men to get to Costington and raid the abandoned town for its supplies.

But first they needed that dynamite.

Five of Sam's men, along with two that were welders, were in a garage in the middle of town working on Henry's other idea. When today was over, if they were still alive, then he was looking forward to seeing what the men had accomplished.

But for now, he had other matters to occupy him.

Over the moaning and wailing of the undead, two engines could be heard drifting to the gate.

Henry watched the highway as the pickup trucks came out of a dip in the road.

They weren't moving very fast, and as Henry watched, a stray ghoul tried to grab the side of the vehicle only to be pulled along beside it until one of the passengers knocked it off with the butt of his weapon.

Then Henry was moving into action.

With a nod askance of him to the guards, they leaned over, tempting the living dead with their live flesh.

Slowly, most of the undead moved away from the gate, but there were many more than before and the trick didn't work as well this time. Swearing under his breath, Henry reached down to the plank beside him and picked up one of the Molotov cocktails and lit its colorful fuse. Then he tossed it into the now denuded, grassy plain below. He quickly retrieved another, and followed that with a third and fourth.

The ground outside the gate erupted into flames, scaring off the stray walkers.

Some weren't as lucky, and when their clothes caught fire, the smell of burning flesh filled the area, the sickly sweet odor lodging in the throat, making gagging an involuntary reflex.

Henry watched the inferno below him, satisfied with the results.

Looking down from the barricade, Henry could clearly see an opening between the flames, a runway for Jimmy and Billy to drive up to the gate and then enter without a hundred walkers following behind.

The channel of fire burned brightly, the trampled, dry grass on the shoulder of the road helping to fuel the flames. The two pickups came over the hill and headed for the small net of safety cushioned between the walls of flames. The guards on both sides of him began firing into the crowd of walking corpses, shooting any down who appeared to be a threat to the pickups.

The ghouls shied away from the flames, the burning barrier more than enough to keep them at bay. But due to the sheer amount of bodies, the pickups were continually jockeying for a better route to the gate.

Bodies bounced off the bumpers of the pickups, the two trucks slowly making their way through. Then two bodies fell to the ground after being struck by the first pickup, their broken and bloody forms lying in the path of the second truck.

Henry watched the driver try to swerve around them, but he was going just a little too fast.

The corpses on the ground became speed bumps to the approaching vehicle and as Henry watched, the truck seemed to jump into the air.

Then it landed back to earth with a hard bounce...and then nothing but a bright light filled the area and a tearing, roaring cacophony of sound ripped the air.

Henry was nearly blown off the barricade; the pickup truck disappearing in a flaming fireball that destroyed every ghoul in a fifty foot radius of the vehicle.

With his ears ringing, he picked himself back up and scanned the area.

Where the second pickup truck had been there was now nothing left but a smoking crater. Henry had to duck when smoking body parts rained down on him and the other men on the wall. A flaming tire bounced off the top of the wall, nearly taking Henry's head with it, and then continued bouncing and rolling down the road until it came to a stop, the rubber still burning.

He looked down and saw the other pickup only seconds away from the gate.

Henry called to the man on watch at the gate, getting the guard's attention, telling him to quickly open the portal.

The gate began to rise with agonizing slowness, and Henry wondered if the pickup would end up getting jammed underneath the bottom of the slowly rising gate.

Thankfully, seconds later, the surviving pickup truck shot through the opening and came to a gentle rest inside the safety of the town. The gate closed, but not before eighteen walkers had found their way inside the opening.

With the help from the other guards on the wall, Henry was able to make short work of the ghouls, and within the space of a minute, they were all either dead or out of action enough to be no immediate threat.

Body parts twitched fitfully, gore a palpable presence, the street and side of the barricade now drenched in red and black ichor.

Henry jumped down to the asphalt and dashed to the pickup just as the driver's door opened.

Relief flooded through him when he saw Jimmy hop out and smile at him. Henry's heart flooded with relief. He hadn't known who had been in the other pickup and had feared the worst.

"So, that was your plan?" Jimmy sneered, gently closing the pickup's door. "You wanted me to drive through a gauntlet of fire with a truckload of dynamite?"

"Yeah, that was it. Why, you didn't like it?" Henry retorted, smiling back, shaking Jimmy's hand.

Sam came running into the area, a concerned look on his face.

"What the hell happened? I heard the explosion, what the fuck blew up?" He yelled, looking at everyone for answers.

"I'm afraid Billy and George didn't make it," Jimmy said, the sadness clearly evident in his voice. "That shit was unstable and all it took was one bump too many. I guess their luck ran out. I'm sorry Sam."

Sam walked up to Jimmy to stand face to face with him, holding out his hand for Jimmy to shake.

"It's not your fault, son, Billy and George knew the risks. Hell, we all do. I'm just glad you made it back in one piece," he said, shaking Jimmy's hand and then slapping him on the shoulder. "Good job, son, and thank you."

A few errant shots rang out above them, the guards taking a few potshots at the now charred walkers. Luckily, the wind was blowing the worst of the smoke away from the town, back down the highway.

"How much dynamite did you get?" Henry inquired, walking to the back of the truck.

"Well, we got all of it. I split it up, just in case it blew up. I figured two trucks would be better than just one. I guess I was right," Jimmy said ruefully, looking over the wall at the rising pillar of smoke from the destroyed truck.

Then he climbed up the ladder and surveyed the carnage first hand.

There was nothing left of the other pickup, the force of the explosion literally ripping it to shreds. Jimmy watched some of the walkers damaged in the explosion crawl around the perimeter of the crater, dragging bent and twisted limbs behind them.

Everywhere he looked, there were bodies, some missing limbs and torsos, others without bottom halves. After a few seconds, he looked away, having seen enough destruction for one day. When he climbed back down from the wall, he was nearly knocked to the ground when Mary flew into his arms.

"Whoa, easy there, you'll break a rib," Jimmy joked while she hugged him happily.

"I can't believe you made it. I was so worried," she said, squeezing tighter.

Then Mary saw Cindy out of the corner of her eye. Letting go, she stepped away, noticing Jimmy had now seen her too.

"Go ahead, go see her, its okay," Mary said, her smile going from ear to ear.

"Thanks, Mary, you're the best," Jimmy said, going to Cindy, where the two hugged and kissed and talked while others dealt with the grim business at hand.

"We need to get that fire out. I don't want it to somehow spread to the town! I've got enough trouble without a plain's fire to deal with," Sam growled to his men from the top of the wall, having climbed up a moment ago.

Henry followed him up, surveying the devastation.

Despite all the walkers destroyed in the ensuing blast and fire, there were still hundreds wandering about. The front of the gate was clear for the moment, the ghouls staying well clear of the fire, but the other ends of the barricade had bodies two and three thick.

Even with the barricade, it was just a matter of time before the walking corpses found their way inside the town. And if that happened, every man, woman and child would be killed in a way Henry wouldn't wish on his worst enemy.

"Well, we got the dynamite, that's what's important. How are your men doing at the garage?" Henry asked Sam.

"I just came from there. Martin said he'll work all through the night if he has to.

They'll definitely be done by morning," Sam said, his face impassive as he watched the undead shuffling about only a few feet below him. Their moans filled the air, grating on the nerves.

"Good, then we'll leave in the morning, sound good?" Henry asked.

Sam pulled his gaze away from the flames and looked to Henry, the sweat flowing generously from his forehead.

"Yeah, that's fine. How many men should we bring?" Sam asked.

"I think eight or ten if you can spare them. Definitely at least six, not including me and Jimmy, that is," Henry suggested.

Sam nodded, the dancing flames seeming to place the large man in a trance.

Their business done for now, Henry climbed back down to the ground to see to his friends. A lot had happened since they'd come to the small town of Pittsfield, but at least they were together again.

With the echoing gunshots of the guards at their backs they all hopped into a security cart and drove back into town together. At least for the rest of the day they could leave the troubles of the world behind them and just enjoy being a group again.

Up on the barricade, Sam continued to watch the flames. As he stared at the twisting, swirling conflagration, he wondered if his town would survive or just end up consumed in the flames, like the fragile grass on the shoulder of the road.

The wind shifted, blowing the smoke into the man's hard visage.

But whether the one small tear rolling down his cheek was from the smoke or something else, no one would ever dare to ask.

# CHAPTER THIRTY

THE SUN SHONE down on the small garage in the middle of the small town of Pittsfield. The morning's dark clouds floated overhead, giving everyone in the group a premonition of the coming rain.

Standing at the large bay door at the front of the building were Sam, Henry and Jimmy. Mary had decided to stay at Sam's house, where she and Cindy had been most of the morning.

Mary had jokingly said that she'd leave the day's work to the men and she and Cindy would spend the time getting to know each other better.

Henry had agreed with her. Although he liked to keep the companions together, Mary wasn't needed today. Plus, her shoulder still wasn't fully healed.

So he'd left her and had gone to meet the rest of the group at the garage.

Now, he stood in front of the small brick building, watching the sun's morning rays spear through the clear spots on the dirty windows of the garage's wide bay doors.

Sitting unobtrusively in the middle of the first bay was a school bus.

Sparks flew from it in different places as Sam's welding crew finished up, laying the last of the sheet metal and bars over the windows.

Once the vehicle was a simple bus for transporting children to and from school, but now the large bus had been transformed into a rolling war machine.

The windows on both sides of the vehicle were covered in a thin layer of sheet metal and holes were cut into this metal to allow a man to fire his weapon through them, if needed.

The top of the bus had a two foot, chicken-wire fence running along the roof, enabling men to be protected from falling off while the vehicle moved across the land. Sandbags had also been placed around the roof for men to lean on.

Lanyards with clips were attached to the railing so men could clip their weapons to it, hopefully to prevent them from losing their gear if the bus hit one bump too many.

In the new world they were living in, firearms were more valuable than gold.

Henry watched the morning rays of sunshine reflect off the small metal spikes that bristled along the sides of the bus.

"What are those for?" Henry asked Sam, the three men moving further into the garage.

His voice was raised to talk over the small gas generator, but was relieved when the motor was cut off.

"To keep the walkers from climbing on the bus, but why don't I let my head welder tell you the rest," Sam said and grinned proudly when a large, Spanish man in his late forties walked up to them, wearing a pair of mechanic's overalls.

His face was covered in soot, and even through the dark welding glasses he wore, Henry could see the man's eyes were bloodshot. The welder's face had countless scars from burns he'd received over the years. One particular scar ran up his cheek, and when he smiled, the scar would bring his lower lip up just a little more, giving the smile a lopsidedness to it.

Walking over to the group, he held his hand out to Henry.

"Hello, I'm Miguel. What do you think of my creation?" He asked with pride.

"It's fantastic, more than I could have hoped. Did you build the metal box on the back of the bus like I asked?" Henry inquired while shaking the man's hand.

"Oh, yes, there's a two inch thick box on the back of the roof. You can't see it from here, but trust me, its there," Miguel smiled.

"What box? What are you guys talking about?" Jimmy asked, staring in awe at the behemoth in front of him.

"Ah, you do not know? Well, then, let me tell you. Your friend here," Miguel said, gesturing to Henry, "told me about how unstable the dynamite is so I built a large metal box on the roof for you to store it in. That way if it goes boom, maybe you all don't go with it, eh?" The welder smiled, showing off one gold tooth situated in the center of his mouth.

Jimmy gulped as he listened, thinking back to Billy and George. The poor bastards probably didn't even know what had hit them.

Sam walked around the bus, careful not to get too close to the six inch spikes.

"Damn, you did a good job Miguel," Sam said, with his eyes still taking it all in.

Jimmy walked closer to the yellow behemoth. "Shit, it looks like something out of Mad Max," he joked.

"Well, whatever it is," Henry said. "It should get the job done nicely.

Henry looked to Sam and asked: "When do we leave?"

Sam gave it the fleetest of thoughts. "I say we go in two hours. That'll give my men enough time to load the bus and get whatever else we need."

Henry nodded. "All right then, let's get to work."

The men began to check the bus over while one of Sam's guards went off to retrieve the men who would be going with them to Costington.

Henry had come up with only one idea to dispose of the walking dead in the other town.

With ammunition low and supplies limited, it had been harder than he thought.

But thanks to Jimmy, the dynamite would hold the key.

Success or failure, either way they'd know in a few hours.


Outside the barricade of old steel and junk cars, the undead horde continued to grow.

More than four hundred of the walking dead now surrounded the town. The walkers had killed all human life in a fifty mile radius of the small town, the other town leaders not wise enough to build a defense against the undead.

Now, like an oasis in the desert, the town of Pittsfield survived

For now.

# CHAPTER THIRTY-ONE

TWO HOURS AND fifteen minutes later the heavy-metal school bus pulled up to the gate of the small town.

There was a total of ten men onboard, including Henry and Jimmy, all hard men who knew how to handle themselves in a fight. Most were on the roof, strapping themselves down with rope so they wouldn't fall off the bouncing vehicle. The rest were in the bus with Sam, Paul, Henry and Jimmy.

Sam had left the younger men in his crew behind to defend the town from the growing horde of ghouls.

If things went well, the bus would return and hopefully take care of the undead. But first they needed to replenish their supplies.

Jimmy smiled from the driver's seat, looking into the big rearview mirror above his head. To him this was nothing more than another adventure.

Henry looked back at him, not at all amused with the situation he now found himself in. Up on top of the bus was half the payload of dynamite Jimmy had brought back to them. The sticks were all carefully and individually wrapped to protect them from jarring, the steel box mounted on rubber to keep the vibration to a minimum. There was another large package up there, as well, wrapped in a sheet to keep it from view of the men. It would be used later once they'd reached Costington.

Sam sat in back, double checking his new weapon, the other guards doing the same with theirs. Old Thomas, the Armorer had given Sam one of his pride and joys, an M-16 rifle with three banana clips, each holding thirty rounds.

Sam was looking at it like a mother to a child, looking forward to the damage he was going to do with the rifle.

Henry was carrying his .38 and his Glock as well as his shotgun, which rested on the seat next to him. His faithful panga was riding his thigh, as always, since he had first acquired the long, shining blade months ago.

Jimmy was upfront with his shotgun leaning next to him, as well as his .38. Spare bullets sat in boxes on the dash and Henry made a point of remembering to tell the young man to stow them away before they got moving.

Up on top of the barricade wall, the guards got ready to draw the undead away from the gate. The trick was losing its originality, but as long as it continued to work, no one was complaining.

Quickly and efficiently the guards moved to both sides of the gate and proceeded to bait the walkers with their live bodies.

When the area in front was mostly clear, two Molotovs went flying to the already scorched road, where they exploded into life, keeping the zombies away from the gate.

In less than five minutes the opening was relatively clear and the guard at the gate began to raise the portal.

Jimmy waited until the gate was almost open and then stepped on the gas. The bus, not necessarily built for speed, started moving and soon began picking up speed.

The top of the bus, now with another two feet of railing-added height, came within inches of catching the lip of the opening gate. Henry slapped his forehead. No one had taken into account the height of the bus and it was just dumb luck the vehicle fit at all.

The bright yellow war machine rolled through the gate, crushing any ghoul unfortunate enough to be in its path. The zombies immediately swarmed around the bus, heedless of the fire, their hunger for meat overwhelming them.

Bare hands slapped at the sheet metal while Jimmy struggled to keep the vehicle on course, the sheer weight of bodies affecting his ability to control the bus.

From the roof came gunshots as the guards shot the walkers when they tried to climb on the sides.

Corpses were ripped to shreds, the steel spikes lining the sides of the bus doing their job well.

Henry stuck his shotgun through a hole in the sheet metal, repeatedly firing until he was out of ammo, then he calmly reloaded and began again. With each squeeze of the trigger another dead face fell away from the bus.

Sam was on the other side of the aisle, spraying bodies with steel jacketed rounds. Walkers shook as bullets ripped loose stinking gobbets of flesh, the bodies collapsing soon after. Paul had placed himself near the back of the bus, his rifle sending bullet after bullet into multiple targets.

One ghoul was knocked to the asphalt, its head falling under the thick tires of the bus. With the sound of a melon exploding, the skull was crushed, blood and brains flying beneath the undercarriage of the bus where they steamed on the exhaust.

Bodies were sent flying in all directions, the unstoppable war machine plowing through them. When the bus was clear of the worst of the undead horde, it continued down the lonely highway.

Henry turned to look out the back window and was pleased to see the gate lowering.

The bus's wide girth prevented most of the walkers from entering through the opening and as the bus crested the top of the incline, the echo of gunshots from the town was already dwindling, the guards disposing of the last undead intruder clever enough to make it inside the town.

Henry saw the frown on Sam's face and called out to him over the rumbling of the engine.

"What's wrong, Sam? You don't look too happy," Henry stated.

If possible, Sam's frown grew more intense when he looked at Henry.

"I'm just wondering if there'll be a town to come back to when we return," Sam said in a hard voice filled with tension.

Thinking of Mary back in town, Henry shrugged off the chill that went down his back at the man's words.

"It'll be there, Sam," Henry said simply.

Sam nodded, then he rechecked his rifle.

In the driver's seat, Jimmy spotted another roamer walking down the lonely highway. Lining up the grille of the vehicle with the walking corpse, he mercilessly ran the ghoul down. The broken corpse rolled for a few seconds and laid still, its insides now on the outside and vice versa.

With gun casings littering the floor, rolling back and forth across the bus, Jimmy continued onward.

The town of Costington was waiting for them, as well as its population.

Only they were now all dead.

*   *   *

About halfway to Costington, Jimmy pulled the bus over to the side of the road with a hiss of tired brakes. Henry looked up from checking his weapon to see Jimmy standing up from his chair.

"What's up? Why'd you stop?" Henry asked him.

"Cause I got to pee, man. With all this running around, I haven't had a chance to go," Jimmy said, opening the bus's door.

With a creaking of unused hinges, the door slid open, bending on its hinges like an accordion.

Jimmy smiled and then hopped down onto the shoulder and turned his back to them while he undid his zipper.

"You know, Sam, maybe we should all take five. Let the men stretch before we get there," Henry suggested, standing up, as well.

"Yeah, okay, five minutes shouldn't hurt," Sam said, walking to the door and moving down the stairs to the outside. Once on the road he called up to the men on the roof.

"If you men want to come down for a few minutes, go ahead," Sam called up.

"Nah, we're fine, Boss," one guard said.

"Yeah, the sooner we get there, the sooner we get back," another of the guards called back down.

Sam nodded. "Fair enough, we'll be moving out in a minute, then."

"Okay," floated back down to him.

Sam walked back to the front of the bus where Jimmy was watching something intently. Sam moved up behind the young man to see what was so interesting, when Jimmy turned to him.

"Look over there, Sam, by that bunch of trees," Jimmy said, pointing, his voice low.

Sam followed Jimmy's finger, and in a moment the shape of what looked like a wolf appeared moving from tree to tree. Sam squinted harder and could make out what appeared to be a human arm in the wolf's mouth.

"Son-of-a-bitch, now that's something you don't see every day," Sam said, the two men watching the animal move about.

The wolf's head turned and looked directly at them, as if it had heard them. Then it bolted from the tree line to be lost amongst the tall grass.

Henry called to them. "Hey, what's so interesting?" He asked.

Sam and Jimmy turned and smiled, sharing something only they had seen.

"Nothin', Henry, just admiring the landscape," Jimmy said while climbing back into the driver's seat as the others climbed aboard behind him.

When everyone was back onboard, Jimmy put the bus in drive, and with a subtle jerk, the bus headed off down the road.

Costington may have only been a few more miles away, but they still had a long way to go.

## CHAPTER THIRTY-TWO

THE FORTIFIED BUS slowed down upon reaching the outskirts of Costington, the front wheel stopping on a corpse left in the road from the last time the men had visited the abandoned town.

After securing the vehicle, Jimmy and the others climbed out of the bus and surveyed the town, the men on the roof keeping watch from their vantage point.

Henry watched the VFW flag fluttering in the wind, looking no worse for wear since the last time he'd seen it.

He scanned the entrance into the town and was pleased to see it was clearly empty. Nothing but the remains of the prisoner Sam had sent to his death lay in the street and that was just some ripped, bloody clothes and a few scattered bones.

"All right then, let's do this," Henry said, walking to the back of the bus.

"I need one stick of dynamite from the box. Oh, yeah, and throw down that corpse, too," he finished.

A moment later with someone up top yelling: "Heads up!" The corpse fell to the asphalt, wrapped in a sheet.

Henry had seen to it that one of the guards had retrieved a ghoul that was still in good shape as it was integral to his plan to take the town back.

One of the guards on top of the bus dropped a rope ladder down the back and then carried the sticks of dynamite as carefully as a newborn baby. By the time the man had set the dynamite down on the road, he was drenched in sweat.

The second he was done, he quickly backed away, his task finished.

Henry then proceeded to drag the corpse to the town limits, with Sam following with the dynamite. His exact spot was the blood-stained street, right where the executed man had died. The scarlet splatter was like a giant X to Henry.

Jimmy followed them both with a one gallon can of gas and some fishing line.

"I sure hope this works, Henry," Sam whispered as they passed the VFW.

Henry ignored him, the weight of the corpse keeping him occupied. In hindsight, he was foolish for not having one of the other men help him.

While the three men walked under the flapping banner above their heads, their eyes were constantly scanning the alleys and doorways for signs of motion.

If the walkers came out of hiding to early, the men would be overrun and never make it out alive.

But luck was on their side.

"This is good, stop here," Henry whispered, letting the corpse fall to the street, almost exactly on the spot the murdered man had stood. Taking the fishing line from Jimmy, Henry quickly tied the line around the corpse's left arm near the wrist. Then he carefully placed the sticks of dynamite next to the body.

Henry then gingerly poured the gas over the corpse, being careful to stay away from the stick of dynamite.

That finished, he shooed everyone away and quickly followed them back to the school bus, unrolling the fishing line behind him.

They all breathed a sigh of relief after escaping the town unscathed, and then Henry waved Paul over to him. Paul was the best shot in Sam's security force so was the obvious choice in the next phase of Henry's plan.

Henry pointed to the corpse lying in the street more than two-hundred feet away and the sticks of dynamite not more than three inches in front of the body.

"Can you hit those sticks from here?" Henry inquired.

Paul sighted the corpse in his rifle's gun sights and then looked back to Henry.

Paul smiled, looking at the men surrounding him. "Yeah, I can hit it. It'll be tough though, it's pretty damn small."

"Yeah, but you can do it, right?" Sam asked.

"Yeah, I can hit it, just give me the word," Paul said, leaning against the front of the bus.

"Good," Henry said. Turning to Sam, he asked him: "We need fireworks now. Have your man do like before and throw them into the road. But make damn sure he doesn't throw them near the corpse."

Sam nodded and went off to gather the fireworks and a man to set them. Meanwhile, Henry ran the fishing line up and over the school bus sign at the top of the bus, giving himself a crude pulley, the other end still connected to the corpse.

By the time he was finished, Sam had returned with a volunteer in tow and fireworks in hand.

"Okay then, just go into town and throw the fireworks into the street, then get the hell out of there. If it works like before, then the streets are going to be full of walkers in less than a minute," Henry instructed the hapless guard.

The guard nodded and jogged away, going back to the town, his countenance one of trepidation. While the guard moved closer to where the corpse lay in the road, Henry gathered everyone together.

"All right, everyone else back on the bus. We need to do this quick. Surprise is our only advantage, as we're totally outnumbered," Henry said, climbing aboard the bus.

A few men stood still for a moment, not moving at Henry's instructions when Sam roared at them. "What the fuck's the matter with you? The man said get on the damn bus!"

The men jumped to it, Sam's control over them still firm.

While this was happening, Jimmy had climbed back in the driver's seat. Looking in the rearview mirror above his head, his eyes met Henry's as the older man climbed aboard the bus.

"You know, if this doesn't work we're all totally fucked, don't you," he said with a sneer.

"Look, I never said I was Patton. I've done the best I could. I didn't see you coming up with any brilliant ideas," Henry replied.

Jimmy held up his hands in surrender. "All right, that's true, I'm just sayin'..." Jimmy wasn't able to finish his sentence. A few hundred feet in front of the bus the guard had lit the fireworks. While running back to the bus the mini-explosives went off in the deserted street behind him. The popping went on for almost thirty seconds, the quiet then descending once more.

Then Jimmy saw movement out of one of the alleyways and soon shambling bodies appeared, the ghouls eager to investigate the noise that had disrupted their undead rest.

Henry reached out of the bus and pulled on the fishing line, the corpse's hand jerking up and down with the movement. From inside the bus, it looked like a living person was lying in the road, possibly wounded.

The walkers continued emerging from hiding, the small Main Street soon filling with rotting bodies.

Flies were everywhere, living and breeding in the rotten flesh of the living dead, and crows flitted from head to head looking for juicy eyes still left in sockets. The zombies would wave their hands in front of their faces, shooing the birds away.

From a distance, it was a familiar gesture for Henry to see and it gave him a shiver to watch.

These things were once human. Once they had hopes and dreams just like him. Now they were nothing more than killing machines. Rotting meat that didn't have the good sense to lie down and die.

Well, in a moment Henry would help them with that.

Henry continued pulling on the fishing line. Outside, Sam was on the roof with his men. He'd said he wanted a bird's eye view of what was going to happen next.

Paul was on the roof, as well. He'd set up on a sandbag on the front of the bus' roof. If Jimmy leaned forward in the driver's seat, he could just make out the barrel of Paul's rifle.

Jimmy watched the walkers covering the corpse with their bodies, the fishing line soon getting tangled in all the legs shambling around the area.

Henry let go of the line as its purpose was finished.

The puppet like hand had been enough movement for the ghouls to investigate, probably thinking in however they still processed thought, that there was another free meal waiting for them.

Well, not this time.

Henry leaned out of the bus's door and called up to Paul.

"Shoot the sticks, Paul. Before the bastards figure out that's just a corpse!"

Paul knocked twice on the roof of the bus, signaling he'd heard him. Then he lined up his target and fired.

The first bullet went an inch wide, the shuffling legs a minor distraction.

With the echo of the gunshot some of the dead faces looked up and out of the town. There were now over a hundred ghouls in the street with more arriving with each passing second.

Noticing the school bus, some turned to investigate.

"Oh shit, they see us," Jimmy whispered, his voice echoing in the bus.

"Just wait for it, Jimmy. Be patient," Henry said.

Another gunshot echoed off the roof as Paul took another shot.

He missed again, this time the bullet ricocheting off the asphalt, sending a few tiny sparks into the gas-soaked corpse.

The body erupted into flame, the walkers starting to back away, their fear of fire apparent.

Henry watched the scene play out, hoping Paul would hit the target this time.

If he didn't then all was lost.

Another gunshot echoed down to them as Paul fired his third shot.

This time his aim was true, the bullet hitting the unstable sticks of dynamite.

The explosion ripped apart the area surrounding the prone corpse, disintegrating any walker unfortunate enough to be at ground zero of the blast.

Others weren't as fortunate.

The bodies were ripped apart as they flew through the air to land in the street with sickening smacks, the lumps of burning and smoking flesh twitching in the morning sun before finally going still.

As if in answer to the explosion, the clouds overhead cracked thunder, sheets of lightning soon following. Henry gazed up at the darkening sky and frowned.

They were in for a rainstorm and soon. They needed to clean up the mess in town before the rain began or they would have to try this all over again on another day.

And Henry didn't want that.

Henry leaned over to Jimmy. "Okay, Jimmy let's go kill us some deaders."

Jimmy smiled back and put the bus in drive. "Hell, yeah, this is what I've been waiting for!"

Henry called up to the roof of the bus through the still open door, the bus slowly picking up speed. "All right, we're going in! Don't get gun happy! Pick your shots! There's sure as hell plenty to hit!"

"We're fine, Henry, you just worry about yourself!" Sam called back down from above.

Henry just grunted and then went and sat down, picking up his shotgun and placing it on his lap.

A few seconds later, the bus plowed into Main St., Costington.

Bodies flew into the air, the front of the bus becoming a massive battering ram.

Within moments the bus was surrounded by living corpses. Henry fired his shotgun through a gap in the sheet metal while Jimmy fired from his small side window with his .38, using his left hand. His right was occupied steering the bus up Main St.

From above his head, Henry could hear the gunshots from the men on the roof.

The bus was surrounded now, and for every ghoul Henry shot, two more would take its place. Soon the bus began rocking, the shear number of animated corpses pushing the large bus on its shocks.

Suddenly, an explosion of fire went off in front of the bus, blasting walkers to Hell with an express ticket. Then Henry saw another bright light behind the bus, followed by a muffled roar. He quickly deduced someone had thrown a Molotov at the horde of walking dead.

Henry kept firing until he was dry, then dropped the shotgun to the seat and pulled his .38.

Indiscriminately firing through the sheet metal, he was soon empty and paused to reload, the weapon hot in his hand. Spent shell casings were everywhere and he tried not to slip on one.

Jimmy was driving the bus in a circle pattern, crushing dozens of ghouls in its path, the bus bouncing on the sidewalk for clearance, due to the width of the street. The bus was rocking and jumping as the wheels ran over bodies and Henry started to worry about the dynamite above his head.

Then the bus slammed to a halt.

Henry ran up front to see why and realized Jimmy was stopped in front of the small crater the dynamite had blasted into the middle of Main St.

The walkers immediately began crawling onto the hood of the bus and Jimmy looked to Henry for an idea.

"We're trapped! If I go in there, we'll get stuck!" Jimmy screamed over the chaos around them,

"Then back the hell up!" Henry yelled back. "It doesn't matter which way you go, just keep moving!"

Jimmy did as he was told, and with a grinding of gears, slammed the bus in reverse. The bus bucked, slowed by the undead bodies behind it, but after a brief hesitation rolled over the corpses.

Unfortunately, with the continuous jerking of the vehicle back and forth, a guard on the roof lost his balance.

The man hadn't strapped himself in but as the bus bucked under him, he fell over the safety railing and into the mass off writhing bodies.

Sam watched helpless as the man tumbled from view, his mouth open in a silent yell.

Sam ran over to the spot the man had fallen from and only caught a glimpse of the man's face, frozen in terror, as the ghouls proceeded to rip him apart.

The guard's shrieks of pain were swallowed by the noise of the walkers feeding, and the bus's engine roaring, while Jimmy fought to keep them moving.

When the guard was gone from view, Sam gritted his teeth.

That was it; he needed to finish this now.

Slowly making his way across the roof of the bus, almost losing his balance in the process and being thrown to the hungry dead as they waited below, he reached the metal box with the dynamite inside.

Carefully opening the box, he pulled out three more sticks.

Then, before he could change his mind, he threw one after another out into the swirling mass of bodies. The explosions from the unstable dynamite rocked the bus, the vehicle leaning hard on its shocks before righting itself.

The windows inside the bus shattered, spraying the men inside with safety glass before they could cover their faces.

After a few moments, the smoke started to clear, a gentle wind blowing up Main Street.

Henry looked out through the sheet metal to see almost all the walkers lying in the street with some if not all of their body parts blown away.

After another moment to gather themselves, the men on the roof continued firing, followed by another Molotov that landed in a particularly large group of walking dead.

The wine bottle smashed at their feet, the flames flowing up their filthy and stained clothing. The smell of burning meat suffused the area, the flaming bodies shambling around the bus.

Paul shot a few in the head, putting them out of their misery, then he stopped firing. Let them burn, he thought.

For the next five minutes only sporadic gunfire came from the roof of the bus, all the men taking a breather and only shooting when necessary.

Sam stood on the roof and surveyed the carnage he and his men had wrought.

The small street looked like nothing more than a battlefield after mortars had blown the ground to Hell and back. Everywhere the man looked, there were writhing, blackened bodies.

Blood and gore were everywhere, the sides of the school bus painted red.

Spotting a ghoul trying to hobble over its brethren and escape into the nearby alleys, so he raised his Colt, and after a second to aim, blasted the pale head with a special delivery of death. The zombie fell to the pile of bodies at its feet, half of its head missing.

Sam barely noticed.

Moving around the roof, he had his men check their ammo and double check they were secured with cables. He didn't want any more men falling off the roof.

Slapping Paul on the shoulder, the dark man looked out over Main St., Costington. With the exception of taking out some stragglers, the town's walkers had basically been destroyed.

Son-of-a-bitch, they'd done it.

Above Sam's head, the thunder continued to roar, threatening him with rain, but harmless for the moment.

Checking to make sure his men had their rain-gear handy, he reloaded his weapon and continued to shoot the closest ghouls that were a threat. From below him in the bus, he heard Henry and Jimmy's weapons firing, as well.

For the next half an hour the men in the yellow and red school bus continued to shoot stray corpses. Then Jimmy drove over the mounds of dead flesh, the weight of the bus pushing through the corpses like mud until they were free from the heart of the devastation.

With their objective accomplished, the bus rolled deeper into Costington.

They needed supplies and ammunition, most of the ammo having been exhausted taking the town back from the dead.

A quarter of a mile later, the bus slowed to a stop in front of a gun store. The sign out front read: Johnny's Army Surplus, Vintage WW2 and other War Paraphernalia.

The sign on the door announced: "COME IN, WE'RE OPEN."

Henry stepped out of the school bus, weapon in hand for any sign of trouble.

Reading the sign, he grinned. "Don't mind if I do," he mumbled.

Sam was at his back now after climbing down from the roof.

"Well, don't just stand there, go," he said. "I want to get what we need and get back to Pittsfield as soon as possible. I'm worried about my town." The Boss of the town was clearly concerned for his residents and Henry's respect for the man grew another notch. They may have started out as slight adversaries, but Sam and Henry relationship had grown into a friendship forged in the fires of battle and blood.

Henry nodded to him, and with Sam following, pushed open the glass door to the gun store. Jimmy and most of the men stayed outside to pick of any stray walkers that hadn't been destroyed in the initial blast.

Jimmy was leaning against the hood of the bus, careful to find a spot free of blood and gore when he heard multiple gunshots come from inside the gun store.

"Shit, there must be deaders in there!" He yelled.

Turning, he ran through the door, praying he wouldn't be too late to help Henry and Sam.

# CHAPTER THIRTY-THREE

JIMMY PULLED THE bulletproof glass door open and darted inside the store with his .38 leading the charge, ready for whatever ghoul was waiting for him.

Instead he stopped in his tracks.

In front of him, standing in the middle of the store were Sam and Henry both with embarrassed looks on their faces.

In the gloom of the store, Jimmy just could make out what was once a mannequin.

The right shoulder and head of the figure was now gone, nothing more than shredded plastic.

Sam still had his Colt raised in his hand, a big smile on his lips.

Henry turned to see Jimmy and raised his hands, motioning Jimmy to relax.

"Everything's fine, Jimmy. Sam shot a rogue mannequin, that's all," Henry said with a grin. "He really did a number on it, too."

"Yeah, sorry, I guess I'm still a little jumpy. Can you blame me? I keep waiting for something to jump out of a corner and bite me in the ass," Sam said.

"Shit, you guys scared the hell out of me," Jimmy said, taking a look around the gun store.

The right half of the store was nothing but old military uniforms, everything from dress uniforms to coveralls.

The left half was nothing but guns and knives.

"Wow, will you look at this place. It's a goddamn goldmine," Jimmy said, his mouth slack as he took it all in.

Sam nodded, "I know, with this much firepower we should be able to keep my town safe for quite a while."

Then Sam hopped over the glass cases and began piling weapons onto the top of the glass counter. Reaching under the shelves, he pulled out box after box of ammunition. There was ammo to fit every weapon imaginable. Shotgun shells, bullets for .45's, .38's and Sam let out a yell like a school girl when he found more ammo for his Colt.

"All right! This place is great!" He exclaimed.

While Sam busied himself with the ammunition, Henry wandered around the store some more.

In the back, behind a faded curtain, was another door with a heavy padlock on it. With his curiosity peaked, he brought up his .38 and placed it near the lock.

"Fire in the hole, guys, it's okay," Henry called out before, blasting the lock to pieces. He pushed the door open, and with his weapon leading the way, slowly entered the hidden backroom.

His jaw dropped, his eyes scanning the walls.

In the wan light coming through the one, small, shaded window, Henry saw all the weapons a civilian was never supposed to own. Scattered on a small workbench were hand grenades and mounted to the wall were M-16's, similar to the one Sam was using. To the side were stacks of boxes. Henry opened one and was pleased to see it contained ammunition for the illegal weapons.

Henry was about to go back to the others when his eye caught something else hanging on the wall by its strap.

Looking closer, he was shocked to see a LAW rocket. The small personnel bazooka was just the thing for the mercenary on the go.

Henry took one last look at all the weaponry and returned to the others.

By now Sam had quite a lot on the counter and Henry walked up to the big man and looked over the pile of ordnance at his protruding head.

"Hey, Sam, if you think there's good stuff out here, then wait until you see what I just found," Henry said with a big smile across his face.

Suddenly, the distinctive sound of gunfire floated into the store from outside. As one unit, the men moved to the door and piled outside, weapons ready.

Paul was there in a relaxed attitude, which immediately calmed the others.

"It's okay, Boss, just a couple of walkers. We took care of them," Paul said, nonchalantly.

"Okay, good job. If it's under control out here then leave two men plus yourself and send the rest into the store. Load up as much ammo and weapons as we can carry in the back of the bus," Sam instructed to his second-in-command.

"We going soon?" Paul asked, the thunder overhead echoing from the roofs of the buildings. The cracking of the thunder was closer now. Soon the storm would be on them and Sam wanted to make sure they were well away from the town and under a roof before that happened.

The sky continued darkening as the storm clouds blocked out the sun, casting the alleyways and doorways into shadows.

"Yeah, we're going soon. I want to be out of here in no less than two hours.

We still have to hit the grocery stores for food as well as check for more fuel.

Plus, there's probably still a lot more walkers around so tell your men to stay sharp. I plan on coming back here again, but I still want all we can carry today. You understand me?" Sam asked Paul.

"Yes, sir," Paul nodded. "I'll get right on it." Then the man started organizing his guards and the men went into the store to gather the ammo, weapons and miscellaneous supplies.

Another gunshot rang out from the roof of the bus and everyone turned to see a ghoul fall to the street not more than twenty feet away. This part of the street was wide open with only a few cars scattered in parking spots along the curb.

That was good; it made it harder for the undead to sneak up on the men.

For the next twenty minutes, the men in the gun store walked back and forth to the school bus with armfuls of ammo and weapons. When Sam was satisfied with the haul they'd acquired, everyone was ordered back onto the bus.

Jimmy then drove slowly down the street, looking for a grocery store.

About ten stores down was a small Mom and Pop convenience store.

After Sam's men had checked it out and cleared the place of danger, Sam had the place stripped of anything edible. The store was the same as the day it closed forever, thanks to the ghouls of the town not being interested in processed foods.

Forty minutes later the place was stripped bare and the school bus was driving off down the road again.

Thunder crackled overhead, sounding like it was right on top of them. Sam had Jimmy pull over and all the guards piled inside the vehicle.

He'd lost enough men in the past few days and he wasn't taking chances with the rain.

Sam stood behind Jimmy in the aisle of the crowded bus, his tall stature causing his head to brush the roof.

"All right, Jimmy, what do you say we head back to Pittsfield? I think we've got all we can carry on this run," Sam said, slapping Jimmy on the back.

"Okay, sounds good to me," Jimmy said, bringing the bus around in a 180 degree turn and heading back the way they'd come.

The going was a little rough when they passed through the beginning of town again. Jimmy slowed down, driving over the bodies of the dead. He came close to tipping the whole bus when it got a little too close to the crater first blown in the asphalt, but after a tense moment the tires were clear and they were out of the town limits and driving back down the lonely highway.

Overhead, the clouds finally opened up, releasing their payload of rain as if the clouds themselves had been waiting for them to leave the desolate town.

The streets ran red with the blood of slaughtered ghouls, washing away the stink of death.

The school bus cleared an incline on the highway and was soon lost from sight.

While the rain washed the streets clear there was movement under some of the piles and pieces of bodies.

Ever so slowly, the walkers that survived the slaughter pulled themselves to their feet or dragged themselves across the wet ground, splashing in the tainted rain that had created them.

As the hours past, the waterlogged ghouls drifted away into the buildings where they would wait for another day to feed.

If it was one thing the dead had, it was patience

# CHAPTER THIRTY-FOUR

ANDY JOHNSON STOOD on the barricade of the town of Pittsfield and watched as the school bus disappeared over the dip in the highway.

It had been close there for a moment, the bus fighting its way through the walkers, but now it was gone.

Leaving the rest of them to fend for themselves.

Ever since Sam had taken over, Andy had been unhappy. He believed he could do a much better job of running the town, but after one of his friends had been threatened to be thrown out of town if he didn't agree with Sam, Andy had quickly learned to keep his opinions to himself...until now.

Now the head of the town, along with his second-in-command were gone, no one even knowing if they'd ever return.

More and more walkers were showing up outside the barricade and it was Andy's opinion it was just a matter of time before the town was overrun with the undead abominations.

That's why he'd been slowly sowing dissent in the ranks of the guards and the town's population and now was the time to act, while Sam and the others were away and couldn't stop him.

Walking to the edge of the barricade, he slipped down the ladder and went to the nearest guard who agreed with his way of thinking.

"Hey, Curt, now's the time to act. Tell everyone to meet me at the fire station in half an hour," Andy told the guard quietly.

"What for?" Curt inquired.

"Because now's the time to leave this sinking ship before we're all dead, now get goin'," Andy snapped at the man.

Curt did as he was asked and ran off into town. He was a good runner and would be at the first building at the town limits in a little less than three minutes.

Sneaking off from his post, Andy was already thinking of the speech he was going to use at the meeting.

How they were doomed if they stayed inside the walls of the town. That the barricade was as much a prison for the town's people as it was a defense against the walkers.

He was going to make the people see reason and join him on an exodus out of town, away from the affected areas, to a place where they could raise their children in peace, without the threat of the walkers always dangling over their heads like a sharpened blade.

If they piled into vans and trucks, they could fight their way out of the gate and escape to a better place.

All they had to do is follow him…to the Promised Land.

Arriving at the fire station, he was pleased to see it was packed. There had to be at least thirty people in the station, squeezed together next to the antique fire truck.

Now that might not have been the whole town, but it was more than enough to make a new start somewhere else…with him as their leader.

Standing on the small podium Curt had set up earlier for him, he started into his speech.

As he listened to himself so eloquently explaining their dilemma, he saw in their faces how they believed him. How they wanted to believe him. They were all so scared they just wanted someone, anyone, to tell them what to do.

And he was that one.

By the time his speech was finished, he saw heads nodding in agreement, his words imparting urgency to their predicament. With his speech concluded, he felt the enthusiasm in the room like it was a palpable presence.

He told his new flock to go home and gather what they needed to take with them on their exodus away from this doomed place.

When they were ready in an hour's time, they would commandeer the vehicles they would need and then they would escape from the walls of confinement and be free to live as God intended.

In the wide open spaces that he Himself would provide in all His glory.

The men and women shuffled out of the fire station talking amongst themselves, their fear of what they could not control helping Andy to sway them to his cause.

When the last man was gone, Andy called Curt over to him and told him to retrieve as many firearms as he could find and to return to the fire house in an hour. He told him to nor be late because the exodus was going to leave, with or without Curt.

Curt nodded and took off at a run to do his bidding.

Andy smiled to himself, enjoying the feeling of power over others.

His patience was now being rewarded. Soon he'd be gone from this prison and they'd all be free.

All they had to do was follow him.


An hour later his flock, as he called them in his mind, had returned.

Moving quickly to the motor pool, it was easy to accommodate the group with enough vehicles for their exodus.

The motor pool was unmanned, every available man and woman now on watch at the wall, desperately trying to keep the walkers at bay until help arrived in the form of Sam and the others.

If they ever returned.

Loading up into a few vans and pickup trucks, the small convoy soon pulled out of the motor pool and headed off to the town's front gate.

He'd wanted to sneak out through the back gate, situated at the far end of town but had found out only hours ago that the walkers had started congregating there, too.

Plus, the amount of guards and men were heavier there and he certainly didn't want to get into a firefight with the heavily armed security guards.

No, he wanted to get away as quickly and cleanly as possible.

He figured if the school bus could do it, then so could he.

Ten minutes later, the first van in line stopped at the portal that only hours ago had allowed Sam and his men to exit through.

His group quickly swarmed up the wall, and before the men on watch could even ask what was going on, they were knocked unconscious, their bodies now lying quietly on the wooden planks surrounding the interior of the barricade.

Two guards were accidentally knocked off the wall to fall into the swarm of undead below. Their screams floated up to Andy as they were ripped to pieces, their wails for help lost amongst the angry dead. Andy ignored their pleas.

The guard on the front gate had been quicker than the others and it was Curt who had slit his throat from ear to ear before the man could call for help.

Andy walked over to Curt, looking down at the hapless guard while his life's blood spread across the asphalt, then he looked into Curt's eyes.

Curt just smiled wanly, waiting for him to say something. Not knowing if Andy was pleased or disappointed.

Then Andy smiled, his white teeth showing through. Slapping Curt on the back, he told him he'd done well. He'd done what had to be done for the welfare of the group.

Then he sent one of the men up to the wall to throw some Molotovs down in front of the gate.

If it had worked for Sam then it would work for him and his flock.


With the Molotovs burning brightly at the front of the gate, Andy had the portal opened and the trucks prepared to leave the town forever.

While the gate slowly rose, Andy could see all the legs milling about, their bodies slowly becoming more visible as the gate continued upward.

"Wait! The fire isn't stopping enough of them!" He screamed; the gate now open to waist height.

But it was too late.

The gate continued upward, the man who'd opened it already back inside his vehicle as he prepared to leave. By the time someone could get to the gate, get back in the car it was attached to and lower it again, the zombies would be inside.

Andy squeezed his jaw tight. Fine, if that's how it is, then so be it.

Standing on the back of the first pickup in line, he raised his rifle to the sky and yelled something encouraging.

The people in the vehicles behind him called back, believing they were doing the right thing.

Then the trucks surged forward out of the gate.

The first truck was almost halfway through the mass of walkers when the sheer weight of bodies surrounding it stopped the truck cold.

The second vehicle in line was a nine passenger van. The van tried to go around the bogged down pickup truck in front of it, but the second the driver hit the brakes to avoid the truck, the van quickly became covered in bodies, with the other vehicles in the convoy behind the van stopping cold, too.

The walking dead beat on the windows and Andy climbed onto the roof of the pickup to try and stay out of those clutching, grasping hands.

From the shaking roof, he was able to see the other vehicles of his flock behind him.

It wasn't pretty.

Every vehicle had been swarmed with the dead. Some of the walkers were on fire after walking through the flames from the Molotovs and they moved about blindly like human Roman candles.

Men and women in the vehicles tried to shoot the ghouls and keep themselves safe, but it was like trying to fight a wave of water with a dishtowel.

For every walker killed, three more took its place.

He watched in horror at the visceral tableaux. All his dreams were being ripped away as his people were pulled from their vehicles, where the undead heathens then proceeded to rip them to pieces.

He looked down at his feet to see a dead face crawling towards him by way of the pickup truck's bed. He shot the fetid thing in the chest, the body falling backward into the mass of walking corpses beyond.

He balanced on the jittery on the roof of the pickup, looking below him. The bodies of the undead were like an undulating wave, swelling forward and backward like the tides in the ocean.

He kicked a dead woman in the head when she reached for him, hearing the cries of his people as they were slowly tortured to death by the hungry dead.

Most of the vehicles were empty now, the people inside nothing more than hunks of meat the surrounding walkers fought over.

Only Curt was still alive, standing on the roof of another pickup truck; two behind himself.

Andy watched the undead begin to swarm up the sides of the truck, rotting hands reaching for Curt's legs. He watched while Curt kicked and screamed, shooting his revolver at the rotting corpses to little or no effect.

Then Curt's legs were pulled out from under him and his body slammed hard against the roof of the truck.

With almost a gentle care, the ghouls pulled Curt to them, where they then began to bite into his flesh, ripping his clothes off to get at the warm meat underneath.

Curt looked back at Andy for a fleeting second, and in that moment the two men's eyes met. Then Curt was lost from sight, overwhelmed by bodies, his screaming form torn apart bit by bit.

Andy jumped into the air when another hand reached for him. Kicking it away, he quickly realized he was heading in the same direction as Curt.

Shaking his head to the mass of moving corpses, he decided he wasn't going out that way.

Shooting a ghoul in the head, he tried to kick the others away, but after a moment he felt his legs pulled out from under him and a second later he was lying on the roof of the truck, the sun glaring down into his eyes through the sparse, dark clouds overhead.

The walkers were pulling him off the truck and he smiled to himself, the horror of his coming death not yet fully realized.

Oh, well, he'd tried and failed. And now was paying the ultimate price for his failure.

Before the ghouls could do any more to him than just tear his clothes off, he quickly placed the rifle under his chin, and although awkward, reached down and squeezed the trigger, expecting the darkness of death to take him.

But instead of the sweet bliss of death, the rifle clicked on an empty chamber.

His eyes went wide with disbelief!

He hadn't kept count of his shots! All he had to do was leave one in the chamber for himself!

The teeth and hands of the ravenous undead pulled him off the roof and his breath left him when he was slammed to the ground.

Then the sun was blocked from his view as the heads of the living corpses leaned over him, and with his shrieks filling his ears, he slowly died in agony.

First his organs were pulled from his warm chest cavity and then his throat was blessedly ripped out, his blood squirting into the faces of the surrounding ghouls until his tank ran dry.

His last fleeting thought was that he should have stayed in the town. Perhaps it hadn't been as bad in there after all.


The front gate was still open, the last vehicle in the small convoy never having a chance to leave.

Other guards showed up after seeing the flames from the Molotovs and were greeted by the undead as they swarmed through the gate and into the town.

One guard tried to lower the gate, but the portal was soon stopped when it struck the roof of the abandoned vehicle. The guard was then attacked and promptly killed and eaten, the rest of the undead moving forward.

The other guards soon realized it was hopeless and abandoned their posts, running back to town to gather their families and somehow escape the unstoppable horde of death.

The empty road leading into town was now covered with the walking dead as they slowly poured through the open portal.

Within a matter of minutes the first walkers would be at the town limits, where the residents went about their business of the day, unaware of the doom to come.

# CHAPTER THIRTY-FIVE

AT ABOUT THE same time Andy was being ripped to pieces by the front gate, across town Mary and Cindy were going for a walk.

The echoes of gunshots coming from the barricade floated across the town, and were now becoming a common occurrence to the two women, so they barely noticed it as they walked along the sidewalk.

People moved around them, going about their business when Mary looked up to see a man in a guard's uniform run by them. Mary only caught a glimpse of his face, but it was long enough for her to see the man was frightened about something.

Then the guard was gone as he turned a corner at the end of the street.

"What was that about?" Cindy asked, her head following the man down the street before he was gone from view.

"I don't know. I hope everything's all right," Mary said with a touch of worry.

"Do you think the boys are okay?" Cindy inquired.

Mary smiled reassuringly. "I'm sure they're fine. If there's one thing I've learned after being with Henry and Jimmy for all these months is that they know how to take care of themselves."

Cindy smiled back. "I like Jimmy, he's a good man." She hesitated for a moment, mulling something over in her head and then spoke up. "Can I ask you something personal?"

"Sure, go ahead," Mary replied.

"How come you and Jimmy never got together and you know..." Cindy said, her words trailing off.

Mary understood what she meant.

"Well, there was a time when we almost did, but then other things happened that changed the way I feel about him. Now he's more like my little brother than anything else," Mary said, a far away look in her eyes as she thought of things in the past.

"Oh, okay, that's good, I guess. I mean, I don't want to step on any toes here," Cindy stuttered out, unsure of what to say.

"It's fine, Cindy, if you want him, he's all yours."

Cindy smiled and the two women continued down the street, enjoying the day.

The clouds overhead were rumbling and they knew they would soon have to return to Sam's house and seek shelter.

They had cut down a small side street which brought them to the end of town.

If they kept walking further, they would be at the barricade's front gate in a little less than ten minutes.

The two women had already decided to turn back when Mary stopped in her tracks.

Cindy's shoulder bumped into Mary, not expecting the other women to stop so suddenly. She was about to ask what was up when she looked across the lonely road leading out of town.

There was smoke coming from the barricade, and while they were a little too far away to see what was happening, they could definitely see the giant crowd of walkers shambling down the middle of the road, the yellow line acting like a trail for the walking dead to follow.

"Oh my God," Mary whispered, taking it all in. "We've got to get away from here now," she stated, backing up down the street.

Cindy followed her, not quite comprehending what was in front of her eyes.

"But how did this happen? We're supposed to be safe in here," she stammered, following Mary.

Mary was now running down the street, yelling at people to get away, to get to their homes and barricade themselves in.

"Where should we go?" Cindy asked, running alongside Mary.

"Back to the house, there's weapons there and I know Henry would look for us there when they get back. We just have to survive until they do."

Cindy nodded, Mary not even noticing. The two women ran for all they were worth until they made it back to Sam's house.

Martha greeted them at the door with a puzzled look at the two out of breath young women, but after Mary filled her in on what had transpired, the old woman had run off to retrieve as many weapons as she could find.

Meanwhile, Mary had Cindy began boarding up the windows and doors with whatever was at hand.

They had no idea when the men would return from Costington. But Mary did know if they weren't rescued soon, then this house would become their tomb.


Outside in the streets, the screams of the townspeople floated to the Victorian house as the undead horde made their way through the streets of the town.

Guards tried to stop the walking corpses, but soon realized there were just too many to stop with conventional weapons.

If Sam didn't return soon with help, then the town would surely be lost.

The ghouls had already begun breaking into houses and killing the residents inside, pulling them out kicking and screaming. Some would run into the streets to escape, only to be overwhelmed by the living dead when they swarmed over their victims.

An old woman ran screaming from her house and right into five walkers. Her screams froze in her throat as the rotting corpses lunged for her, pulling her to the ground in an instant. Teeth and nails went to work, ripping the wrinkled skin apart so they could get at the soft organs within. Spitting blood, the old woman's eyes nearly jumped out of her sockets in pain before she passed out.

Within moments her body was ripped from head to feet, the shambling ghouls moving away to feed with whatever piece of gore they had managed to retrieve from the now lifeless corpse.

The townspeople were slowly being slaughtered one house at a time as the unending numbers of the dead swarmed into the town.

Mary looked out through a boarded window while the walkers flowed across the street like a wave, pulling people to the street where they began to feed amid the screams of their victims

In a few moments the undead horde would be banging on her front door and windows.

With her .38 in her hand, she set her jaw.

She was ready for whatever came next.

And though it seemed more and more likely help was not coming, she still hoped the men would return soon and save her.

She couldn't think they wouldn't come for her and Cindy, because if she did, then she might as well eat a bullet now and save the walkers the work of chasing her down.

# CHAPTER THIRTY-SIX

THE SCHOOL BUS continued down the highway no more than fifteen minutes away from the barricade of Pittsfield.

Inside the bus, Sam continued to try and raise someone on the two-way radio, but all he received in reply to his calls was empty static.

"Damn it, I knew something would happen if we left," he said, throwing the radio to the seat next to him.

"What do you think it could be?" Henry asked from the front of the bus.

The rain had stopped for now, but Sam had decided to keep everyone inside the vehicle. They'd spent enough time away from Pittsfield and he wanted to return as soon as possible.

"Could be nothin' or it could be somethin', either way we'll know in a few minutes," Jimmy said, pressing the gas pedal down to the floor a little more.

The engine revved louder, the bus picking up speed. Jimmy knew the patch of highway they were now on and wasn't worried about wrecks or abandoned vehicles in his path.

The road ahead was clear.

Coming over a slight rise in the highway, Jimmy slowed the bus, surveying the barricade in the distance, not more than a few hundred feet away.

"Ah guys, I think you need to see this," Jimmy said, the worry in his voice apparent.

Sam and Henry moved up to stand next to Jimmy's seat, while the men in the back of the bus tried to steal a peek around them.

The growing murmuring as the guards discussed what was going on became louder until Sam turned to look at them, his face set in stone.

The voices grew quiet, then Sam turned back to look out the front windshield.

He wasn't pleased with what he saw. The front gate to his town was nothing like he'd left it.

There were six vehicles spread out from the gate with one stuck under the large metal portal.

When they had left that morning, there were hundreds of walkers outside the wall. Now, they were gone, with the exception of a few stragglers who appeared to be feasting on the remains of people.

The top of the barricade was empty, his guards evidently having abandoned their posts.

But why, what had happened here?

"What the hell happened here?" Henry asked, echoing Sam's thoughts.

Sam looked at the gate and the vehicle stuck underneath it.

"Well, whatever the fuck happened here, the first thing we need to do is get that pickup truck out of the opening so we can bring the bus in," Sam said.

"Fine, there doesn't seem to be a lot of deaders around, so why don't we have a few guards cover one of us so we can move that truck out of there?" Henry asked.

Sam grunted in agreement and had Paul pick the men he wanted to use when they were closer.

"Okay, Jimmy, move us closer," Henry told him, patting the younger man on the back. Jimmy nodded and placed the bus in drive, then slowly drove the rest of the way to the gate.

The feeding ghouls looked up at the sound of the approaching bus, but weren't that interested in it, just happy with the meat they had in front of them.

While the bus moved closer to the open gate, Henry did a quick count of the remaining walkers. He stopped at twenty, although there was probably a few more.

"You know if all the deaders went inside the town…" Henry thought out loud.

"Yeah, I know, what about Mary? Do you think she's all right… and Cindy?" Jimmy asked, driving around the first pickup sitting in the road.

"Yeah, Jimmy, I was thinking it, too. But she's smart. I'm sure she'll hole up somewhere waiting for us. You'll see, they'll both be fine," Henry said, not sounding very sure of his own words.

When the bus was right on top of the gate, Jimmy stopped it and placed the transmission in park. The group of guards filed out of the bus with Sam in the lead.

Without hesitation, Sam went to the vehicle trapped under the gate while two more guards went inside to raise the portal again. Sam frowned when he saw the keys still in it and the thick coating of blood over everything. The seat, dashboard and headliner were now stained a dark crimson, with droplets dripping from the roof. Turning the ignition, he saw it still had gas.

Slamming the vehicle into drive, he drove it onto the road next to the pickup in front of it. A ghoul shambled into view, a half an arm in its teeth as it chewed merrily.

Sam swerved into the feeding corpse, knocking the body to the asphalt. Then he drove over the flailing ghoul a few times, slamming the truck into drive and reverse as he crushed the rotting body into the street like it was a worn out squirrel not fast enough to cross a busy highway.

Stepping out of the truck, he then walked back to the gate.

Another ghoul lurched from around one of the vehicles and Sam pulled his Colt and shot it in the head in one smooth motion. The body crumpled to the earth as Sam kept moving, barely slowing his stride.

Two more vehicles had to be moved before the bus would be able to maneuver through the gate, so Sam quickly jumped in each one. They all had keys, and despite the blood covering every surface of the inside of the vehicles, appeared to be working fine.

A gunshot rang out and Sam heard a body fall to the ground next to him, as he sat in the driver's seat of an old van, the door still hanging open.

Looking up, he saw Paul lower his rifle.

Sam waved to him in thanks and then finished moving the last vehicle.

More gunshots rang out inside the gate as the guards finished off a few more stray walkers.

Henry stood by the entrance to the bus, firing his shotgun at the feeding ghouls. One at a time the zombies fell to the dirt with some part of their heads blown away.

Henry caught movement in his peripheral vision. Turning, he saw one lone walker lurching towards him. Its chin and upper chest was covered in a red viscous liquid that was obviously blood.

Henry slung his shotgun over his shoulder and reached for his Glock. He hadn't used it much on the past outing and it still had a full clip.

He waited for the shambling corpse to get closer, and when it was no more than two feet away, he shot it through the chest and stomach twice.

He knew it wouldn't stop it, but he just wanted to make the bastard suffer. Although he wondered if the dead bastards even felt pain.

The 9mm rounds blew the chest of the walking corpse apart, its intestines and organs dripping onto the dirt at its feet, the visceral scene enough for Henry to begin to taste bile in his mouth

Then Henry brought the Glock up even with the ghoul's head, and with a gentle squeeze of the trigger, put two more bullets into its head. The body fell back to the dirt with the force of the impact where it stayed motionless forever, the reanimated spark snuffed out for good

Then he entered the bus again, seeing Sam coming back, his task finished.

So far they had more than enough men to handle the undead threat.

The clouds crackled with thunder, forewarning the group of survivors that more rain was on the way. They had been caught in the storm and had then outrun it, but now it was closing in on their trail again.

Quickly, Sam and the others boarded the bus and Jimmy slowly drove through the gate.

Henry had an idea of what they were going to find inside the town, but he wasn't relishing it, and at the back of his mind he kept hoping Mary was okay.

The bus slowly rolled into the town with the crunch of bones under its already blood-covered tires, and no matter what was coming next, Henry knew he would find out soon enough.

# Chapter Thirty-seven

Mary stood as still as she could while the reanimated corpses walked around on the front porch of the house.

Behind her stood Cindy, holding an aluminum baseball bat she'd found in a hall closet.

Off the foyer, Martha sat in one of the dining room chairs. The woman was in total denial of the situation she now found herself in.

Mary watched over her shoulder while the old woman silently talked to herself, saying how everything was going to be fine. That it was all just a big mistake and in no time the master would be home and would fix everything.

Mary shook her head. She'd seen it countless times.

Some people just couldn't accept their new reality.

Usually those people were the first to die.

One of the front windows broke with a crashing of glass, the ghouls trying to gain entry.

Mary backed up a step, bracing herself for the inevitable.

She and Cindy had found a few pieces of wood to board some of the lower windows up, but they had fallen far short of the quota needed to firmly secure the house. Instead, they had thrown up the wood haphazardly in the hopes of deterring the undead long enough for help to come.

Unfortunately, with the walking corpses fighting their way into the house, Mary was slowly losing hope that rescue would arrive in time. Squeezing her .38 just a little tighter, she had already resolved to save three bullets for each of them, just in case.

A dining room window exploded inward when a ghoul attempted to climb inside, pieces of the window frame splintering and falling into the room.

Martha looked up at the window, seeing the hands reaching for her, and as Mary stared in mystified shock, the old woman raised herself from her chair and walked over to the window.

Mary could hear her mumbling aloud about how they could reason with the walkers, how if they understood they just wanted to live in peace, they would leave them alone.

Obviously, the woman had snapped, Mary thought.

Martha walked up to the window, and before she could utter another syllable, a pair of desiccated hands reached out and grabbed her head by the ears, one hand on each ear.

Martha screamed and tried to pull away, but the death grip was too tight.

With a speed that surprised Mary, the hands pulled Martha's head onto a large wooden splinter from the window frame. The old woman's left eye was sliced down the middle as her eye was impaled on the sharp wooden spike.

The hands continued to pull Martha's face forward until her head was against the window frame.

Mary watched in horror as the splinter punched its way out the back of the old woman's head. Then a rotting face stuck its head inside the room and bit a chunk of Martha's cheek clean off, although by this time Martha was beyond caring, her lifeless body sagging against the lower half of the broken window frame.

Cindy screamed in horror while the old woman was ripped apart by grasping hands.

Mary shot a ghoul passing by the window in the foyer, but she'd doubted it was a killing shot.

From the side of the house, breaking glass floated to her ears.

"Damn it," she said. "I can't believe the bastards are getting in here so quick."

Backing up, she headed for the stairs, only pausing long enough to grab Cindy's arm.

"Come on, if we stay here we're dead. There's too damn many of them. Our best chance is to barricade ourselves into one of the upstairs bedrooms and hope help arrives," Mary said, anxiously.

"But what if it doesn't get here?" Cindy asked.

Starting up the stairs, Mary threw her answer over her shoulder.

"Then we're both dead and all our problems will be solved."

"But what about Martha? We have to help her?" Cindy pleaded.

"I'm sorry, Cindy, she's past help. And so will we if we don't get upstairs now!"

To punctuate her statement, the last window on the first floor blew in, glass and wood covering the lush carpeting.

A heartbeat later, ghouls began piling through the window, pushing and shoving each other to be the first to reach the live meat in front of them.

Now firmly dragging Cindy up the stairs, the two women climbed using hands and feet in their haste to reach the top. Mary turned around at the top landing to glance back down the stairs and was shocked to see the foyer already filled with bodies.

The first ghoul that saw the two women turned and began moving up the stairs. Mary took enough time to shoot it in the head, the now lifeless corpse falling backward to land on its brethren. Then the stairs were gone from view as she dragged Cindy to the nearest bedroom off the hallway.

She was pleased to see the door was made out of a heavy wood, oak perhaps, when she slammed it closed and turned the lock.

Then with Cindy's help, they pushed the bed against the door and piled the other furniture in the room on top of the four-poster bed. That done, she moved to the window.

Brushing aside the curtain with the nose of her .38, her heart sank into her stomach. The street was wall to wall walkers, the undead roaming around looking for meat, their incessant hunger driving them on. Stepping away from the window, she collapsed to the floor and put her head in her hands.

"What's wrong, we're gonna get out of here, right?" Cindy asked, plopping down next to her on the floor.

Mary brushed a stray hair from her forehead and turned to look at Cindy.

The blonde girl's face looked so innocent while she waited for Mary to tell her everything was going to be okay.

A crash outside the door made the two women jump, and they leaned closer to each other, taking comfort in another person. Mary heard Cindy whimper in fear, so she put her arm around the young girl's shoulder.

"Don't worry, they'll be here to rescue us, you'll see," Mary said, trying to console the girl.

Another crash seeped through the thick door from outside in the hallway and Cindy buried her head in Mary's shoulder, shivering in fear.

Mary squeezed her .38 so hard her hand began to turn white.

She whispered to the ceiling, hoping to mentally signal Henry and Jimmy from wherever they were.

"You hear that, guys? Hurry the hell up and save us."

## CHAPTER THIRTY-EIGHT

JIMMY WAS HOLDING the steering wheel so tight his hands began to hurt. Not realizing it, he loosened his grip.

When the bus entered the beginning of town, it was terribly obvious everything had gone to Hell fast.

Inside the bus, Henry, Sam and the guards all sat silently and watched the roaming ghouls while they shuffled around the streets of Pittsfield.

The only noise to break the silence other than the rumbling engine was the thumping sound every time Jimmy would hit another walker in the street.

The bus slowly crawled its way through the crowd of undead until Jimmy was really beginning to worry about getting trapped by the writhing masses of arms and legs.

As if in answer to his thoughts, Sam walked over to Jimmy, his body swaying with the rhythm of the vehicle each time it ran over the countless bodies.

"Okay, I can't believe this shit is happening, but there's no time to cry about it now. Right now we need to save as many survivors as possible," Sam snapped, upset at having to watch his town crumble in front of him.

Jimmy nodded in agreement. "I've already been looking, but so far, nada," Jimmy replied.

"Well, shit, there has to be some survivors," Henry said. He thought about it for a moment and then an idea struck him. "Hey, Jimmy, head over to our boarding house, maybe Mary's there. I know she'd go somewhere that we all knew about."

"Okay, it's a good place to try as any," Jimmy replied.

At the precise moment Jimmy started to turn the wheel to work his way down another street, a shout rang out that cut through the din surrounding the bus.

Jimmy slowed the bus to a crawl, looking out his windshield.

"Did you guys hear that?" Jimmy asked.

"Yeah, I heard it, too. A survivor, maybe?" Henry suggested.

"There! Over there!" Sam yelled, pointing out his window at a small, one-story hardware store on their right side.

There was an older couple and a young woman on the roof of the store, waiving frantically at the bus.

"Jimmy, can you pull the bus onto the sidewalk so they can jump onto the roof?" Sam asked.

"Yeah, sure, why not? My driving instructor always said pedestrians needed to stay off the sidewalk when I was driving," he quipped, although no one laughed.

Jimmy frowned, studying the faces in his rearview mirror.

"Wow, tough crowd," he said, turning the steering wheel so he was now driving along the sidewalk.

Parking meters and newspaper kiosks, now worthless relics from another time, went flying as the heavy bus barreled down the sidewalk. Walkers were sent crashing into storefront windows where they would flail around, rebounding off the steel bumper and metal grille.

By that time the bus was past them, the zombies forgotten, until the next group of walking dead was sent flying or run down to be crushed under the balding tires of the yellow bus.

Jimmy slowed when he was even with the building the three survivors were on and said: "That's as close as I can get, guys, it's now or never."

The instant the bus stopped, it began rocking, the horde of undead beating on the sides of the vehicle, the metal spikes barely slowing then down.

They knew there was meat inside and wanted access to it badly.

The guards in the bus started shooting through the holes in the sheet metal, attempting to keep the worst of the dead away. But it was hopeless. For every one ghoul shot, three and four more would fill the gap, their milky-white, dead eyed, slack jawed faces staring off into the void of Hell.

Sam had knocked one of the side windows out of the back of the bus and had managed to pull his massive frame through the window to climb onto the roof.

Sam swayed to the shaking of the roof while the ghouls below banged and pushed. He felt like he was on a boat in rough seas as he carefully made his way to the other end. Upon reaching the edge, he then looked up at the geriatric couple and the woman.

"You'll have to jump. It's the only way!" Sam yelled to them.

The old woman shrank into the man's arms, shaking her head no.

Due to obstructions on the sidewalk and on the building's façade, Jimmy was still a few feet away from the building. Not that far if you were a young, twenty- five year old, but if you were in your sixties, the gap appeared a lot more daunting.

"Listen, we don't have a lot of time!" Sam yelled over the gunshots floating up below him. "It's either now or never!"

The man pulled his wife apart from him and then turned to look at her. Sam watched the man say something to her. Then she nodded in agreement and turned to Sam.

With a look that said the woman was scared out of her mind, she backed up a little and then jumped over the gap.

If Sam hadn't been there to catch her, the old woman would have continued over the side of the bus and into the waiting arms of the ghouls below, but he was there, and he grabbed her, slamming her to the roof of the bus to slow her momentum.

The woman moved to the side to make room for her husband.

The man disappeared from view for a moment and then, he too, flew across the gap, landing in a disheveled lump on the roof of the bus, the safety railing preventing him from falling over. The young woman followed soon after, her youth making the leap easy, even in her present state of terror. She landed smoothly and moved to the side, her eyes wide with fear as she stared at the undead below her, their arms reaching up, wanting her to jump into their waiting embrace.

Sam helped the old man to a sitting position and then banged three times on the roof.

"All right, I've got 'em, let's go!" Sam yelled down to Jimmy.

Sam received his reply, the roof bucking underneath him as Jimmy began driving through the swarms of bodies surrounding them.

The bus acted like a snow plow, pushing its way through the hordes of the undead.

Inside, Jimmy prayed to every god he could think of for the bus to keep running. If the engine died on them now, there'd be no way of ever escaping…except death.

Slowly turning a corner at the next intersection, Jimmy spotted two women and a child.

They were trapped on top of an old delivery truck parked haphazardly on the side of the street. The truck had broken down just before the contaminated rains had first come and no one had cared enough to move it.

Now it was an island in an ocean of the dead, the ghouls trying to reach the three humans.

One of the women was guarding the front of the truck where the engine was and every time a zombie managed to climb up onto the hood, she would kick it back to the street.

Jimmy wondered how long she'd been doing that until the bus had arrived, but pushed the thought away while he maneuvered closer to the three survivors.

"Henry, check my right side and tell me how close I am," Jimmy told him.

Henry just grunted, leaning over his seat to watch the bus creep closer.

Jimmy was able to get so close the metal spikes on the side of the bus scraped against the derelict truck.

Any walker having the misfortune to be caught in the middle as the two vehicles connected was ripped to shreds, the blood splashing against the sides of the bus, adding to the already new vermilion and yellow paintjob.

Sam was still balancing on the roof, and as the bus pulled close enough, he reached out his hand to the frightened survivors.

"It's okay, honey. Just jump and we'll get you out of here," Sam said in a reassuring tone.

The women sent the child over first and then soon followed, all without incident.

Sam hit the roof three times and Jimmy pulled away into the street again and turned a corner to get the bus to the boarding house.

The yellow school bus moved through the walkers like it was driving through molasses, but after another fifteen minutes they pulled up to the boarding house.

Henry was already at the window of the bus looking for signs of Mary, but his heart sank when he could see nothing but the living dead.

On the stoop of the boarding house, Henry saw a ghoul munching on an upside down head. Inverting his head a little, he recognized the face on the severed head. It was Susan, the woman who had run the boarding house.

Jimmy blared the horn, hoping Mary would hear it, but after five minutes had passed, he gave up.

"Shit, Henry, you don't think they got her, do you?" Jimmy asked, not wanting to admit it.

Henry looked him straight in the eyes, his face as hard as stone, his jaw taut with anxiety.

"Don't think like that, Jimmy!. Don't even say it. I know she's alive." He pondered his options for only a second before his face lit up. "Wait, I can't believe I didn't think of this before! She's probably at Sam's house. Jimmy, head to Sam's house, now!" Henry said, with excitement in his voice.

"Well, that's great, but I don't know where the hell we are. How do I get there?" Jimmy asked as he studied the streets around him.

The street forked off to the right and left and Jimmy didn't remember the part of town he now found himself in. Besides, the town had been a little quieter the last time he'd seen it, less dead people were walking around then, anyway.

Henry hit the roof with the butt of his shotgun to get Sam's attention.

The next moment Jimmy nearly jumped out of his seat when Sam's face popped into view on the front windshield.

"What do you want? I'm a little busy up here," Sam called to them.

"Where's your house. I don't know how to get there!" Jimmy yelled back.

Sam started running off a few lefts and rights, trying to point upside down. Jimmy just nodded, and when Sam pulled his head away, he turned to Henry.

"I didn't get any of that, did you?" Jimmy asked.

Henry frowned and slapped him playfully on the back of the head.

"Yeah, I did, just go and I'll tell you when to turn," Henry said.

Behind them the guards continued shooting walkers from the bus, but Henry had already decided it was a waste of time.

They needed to rescue as many people as they could and then get the hell out of Dodge, in that order.

*     *     *

The bus continued onward, leaving crushed corpses behind it while it drove through the streets.

Along the way, they had managed to save another fifteen survivors, the roof of the bus getting severely crowded.

Half an hour later, the bus rolled up the driveway to Sam's house. Henry looked out through the sheet metal to see the door was kicked in and the windows were shattered.

Jimmy laid on the horn, the blaring noise one continuous note.

After a full minute passed, he let off and sat there with his fingers crossed.

Then a window opened on the second floor and Henry felt relief flood through him when he saw Mary's head peek out.

Sam was still on the roof and he told her to jump to them. She nodded and withdrew her head, a moment later coming back out with Cindy in tow.

Jimmy smiled from ear to ear when he saw the pretty, blonde girl with Mary.

He hadn't wanted to entertain the thought she was dead, figuring Mary would have kept her close when things had started getting bad.

He watched helplessly from the driver's seat as the two women jumped to the bus.

Cindy jumped first, making the distance without any problem, the crowd on the roof of the bus helping her when she landed. Then Mary jumped. Her arm was still sore from her wound and she was off balance as she leapt for the bus' roof.

Her foot slipped and she missed the railing by a good three inches. Starting to fall, she saw the hungry faces of the undead waiting to rip her to shreds.

She closed her eyes and waited for what she knew would be next. Unbearable pain when the teeth and dead hands of the dead tore her apart to then feed on her still warm organs.

Then she was jarred to a halt. Her arm was almost pulled from its socket and then she felt herself being raised back up to the roof of the bus. She looked up to see the handsome brown face of Sam lifting her to the roof and gently lying her down with the help of a few other survivors. Mary breathed in the musty air from all the bodies near her, but it was the sweetest air she'd ever tasted.

Rubbing her shoulder and thanking God it hadn't been the one with the stitches, she looked up at Sam and smiled weakly.

"Thank you," she whispered, lying amid the legs of the other survivors.

"My pleasure," Sam grinned back.

Sam slapped the roof three times and yelled over the front of the bus.

"Okay, that's it. There's no more room up here, lets get the hell out of here!"

Inside the bus, Henry slapped Jimmy on the shoulder, the smile on his face hard to miss.

"You heard the man. It's time to go. Get us to the gate and then far away from here," Henry told him like he was the captain of a ship.

Jimmy nodded and cut the wheel hard. Spinning the bus around, he began driving for the gate again.

Up above on the roof, the bus rocked to the jerking motions of the vehicle with the survivors watching the living dead moving below them. To say it was unsettling would have been a vast understatement.

Sam had to cover his nose, the stench of all the decaying bodies finally getting to him. Breathing through his mouth made it a little better, but not by much.

After another half an hour Jimmy had made it out of the worst of the undead horde and was almost back to the gate. The opening had just come into view when Sam slapped the roof for Jimmy to stop.

The area was clear, so Jimmy pulled over and placed the bus in park, the engine rumbling while it idled.

Sam climbed down from the roof and stopped at the door of the bus.

The door was opened and Henry and Jimmy noticed something in his hand.

"Send Paul out here and then drive through the gate and wait for us, will ya?" Sam asked.

"Sure, man, no problem," Jimmy replied, calling for Paul to come up front.

After Paul had disembarked from the bus, Jimmy drove through the gate and stopped the vehicle alongside the first abandoned pickup truck.

Then they waited for Sam and Paul to return with a few guards keeping an eye out for any stray ghouls.

About five minutes later, the two men walked through the opening and when they were back near the bus, Henry asked: "What was that about. What did you two do?"

"Watch and learn, my friend," Sam said simply and then patted Paul on the back while nodding to the open gate.

Paul walked over to one of the pickups and placed his rifle on the hood. Then after a moment to sight his target, he fired one shot.

A split second later, before the echo of the rifle shot had faded from the area, the front barricade of the town went up in a fiery explosion that ripped the gate off its rails and sent the surrounding piles of metal and steel crashing to the ground.

One of the abandoned vehicles was hit by flaming wreckage and after another minute, it too, went up in flames, the body of the truck flipping over in the air before it came to rest again on the asphalt.

The opening was now blocked by a flaming mass of steel and other remnants of the makeshift barrier. The smell of burning rubber and gasoline filled the area around the bus with the shifting of the wind.

"Whoa, what the hell did you do?" Jimmy asked.

With the fire reflecting in his eyes. Sam answered in a low subdued voice.

"I used the last of the dynamite to blow the gate. If those dead bastards want my town so bad, they can have it. And I've just made sure they'll never leave."

Henry just stood there and watched the licking flames. There was nothing he could say. The man standing next to him had lost everything. His house, his town and all the people who had trusted him to save them were now dead.

Turning, he looked up at the survivors of the town still clustered on the roof of the bus. Only a handful had made it compared to what the population of the town once was. A handful from what had been almost six hundred people, until the undead had come and destroyed them and everything they held dear in this earthly life.

That's why Henry and his friends kept moving. If you stayed still too long, the dead always caught up to you. No matter how hard you tried, you couldn't stop death; but you could stall it for as long as possible.

Overhead in the sky, the clouds rumbled again, threatening to drop more rain on them at any second. Mary had climbed down from the roof, and after hugging Jimmy and Henry, she went to Sam.

Placing her arm on his broad shoulder, she looked up at him. "Where will you go now?" She asked.

He chuckled to himself, and then looked at her. "You know, I have no idea. But we have the supplies from Costington and that town is pretty much empty of walkers, so maybe I'll go there. Start over again fresh."

He looked at Mary and then shifted his gaze to Henry and Jimmy.

"My offer still stands. You could join us. You're needed now more than ever," Sam offered.

"Thanks for the offer, Sam, but I don't think so. Besides, we were heading further north when we met you and I think we'll continue that way. Way I figure it, winter's coming and the deaders shouldn't fare so well in the frigid temperatures. So at least we'll get a few months relief until the snow thaws.

Sam mulled that over for a few moments.

"Yeah, that's not a bad idea, but this is my home and I'll be damned if I'll let those dead bastards run me out of my own state. Besides, it can get pretty damn cold here, too."

Henry nodded, not wanting to get into the semantics of why the three companions kept moving.

Besides, it just didn't matter.

They all stood quietly for a time, watching the fires burn until another crack of thunder broke them out of their stupor.

Then they all gathered together and worked out the next plan of action.

Sam would give the companions one of the abandoned vehicles that were spread out around the gate and he would take the rest.

Then, after giving the companions a small share of the ammunition found at Costington for their weapons, they would part ways, with Sam driving off with the school bus and the other survivors to an uncertain future.

\*  \*  \*

An hour later, with the first signs of raindrops preparing to fall, Henry shook Sam's hand.

"Thanks again for all the help you gave us with Mary, despite the threats,"

Henry said.

Sam smiled back. "Yeah, I'm sorry about that, but I had to do whatever it took to save my town," Sam replied.

"Oh, yeah, and how did that work out for you?" Jimmy quipped next to Sam.

Sam opened his mouth to say something and then let it go when he saw the smile on Jimmy's face.

"I'd like to say I'll miss your wiseass remarks, but I'd be lying," Sam said to Jimmy.

"That's okay. I have that effect on people. Good luck, Sam," Jimmy said, holding out his hand.

Sam shook it and then turned to Cindy. "You sure you want to go with them?" He asked her.

She just nodded and moved a little closer to Jimmy.

"All right then, go," he said.

Mary walked up to Sam and kissed his cheek. "Thank you for everything and I hope I see you again," she whispered into his ear.

"Someday you will, I promise," he whispered back.

Then the first rain drops began to fall and everyone ran for cover, cutting the goodbyes short. Far more would happen if they were foolish enough to get wet.

When everyone had made it safely to their vehicles, the clouds opened up and sent a deluge of rain onto the wayward convoy.

Henry was in the driver's seat and he turned the key, the six cylinder engine turning over on the first try. Flicking the windshield wipers on, he was pleased to see them moving smoothly across the glass.

He checked the gas tank and frowned when he saw it was less than half a tank.

Oh well, at least it would get them far away from where they were now before the tank went dry. And who knows, maybe they'd find some more gas on their way, it had happened before, although more infrequently with every passing day.

The bus drove off, blaring its horn in a loud goodbye. Henry hit his horn a few times, returning the favor, and then drove on, following the last vehicle in the convoy.

He followed the convoy of vehicles for another few miles until he turned onto the onramp for Interstate 95. He knew from past vacations with his wife that this interstate would bring him all the way to New England.

Hell, if they found more gas and drove all the way there they might even get to see the leaves change.

He looked in his rearview mirror to see the faces of Jimmy and Cindy as they sat close together in the back seat, talking quietly about something. Their hands were entwined and it reminded Henry of how a father drives his young son and his date to the movies.

Askance of him, in the passenger seat, was Mary. She noticed him looking at her and she reached out her left hand and rubbed his shoulder gently.

He took her hand in his and held it as he drove.

Leaning back in his seat, with his friends around him, he continued down the highway until the vehicle was lost from sight, while the rain continued to fall, washing the world clean one raindrop at a time.

# *AFTERWORD*

RECENTLY, A MEMBER of my family passed away and although he and I weren't close, he still held a special place in my heart.

When I think of someone dying, I think of the little things that the person will now miss.

When the skies are overcast and it rains for a week straight here in New England, I will always find myself feeling miserable as I stare at the dreary weather.

But what if I had just died and survived as some form of ghost or ethereal being?

I'll bet you that with every fiber of my essence, I'd wish I could be alive again to enjoy one of those dreary days.

The things in life that get to us and bother us really just don't matter because at any time we could cease to exist; except in the hearts of our loved ones.

When you go to a funeral and everyone's crying and sad about the passing of a loved one, exactly who are they crying for? Surely not the deceased, as they now feel no pain, in fact, all their problems are over. No, we cry for ourselves because that person won't be around anymore to answer the phone when you call to wish them a Happy Birthday once a year, and the fact that sooner or later, we too, will be joining them in the darkness of death; whether it takes four years or forty.

Which brings me to the main subject of this story; zombies

When a character opens a door in a horror movie to see a zombie standing before them to me they see much more than a reanimated corpse. They see what we all will eventually become; unless you choose cremation.

When you look into the face of a zombie, it's like looking into the face of death itself.

And no matter how hard we struggle, rich or poor, famous or an average Joe, eventually we all lose the fight. Death is the great equalizer. That's why all of us need to make our mark in this world. Because, with a snap of a finger it can all be gone; and unfortunately there are no do-overs.

So when you read a book or watch a movie about zombies (although when you die you may not be walking around and trying to eat your neighbors) you may not realize it, but you ultimately may be seeing a part of yourself you'd rather not know could exist.

A. G.
Dec. 2006

THE NEXT EXCITING CHAPTER IN THE DEADWATER
SERIES!

**DEAD CITY**
By Anthony Giangregorio


NEW PERILS IN AN UNDEAD WORLD

After narrowly surviving an attack by a large pack of blood thirsty,
wild dogs, Henry and his companions stumble upon an enclave that
has made its home in an abandoned shopping mall.

Hoping for a respite from the perils of the walking dead, Henry and
the others plan to settle down for the winter, safe in the company of
fellow survivors of the zombie apocalypse.

But unknown to the group is the dark secret the enclave keeps, a secret
that could threaten to destroy the companions and anyone else
unfortunate enough to be caught in the trap.

In a dead world the only thing still living… is hope.

# DEAD RECKONING: DAWNING OF THE DEAD
## By Anthony Giangregorio

### THE DEAD HAVE RISEN!

In the dead city of Pittsburgh, two small enclaves struggle to survive, eking out an existence of hand to mouth.

But instead of working together, both groups battle for the last remaining fuel and supplies of a city filled with the living dead.

Six months after the initial outbreak, a lone helicopter arrives bearing two more survivors and a newborn baby. One enclave welcomes them, while the other schemes to steal their helicopter and escape the decaying city.

With no police, fire, or social services existing, the two will battle for dominance in the steel city of the walking dead.

But when the dust settles, the question is: will the remaining humans be the winners, or the losers?

When the dead walk, the line between Heaven and Hell is so twisted and bent there is no line at all.


# RISE OF THE DEAD
## By Anthony Giangregorio

### DEATH IS ONLY THE BEGINNING

In less than forty-eight hours, more than half the globe was infected.
In another forty-eight, the rest would be enveloped.
The reason?
A science experiment gone horribly wrong which enabled the dead to walk, their flesh rotting on their bones even as they seek human prey.

Jeremy was an ordinary nineteen year old slacker. He partied too much and had done poorly in high school. After a night of drinking and drugs, he awoke to find the world a very different place from the one he'd left the night before. The dead were walking and feeding on the living, and as Jeremy stepped out into a world gone mad, the dead spotting him alone and unarmed in the middle of the street, he had to wonder if he would live long enough to see his twentieth birthday.

BOOK 6

# DEAD UNION

By Anthony Giangregorio

### BRAVE NEW WORLD

More than a year has passed since the world died not with a bang, but with a moan.

Where sprawling cities once stood, now only the dead inhabit the hollow walls of a shattered civilization; a mockery of lives once led.

But there are still survivors in this barren world, all slowly struggling to take back what was stripped from their birthright; the promise of a world free of the undead.

Fortified towns have shunned the outside world, becoming massive fortresses in their own right. These refugees of a world torn asunder are once again trying to carve out a new piece of the earth, or hold onto what little they already possess.

### HOSTAGES

Henry Watson and his warrior survivalists are conscripted by a mad colonel, one of the last military leaders still functioning in the decimated United States. The colonel has settled in Fort Knox, and from there plans to rule the world with his slave army of lost souls and the last remaining soldiers of a defunct army.

But first he must take back America and mold it in his own image; and he will crush all who oppose him, including the new recruits of Henry and crew.

The battle lines are drawn with the fate of America at stake, and this time, the outcome may be unsure.

In a world where the dead walk, even the grave isn't safe.


# THE DARK

By Anthony Giangregorio

### DARKNESS FALLS

The darkness came without warning.

First New York, then the rest of United States, and then the world became enveloped in a perpetual night without end.

With no sunlight, eventually the planet will wither and die, bringing on a new Ice Age. But that isn't problem for the human race, for humanity will be dead long before that happens.

There is something in the dark, creatures only seen in nightmares, and they are on the prowl.

Evolution has changed and man is no longer the dominant species.

When we are children, we are told not to fear the dark, that what we believe to exist in the shadows is false.

Unfortunately, that is no longer true.

# DARK PLACES
## By Anthony Giangregorio

A cave-in inside the Boston subway unleashes something that should have stayed buried forever.

Three boys sneak out to a haunted junkyard after dark and find more than they gambled on.

In a world where everyone over twelve has died from a mysterious illness, one young boy tries to carry on.

A mysterious man in black tries his hand at a game of chance at a local carnival, to interesting results.

God, Allah, and Buddha play a friendly game of poker with the fate of the Earth resting in the balance.

Ever have one of those days where everything that can go wrong, does? Well, so did Byron, and no one should have a day like this!

Thad had an imaginary friend named Charlie when he was a child. Charlie would make him do bad things. Now Thad is all grown up and guess who's coming for a visit?

These and other short stories, all filled with frozen moments of dread and wonder, will keep you captivated long into the night.

Just be sure to watch out when you turn off the light!


# ROAD KILL: A ZOMBIE TALE
## By Anthony Giangregorio

### ORDER UP!

In the summer of 2008, a rogue comet entered earth's orbit for 72 hours. During this time, a strange amber glow suffused the sky.

But something else happened; something in the comet's tail had an adverse affect on dead tissue and the result was the reanimation of every dead animal carcass on the planet.

A handful of survivors hole up in a diner in the backwoods of New Hampshire while the undead creatures of the night hunt for human prey.

There's a new blue plate special at DJ's Diner and Truck Stop, and it's you!

# THE MONSTER UNDER THE BED
By Anthony Giangregorio

Rupert was just one of many monsters that inhabit the human world, scaring children before bed. Only Rupert wanted to play with the children he was forced to scare.

When Rupert meets Timmy, an instant friendship is born. Running away from his abusive step-father, Timmy leaves home, embarking on a journey that leads him to New York City.

On his way, Timmy will realize that the true monsters are other adults who are just waiting to take advantage of a small boy, all alone in the big city.

Can Rupert save him?

Or will Timmy just become another statistic.

# SOULEATER
By Anthony Giangregorio

Twenty years ago, Jason Lawson witnessed the brutal death of his father by something only seen in nightmares, something so horrible he'd blocked it from his mind.

Now twenty years later the creature is back, this time for his son.

Jason won't let that happen.

He'll travel to the demon's world, struggling every second to rescue his son from its clutches.

But what he doesn't know is that the portal will only be open for a finite time and if he doesn't return with his son before it closes, then he'll be trapped in the demon's dimension forever.

# DEAD TALES: SHORT STORIES TO DIE FOR
By Anthony Giangregorio

In a world much like our own, terrorists unleash a deadly dis-ease that turns people into flesh-eating ghouls.

A camping trip goes horribly wrong when forces of evil seek to dominate mankind.

After losing his life, a man returns reincarnated again and again; his soul inhabiting the bodies of animals.

In the Colorado Mountains, a woman runs for her life, stalked by a sadistic killer.

In a world where the Patriot Act has come to fruition, a man struggles to survive, despite eroding liberties.

Not able to accept his wife's death, a widower will cross into the dream realm to find her again, despite the dark forces that hold her in thrall.

These and other short stories will captivate and thrill you.

These are short stories to die for.

# DEADFREEZE
By Anthony Giangregorio

THIS IS WHAT HELL WOULD BE LIKE IF IT FROZE OVER.

When an experimental serum for hypothermia goes horribly wrong, a small research station in the middle of Antarctica becomes overrun with an army of the frozen dead.

Now a small group of survivors must battle the arctic weather and a horde of frozen zombies as they make their way across the frozen plains of Antarctica to a neighboring research station.

What they don't realize is that they are being hunted by an entity whose sole reason for existing is vengeance; and it will find them wherever they run.

# DEADFALL
By Anthony Giangregorio

It's Halloween in the small suburban town of Wakefield, Mass.

While parents take their children trick or treating and others throw costume parties, a swarm of meteorites enter the earth's atmosphere and crash to earth.

Inside are small parasitic worms, no larger than maggots.

The worms quickly infect the corpses at a local cemetery and so begins the rise of the undead.

The walking dead soon get the upper hand, with no one believing the truth.

That the dead now walk.

Will a small group of survivors live through the zombie apocalypse?

Or will they, too, succumb to the Deadfall.

# DEAD HARVEST

By Anthony Giangregorio

Lost at sea and fearing for their lives, a miracle arrives on the horizon, in the shape of a cruise ship, saving Henry Watson and his friends from a watery grave.

Enjoying the safety of the commandeered ship, Henry and his companions take a much needed rest and settle down for a life at sea, but after a devastating storm sends the companions adrift once again, they find themselves separated, exhausted, and washed ashore on the coast of California.

With each person believing the others in the group are dead; they fall into the middle of a feud between two neighboring towns, the companions now unknowingly battling against one another.

Needing to escape their newfound prisons, each one struggles to adapt to their new life, while the tableau of life continues around them.

But one sadistic ruler will seek to unleash the awesome power of the living dead on his unsuspecting adversaries, wiping the populace from the face of the earth, and in doing so, take Henry and his friends with them.

Though death looms around every corner, man's journey is far from over.

# LIVING DEAD PRESS

## Where the Dead Walk

www.livingdeadpress.com

Book One of the *Undead World Trilogy*

# BLOOD
## OF THE
# DEAD

A Shoot 'Em Up Zombie Novel by A.P. Fuchs

"*Blood of the Dead* . . . is the stuff of nightmares . . . with some unnerving and frightening action scenes that will have you on the edge of your seat."

- Rick Hautala
author of *The Wildman*

Joe Bailey prowls the Haven's streets, taking them back from the undead, each kill one step closer to reclaiming a life once stolen from him.

As the dead push into the Haven, he and a couple others are forced into the one place where folks fear to tread: the heart of the city, a place overrun with flesh-eating zombies.

Welcome to the end of all things.

**Ask for it at your local bookstore.
Also available from your favorite on-line retailer.**

ISBN-10   1-897217-80-3 / ISBN-13   978-1-897217-80-1

**www.undeadworldtrilogy.com**

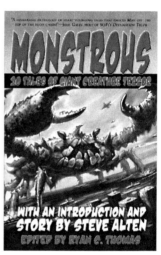

Printed in the United Kingdom by
Lightning Source UK Ltd., Milton Keynes
139624UK00001B/158/P